FATAL ASSASSIN

THE FATAL FAE SERIES: BOOK TWO

TEACUP
DRAGON
PUBLISHING

To those who came before and challenged me to be better. To those who came after and inspire me to reach higher.

BOOKS BY TAMERI ETHERTON

Song of the Swords *

The Prince of Dragons

The Stones of Resurrection

The Temple of Sacrifice

The Ruins of Betrayal

The Veils of Deception

The Fatal Fae *

Fatal Illusion

Fatal Assassin

Fatal Legacy

Court of Stars *

Sunset in Shadow

Chronicles of Eidyn *

Child of Fire

Dragon Mage

Short Stories

UnBroken

Wicked Shorts

One Wicked Night

*Books that are part of the Aetherverse: The fantastical realms of Tameri Etherton. Characters and storylines intersect within the books with magical consequences.

FATAL ASSASSIN

THE FATAL FAE SERIES: BOOK TWO

USA TODAY BESTSELLING AUTHOR

TAMERI ETHERTON

Dead witches tell no lies.

Cian MacNair crouched over the withered body of the enchantress, hope creeping away with every passing second. His sister's dagger lay among the rotting detritus and he carefully retrieved it. When he had a moment to think, he'd have to ask Rori how she managed to hit her mark without seeing the target. Acelyne had been behind a tree when Rori cast the dagger toward the enchantress. Cian blew out a breath, impressed with his baby sister, and equally concerned for her well-being.

When she'd stormed off into the forest, he'd waited with the two queens of Faerie, Eirlys and Midna. They'd planned it all from the start—upsetting Rori enough that she'd confront Acelyne—but what they hadn't counted on was Rori's skill as an assassin. Yes, they'd used his sister as a trap. Hell, it had been his idea, after all. Not that he was proud of it, but he'd known Rori would seek refuge in the forest and he'd also known she'd be drawn to Acelyne just as much as the enchantress was drawn to her. There was a connection between Rori and Acelyne beyond the glass prisons; he needed a hot second to figure out what.

Cian wiped the dagger on a tuft of grass, noting the elegant lines of the blade, the script scrawling from hilt to tip. It wasn't a weapon he recognized. He was reminded how much his sister had matured since the Academy. How much time had passed since either one was anything other than a spy. In truth, neither of them had ever had a choice in their career. Not since their father's death. Cian had watched his sister emotionally shut down when she'd heard the news and he'd known at that moment she'd follow in their father's footsteps.

That was a long time ago and now Rori was one of Queen Eirlys's favorites. A begrudging smile strained his lips. He was damn proud of his sister. He just wished she'd be more careful.

"The enchantress will not take her secrets into the darkness." Queen Eirlys muttered low enough only he heard. The Seelie queen moved in front of him, her arms outstretched. "Will you help me, Midna?"

Cian rose and backed away, allowing Eirlys and Midna room. The Unseelie queen stood on the other side of the decaying body and arched her arms toward Eirlys. Together, they chanted an ancient spell, one of dark magic Cian knew to be forbidden. Except for queens, apparently. He knew most of the spells of dark and black magic—had been taught them as a young lad, always with the condition he never used them. Knowledge, he'd been taught, was power. Using black magic was dangerous not just to the cursed, but to the spellcaster as well. Cian had taken the warning to heart and rarely, only when absolutely necessary, delved into the dark arts. And he never, ever told anyone about his secret knowledge—not even Rori.

The queens' voices rose and lowered in a convoluted melody he tried hard to follow. Their words mingled together, becoming one long string, a single syllable stretching to the end of time. The witch's features filled in, flesh returned to rotted bones. She no longer resembled the attractive woman she'd been, but now had the appearance of an aged crone.

Hope bloomed in his chest. Perhaps he could get answers after all. He moved beside his sister and returned her dagger. She took it, her face screwed into a look of confusion. After a moment, she slid the dagger into the sheath strapped to her thigh.

"I don't understand," Rori half-whispered.

"Nor do I," Midna's expression was one of concern, "but we've done our best to preserve her mind. I'll send her to my necromancer to see if there's anything yet to learn."

Midna signaled to her soldiers, dressed as courtiers for surreptitious guard duty, to take the enchantress away. Cian debated following them, to keep the body in his sight for fear of losing an opportunity for answers, but chose to stay with the queens. The elven thief Therron stood by Rori as she and her friend Tug chatted with Meg. The healer's haggard appearance had been erased. In its place was the face and body of a young woman. He overheard her saying Acelyne had been stealing her youth for years and a bitterness wedged itself in his heart.

Stealing Meg's life force, kidnapping fae, and endangering his sister were the crimes Cian knew about—what else had the witch done? He strode to the body of Dorchmeir, one of Queen Eirlys's guard, and withdrew Rori's dagger from his throat. His gaze slid to Esme, who stood with Rori's small group. If memory served, she was Dorchmeir's betrothed. She and his sister had answers he desperately needed. Two dead bodies, both with Rori's daggers sunk deep in their flesh. How had Dorchmeir slid under Eirlys's radar—or had he? Was he working as an informant? Too many questions—the kind that made him lose sleep at night—plagued his thoughts.

He cleaned the weapon and placed it in his pocket for the time being. Daggers weren't really his style, but seeing how lethal his sister was with them, he made a mental note to get in some target practice. A soldier wrapped Dorchmeir's sword in a blanket and took it away to be analyzed. Cian gestured to another soldier to take the body along with Acelyne's to the necromancer. Perhaps more answers could be found.

He left the stench of death behind and stepped through the woods to the vale and inhaled deeply. Fresh, clean air filled his lungs. Sunlight warmed his skin and he nodded that all would soon be as it should. He'd make certain of it.

Queen Eirlys turned from the Unseelie queen and sighed. "This day has been one I had hoped would never come to Faerie, yet here we are. There is malevolence growing all around, and we need to stop it before it destroys every last one of us. Rori, I should like you to go to the human realm and gather what you can about the amulets. Meg, get her healed and fit. Cian, continue doing the good work you've started here. Midna and I will do what we can to uncover who is behind all of this."

Cian heard his queen's words like a blow to the gut. This should've been his assignment. After all, hadn't it been him who had worked for months tracking down Malcolm Dagniss and every scrap of information about Malcolm's company, SIRE Unlimited? Malcolm was in the human realm, where Cian should be, not Rori. He could continue investigating SIRE while searching for clues about the amulets and who might be involved. Eirlys had hinted at the possibility of war in the past, but he'd not heard even a whisper of discontent in Faerie. The fact that she followed up her musing of malevolence with sending Rori to the human realm gave Cian the idea she meant the friction was coming from there. So why keep him in Faerie?

His gaze flicked to Midna. If this was a ploy of hers to keep him at her court, he'd make sure she understood his displeasure. To date, he'd avoided her bed, but another month and his resolve might crumble. She was voracious in her appetites, including wanting him to father her heir. Midna looked the picture of innocence as she held Eirlys's hand and nodded her agreement with what the Seelie queen said. He tore his gaze from her and met Rori's apology-laden stare. At least his sister understood this should be his mission. But there was nothing to be done. The queens had made their decision.

He tilted his head and cracked his neck, his mind churning. If he had to stay at the Unseelie palace, so be it. He would, as Eirlys said, continue doing the good work he'd started. Bastards and rubbish. If it was such good work, then why did it feel like a demotion?

He followed the queens into Rowan's cottage and hung back, not wanting to be too near them for fear of saying something that might be regarded as treason. Rori ambled in, Therron supporting her as best he could. Cian studied them, saw the subtle flush of his sister's cheeks. He mentally flipped a coin whether to tell her all he knew of the elf. She wasn't a child anymore—it wasn't his job to protect her, but still he felt obligated to tell her who Therron was, and what he'd learned about him at the Unseelie Court. He took a half step and paused. Rori had to learn her own lessons. He'd say nothing for the moment. Instead, he'd keep a close watch on the pair.

Rori cleared her throat and said in a firm voice, "I'd like Cian to go to the human realm to seek out the miscreant who is kidnapping fae." She dropped a low curtsey and winced.

Cian stared at his sister as if she'd grown a dragon's tail and shook it like an exotic dancer.

He barely heard as she continued, "If you approve, Your Majesties, I would like to convalesce with Queen Midna for an undetermined amount of time. Once healed, I'd like to learn everything she can teach me."

The room quieted as if everyone crowded into the space held their breath. He glanced at the two queens, who each raised their eyebrows at Rori's request. Cian's gaze swept to his sister and even she looked shocked at her words. Surely she knew what she was asking, but did she understand what exactly Midna would expect from her? This was one time Cian wished Rori wasn't his sister. He didn't want to know what she'd be doing at the Unseelie

Court. Didn't want to know what education she meant. Fuck it all, but he *did* know. Knew only too well what Midna would do to Rori and there wasn't a damn thing he could do to stop it.

Eirlys turned to Midna, a coy little smile tugging the corners of her lips. "Well, sister of my heart, do you consent to taking my Rori on as a foster?"

"Only with your approval."

"Then you shall have it." Eirlys scanned above the heads of those gathered and met Cian's look with a silent challenge. "Cian, what say you to your sister's request?"

What could he say? *No? Hell no? Stay the fuck away from my baby sister?* None of those words passed his lips. In fact, for once in his life, he honestly wasn't sure what to say. If Rori wanted to stay at Midna's court, the least he could do was get the hell out of Faerie.

"I'll take that as a yes." The queen giggled when she turned toward Rori. "You'll have your education, dearest. Learn well, but learn quickly. I have a feeling your brother will be needing your assistance soon enough."

With what? What assistance did Eirlys think he'd need from Rori? Cian was accustomed to Midna playing games, but now it seemed Eirlys was infected with the tiresome habit. Before he turned to leave the room, Therron caught his attention. The fool elf held Rori with a strong arm wrapped around her waist. That wasn't what stopped Cian from storming out like a wounded child. It was the look deep in Therron's eyes that stopped Cian.

There, in the murky darkness, he saw a silent request.

Therron was asking for Cian's permission.

Bloody hell and codswaddle. The man was insufferable. Rori shifted as if to maneuver herself away from the queens, and Therron looked away from Cian, his focus entirely on Rori. Something passed between the pair. An electric current even Cian couldn't deny. If Rori chose Therron, he'd have to give his blessing at some point, but he would prefer it to be later rather than sooner. Conflicting thoughts raged in his mind—why would Rori asked to be one of Midna's álainn obedience if she had feelings for Therron? Certainly, she wouldn't expect the elf to stand by while she explored her sexual desires with the queen? Unless, of course, there was another reason Rori sought Midna's teachings.

I'll take care of her, my sweet. Never fear, for what she discovers in my court will make her stronger in all things. Compassion, caring, even killing. Do you deny this?

Midna's words brushed his thoughts, and his jaw tightened at the truth of them. He knew what Rori would go through at Midna's palace, and he agreed it would make her one of the finest assassins Faerie had ever known. But she was his sister.

Aye, I can't deny the truth of your words, but I don't have to like them either.

I suppose this means your stay with me is at an end.

Their eyes met and he saw not sadness, as he thought he might, but a challenge in Midna's glorious eyes. A smirk twisted her lips. Insufferable. Every night, he'd denied her request to join in the sexual festivities and now, he realized she'd known all along he would. Her constant prodding and begging him to bed her was nothing but foreplay. Rori would indeed be safe with the queen. She'd not make his sister do anything she wasn't comfortable doing. He shook his head and laughed, a full-chested chortle that caused several courtiers to jump in surprise.

Cian strode to the queens and bowed low at the waist. "Your Majesties, I am ever your servant. If you'll excuse me, I've preparations to make. I should be leaving Faerie by sundown."

Eirlys eyed him suspiciously while Midna continued to grin with an irritating, all-knowing expression.

"We shall miss you, Cian." Eirlys took his hand in her own and gave him a meaningful stare. *My daughter lies in slumber, but for how long, we can't be certain. Even Meg is unsure how to wake her, nor do we know how to release the others. Be swift and sure in your investigations. If you encounter any opposition, you have my permission and blessing to do what's needed.*

"I shall miss you, as well. You'll both have regular updates on my progress." To Eirlys alone, he replied, *Arianna will be avenged, my queen.*

Midna was less eloquent.

"If you find whoever is responsible for the kidnappings, kill them in a most brutal way. I wish to know all the details when you return." Her eyes, ever shifting and changing in color, much like her hair and wings, bore into his. "I can't shake the unsettling feeling Mairead is there, with the humans. Please find her." The last was said in a near whisper, with enough emotion behind the words to knock Cian sideways.

No one could deny the Unseelie queen's love for her sister, nor could they question Mairead's loyalty to the throne. That's why those who knew of her disappearance were concerned—Mairead would never venture out of Faerie on her own.

"If she is in the human realm, I'll find her. That I promise you."

But how, was the question. Faerie was tiny compared to Earth, perhaps the size of North America, with a fraction of the population. Those who had never traveled beyond the doorways had no way of knowing how vast and overflowing with people the human realm was. Finding Mairead might be damn near impossible. At least Cian had a clue where Malcolm Dagniss and SIRE were located.

Edinburgh.

The only city where Cian had vowed never to return.

Everything hurt, as if hellfire burned in her veins and a troll was squishing her guts. Yet Rori gave no outward indication of how difficult it was to walk beside Therron. With too much effort, she kept her head held high as she left the queens and their confusing words. Although, she'd surprised even herself with the admission that she wished to return to Midna's court.

She glanced up at the elf, and the intensity of his gaze spun through her solar plexus. This was no illusion. At least, she hoped it wasn't. Hoped what she saw burning in those depths was the same desire she felt. What delicious torment he could unleash upon her and how ready she was to accept it. A shiver of lust tickled down her spine, and Therron tightened his grip.

"You're in shock. We need to see to your wounds."

It wasn't shock she felt, but well, maybe it was. She had lost a lot of blood, and her hand throbbed from where she'd broken it punching Dorchmeir's ruddy face. It had been totally worth it to see the surprise in his eyes, to know that he would never again hurt anyone, especially Esme. A fresh tremble—this one of rage

—rattled her bones. Therron pulled her close and she inhaled his scent, imprinting him firmly in her mind.

"I'm starving." Her stomach growled its empty state.

"Later. First, healing." Therron caught Meg's attention, and Rori felt rather than saw him tilt his head toward the bedrooms.

The next thing she knew, Tug lifted her into his arms. Indignant to be coddled like a child, Rori started to protest, but the giant rolled her against his heavy chest, silencing her objections.

"Let us help, Aurora."

Tug's soft voice held a note of concern and she relaxed into him. Who cared if the entire court saw her being treated like a baby. It wasn't as if her reputation were at stake or anything.

"I'm actually surprised she's not fighting you, Tug."

"Shut it, Meg." Rori tried for anger, but they were right—there was no need to fight them and she was in pain. The sooner she let them heal her, the sooner she could eat. Fighting them would only cause more injuries.

Tug laid her on a bed and her body immediately went limp, as if she could sleep for a year.

"That's more like it. Therron, Tug, could you please give us some privacy?"

The men left, but not entirely willingly. Meg's stern glare might've had something to do with it.

"Take this." Meg handed Rori a vial and she sniffed it. "It's the burdock root mixture you made yesterday. It will help with mending your broken bones."

Rori propped herself up on the pillows and opened the stopper. "Gah! It smells like ass. I thought you said this was for curing blood in urine."

"I told you that in case Acelyne was listening, remember? If she knew this potion could heal broken bones, she might've stolen it as well. Down it goes, that's a good girl."

The vile liquid coated the back of her throat as it slithered to her gut. A loud gurgle came from her innards and she would've retched the foulness up had it not been for the emptiness of her stomach.

"That was disgusting."

The room tilted to one side, then the other, and Rori closed her eyes against the dizziness.

"Just relax, Rori. This might sting a little." Despite the words spoken, Meg's gentle tone lulled Rori into a sense of complacency.

She settled into the pillows, imagining they were puffs of clouds and she a goddess with hair of silver. The woman from her illusion.

"She's not just beautiful. She's life," Rori murmured.

"Who is, darling?" Meg's soothing voice came from far away.

A pinch against her thigh, then another, followed by several more, were disturbing her peaceful gliding upon the cloud. With each, she fought off a wince and forced her mind away from what Meg was doing to her leg.

"Taryn. Her name was Taryn. She said so much, yet so little. It was terribly confusing."

"Is she someone from the human realm?"

Rori drifted on the cloud, happy to be off her feet. Relieved to be done fighting for the moment. "I don't think so. She said she was in her mother's palace in Talaith. I've never heard of such a place, have you?"

"Hmmm, I don't think so." Meg sounded closer now, but distracted.

Eyes still closed, Rori tried to recall the exact conversation she'd had with the silver-haired woman in the illusion. "I suppose I could've imagined it all. She called Arianna her daughter. Kind of like how the queen says we're all her children. That must've been what she meant. Ouch!" Rori glared at Meg, who hunched over her leg with a needle hovering close to her skin. "What the fool hell are you doing?"

Meg ignored her and tied off a stitch. "There. Now, please,

Rori. Be gentle. This was a deep wound and that man's sword was poisoned. You really should be dead, you know. The amount of blood you lost alone would've crippled a giant like Tug. Promise me you'll take it easy until this wound is healed."

Tiny black threads crisscrossed the five-inch gash Dorchmeir had given her. Angry red skin surrounded the wound. Meg spread one of her tinctures across the infected area with the precision of a surgeon. When she finished with Rori's leg, she poked and prodded the rest of her body to be certain there were no further injuries. Aside from the mostly healed cut she'd received when she broke out of the amulet, and her broken hand, and maybe some bruised ribs, she was fine.

"Well?" Meg gave Rori her best stern glare.

"Well what?"

"Do you promise to let your wounds heal before racing after your brother?"

"Yes. I promise." Rori held out her hand, surprised to see it bandaged. "When did you do that?" She wriggled her fingers, the only part of her hand still visible. There was no jabbing pain, nothing to indicate the bones had been broken.

"While you were dreaming of goddesses with silver hair."

She peered out the window at the shadows creeping toward the west. They must've been in the room several hours. "Thank you, Meg."

Meg rose off the little chair beside the bed and faced Rori. "I don't pretend to know what it is you and Cian do, and honestly, I don't want to know. It's for the good of Faerie and that's enough for me." She scooted onto the bed and ran her fingertips across Rori's brow. "Your father was a good man. I used to treat him the same as I treat you now. Whatever is happening to Faerie, I have a feeling he's involved. Mairead, too."

"You think my father's alive?" Hunger, fatigue, and the potion Meg had given her churned her thoughts into spirals of anxiety and terror. If her father was still alive, where was he and why hadn't he tried to contact them?

"I don't want to give you false hope. They're just glimpses I saw in Acelyne's mind. Fragments of images." Meg took Rori's hands in her own and squeezed. "Wherever they are, they aren't in Faerie, this I know for sure. But Faerie's future depends on you finding them. You and Cian."

A sheen of sweat covered Rori's skin, chilling her in the warm room. An image of her father in chains somewhere dark and musty lodged itself into her mind and tears stung the backs of her eyes.

"In the forest, when she was dying, Acelyne said I was perfect. Do you know what she meant?"

"I'm sorry, lass, I do not."

Her accelerated heart rate burned away the last vestiges of Meg's potion and her thoughts came quickly, too quickly to process. Questions, plans, and actions all twisted together until she was too overwhelmed to focus. Yet a single thought stayed clear—the silver-haired woman said to trust Therron. That she needed his help.

Yet how he could help if her father wasn't in Faerie, she had no idea. It was riddles and conundrums. *Bloody flippin' hell.*

Rori's stomach gave a vicious growl, surprising both women.

"Before you do anything, I think a good meal is in order."

Pain shot from her toes to her nose when Meg slid off the bed and offered her hand to help Rori stand. Her ruined jeans hung limp as she tentatively put weight on her injured leg. Fresh waves of hellfire raced through her blood and Rori bit back a scream.

"Why does it hurt so much more now that you've stitched me up?"

"I put medicine inside the wound and it's seeping into your bloodstream. It'll pass."

Meg opened the door and there stood Tug and Therron, looking like two men expecting news of the worst sort. When they saw Rori, twin looks of relief swept over their faces. The care they displayed knocked her back a step. Meg steadied her, a fierce display of worry on her features.

"I'm fine, just recovering from the shock, I guess."

"I was serious, Rori. Take it slow. Let your body heal completely." To Therron, Meg said, "Whatever education she seeks at the Unseelie Court, make sure it isn't physically demanding. Her body has suffered enough."

Mortification, raw and pure, washed over Rori. She'd only meant to go to Midna's palace to learn to control her emotions, but the way everyone was behaving, they must all assume she meant to become an álainn obedience.

She was about to rebuke Meg when Therron answered mildly, "I'll make sure the queen is aware of her limitations." The fool man was grinning! And they called themselves her friends. Traitors, the both of them! Despite her better judgment, their amusement at her situation caused a stir in her heart.

Pretending otherwise, Rori brushed past both of them, ignoring the jolt of pain in her leg. Tug caught her and wrapped an arm around her waist for support. Thank goodness for Tug.

"Take me to the kitchen, please." Her request came out more breathless than she would've liked, but Tug didn't argue. He steered her to a large table set near Rowan's kitchen.

Once certain she was settled, he lumbered off to find her nourishment. Therron joined her on the right, and Meg on the left. The pair wore identical smirks. She would ignore them until she'd filled her belly and could think of an appropriate response to their plotting. Right now, her mind was a flurry of confusion, and not just from what Meg had said. She had to find Cian before he left and warn him that their dad might be alive. But should she? Would that alter the course of his assignment? Would it alter hers? She chewed the inside of her lip. If their father were alive and in the human realm, Cian would drop his mission and go looking for their dad. Hell, she was half tempted to screw her healing and go with him. After she ate, she'd seek out the queen for advice. But first—food.

Rori ate whatever they placed in front of her, neither caring what the food was, nor how it tasted. After the bizarre few days she'd had, she was grateful for a hot meal and company to share it with. Although, Tug wasn't eating much and Therron was too busy watching her to fill his own belly.

Spooning porridge into her mouth with a broken hand proved more difficult than she'd thought, but trying to feed herself with her left hand was like walking upside down while drunk. She could; it just didn't feel right. A dribble of wet oats stuck to her chin and after several attempts to lick it off, Therron reached over with a cloth and wiped her face. The words that came to her lips never left them, but irritation simmered in her thoughts. She was more than capable of taking care of herself— hadn't she been doing exactly that for over a decade? *They really must stop babying her.*

Two more bites of egg and she was stuffed. She couldn't possibly fit another morsel in her belly even if paid to do so. With a satisfied pat to her midsection, she pushed away from the table. A pair of strong hands gripped her shoulders, helping her stand. Rori was about to let the insults loose when she realized Therron hadn't stood, nor had Tug. Someone else had given her assistance. She turned to gaze up at her brother and immediately softened.

"Feeling better?"

The concern in Cian's eyes melted her ire. She missed him.

"Much, thank you."

"You missed a spot."

"If you wipe my face, I swear I'll dick punch you right here in front of everyone."

The wince he tried to hide made her giggle. She bent to wipe her face on the hem of her shirt and it was then she noticed he wore a dark wool traveling cloak. Unlike her, he always wore

Faerie clothes when home. Seeing him dressed for travel made her nerves tangle like a pot of noodles.

"You're leaving so soon? I thought you'd wait to hear what the necromancer had to say."

"I intended to, but that's your job now." He pressed his lips to her forehead and breathed deeply. "Please try not to get injured while I'm gone. Or kidnapped again."

Her chuckle was muted by his close proximity. "I'll do my best." She wrapped her arms around his waist and rested her cheek against his chest. "Be safe. I'll join you as soon as I can."

They'd never worked a mission together and the thought thrilled her. He was the best. She could learn much from him.

"Take the time you need to heal. For real, Rori. Meg told me of your injuries and limitations."

"And I suppose you told Midna?"

"I did. Trust me, you'll thank me later that I did."

Rori pulled away from Cian to read his features. "If you have any reservations about me going to Midna's palace, now's the time to voice them."

Several emotions flickered across his face, only one of which caused her concern: remorse.

❧ 3 ❧

Cian took in the cuts on Rori's face, noted the pain lingering in her eyes. He'd never doubted his sister's abilities. Far from it. He knew from a young age that she was a bigger badass than him and he'd quietly worked hard to prove to the world otherwise. The fact that everyone thought he was the more lethal of the pair was exactly the result he'd sought, but it came at the expense of outshining his sister. Even she bought into his superiority. She could take whatever Midna would give her—that wasn't what caused his gut to pinch.

He kept his gaze trained on her, ignoring the others in the room. Especially that blasted elf.

Her eyes were pools of trust. Love. Despite her best effort, the love she had for Cian shone clear. He could see it in the slight crinkles of worry at the corners of her eyes. Saw it in the way she tossed her hair as if challenging him, but kept her gaze just as focused on him as he was her.

"You know, I can change my mind and tell Eirlys I'll go to the human realm and you can return to the Unseelie Court."

Just as he knew she had to go to Midna's, he also knew she'd lose a part of herself from the training she'd receive. To be sure, it was sentimental to mourn that loss, Cian knew.

"I'll be fine, Rori. You know me." But something else lingered in her blue depths. "What aren't you telling me?"

"Nice deflection, brother mine. What's so terrible about Midna's court?"

"I have no qualms about you going to the Unseelie palace. You're an independent woman. You can do what you like. I just don't ever want to hear about it. Agreed?"

A furious blush stained her cheeks, but she kept a scowl firmly in place. "Like I'd tell you anyway. Besides, it's nothing you haven't done."

Now it was his turn to blush, but he hoped he kept his chagrin a little less obvious. Cian bent low to whisper in Rori's ear, "I never slept with Midna, nor anyone at her court." A slight gasp tickled his cheek. "Because I didn't need the education."

Rori whirled back and slapped his arm playfully. "You're incorrigible!"

"I know." He cocked an eyebrow and smirked at his sister with his best, most wicked grin. "I have to go soon. Take care of yourself, will you?" He brushed hair from her forehead and tucked the strand behind her ear. "Visit Mum. Wait until you've healed, but go see her."

"I will." A slice of indecision cut across her face, then she reached for his hand and squeezed it. "Cian, there's something you should know." She moved closer to whisper low, "Meg thinks Dad's alive. That he and Mairead are caught up with what's going on."

If not for his training, Cian might've staggered at his sister's words, but instead he remained upright, aloof. "Interesting. I'll have a chat with her before I leave. Anything else you think I should know?"

Confusion flicked across Rori's face. She still wore her emotions too easily. Yes, Midna's palace would be good for her.

The Academy could only train their agents so much; the rest of their education would come from life. Someday Rori would be hardened and able to school her features into a mask of indifference. For her sake, he hoped soon. Being vulnerable was only an option if it garnered information.

"Did you hear what I said? She thinks our father is alive. Not in Faerie, but the human realm. Don't you care?"

"Of course I care." He practically dragged her against his chest to crush her in a hug. "Tell no one what Meg said. If rumors spread about Dad being alive, just think how Mum will feel. She never got over the shock of losing him." Cian hoped that would subdue his sister.

"You're right. I wasn't thinking. Will you look for him?"

He kissed the top of her head, holding back his reasons for hating having to return to Edinburgh. "Absolutely. If he's alive, I'll find him."

"I'll join you soon. A few months, maybe?"

"Take your time to heal. And learn."

If she didn't learn to quiet her emotions, she'd never make it as a spy in the human realm. The missions Eirlys had sent Rori on so far were simple enough. He'd done all the research he could in Faerie. It was time to leave and uncover what he could in the human realm. What Cian saw coming was nothing short of gang warfare between Faerie and the humans, if his intel and Meg's predictions proved correct.

"I'll miss you, Scrapper."

"Yeah, well, try not to do anything stupid before I get there. And stop calling me that."

Cian kissed his sister's temple and motioned for Meg to join him. He left his sister in Tug's capable hands and followed Meg to a small alcove off the kitchen. He adjusted the heavy traveling cloak, the only article of clothing he wished he could trade for human apparel. Not that he minded wearing Faerie clothes when home. The one thing he insisted upon was that the clothes were comfortable—and he refused to wear anything but his bespoke human-made shoes. He understood Rori's affection for jeans and T-shirts, even if he didn't share her clothing aesthetic. Movability was key in their profession, but so was blending in—which was why Cian chose to wear Faerie kit at home. Another lesson Rori would need to learn.

Meg waited for him to speak, her features calm, her lips soft.

"Rori tells me you think our father is alive."

"As I told her, it was a fragment stolen from Acelyne's memory. I believe Mairead is in the human realm, and if your father is alive, he as well. Both have something to do with what's been happening in Faerie, but beyond that, I can't give you more. I'm sorry."

"Please don't mention this to anyone else."

"You have my word."

Cian touched the healer's cheek with his fingertips. "Mum misses you. Take Rori to see her, please."

Meg's eyes filled with tears and she nodded. He knew the mention of his mother would silence her from telling anyone else about his father. Without another word, he turned from the kitchen toward Rowan's study.

As much as he liked Rowan, the sorcerer's cottage held nothing for the spy. All he needed was the use of Rowan's doorway to the human realm. As far as Cian was aware, no other wizard or sorcerer in all of Faerie had their own personal doorway to other realms, but Rowan had made his with the permission of Faerie's rulers more than one hundred years earlier. The two present queens knew of his portal and kept surveillance on it, but didn't expressly condone or prohibit its usage. Even now, with Cian's assignment necessitating his arrival in the human realm with haste, the queens would pretend ignorance of Rowan's doorway.

They could be exasperating, his queens.

Well, what they didn't know wouldn't kill them. Cian took

the back stairs two at a time, hoping not to encounter anyone on his way to Rowan's study. His hopes were dashed at the landing when Therron's tall frame blocked his path. If Cian were a betting man, he would've put money down that the elf purposefully tried to catch him before he left.

"Excuse me." He did his best to sidle past, but Therron refused to move.

"A word, MacNair, if you please."

"Just one."

The elf's eyes narrowed and his lips twitched. With an unkind remark he wouldn't dare say, most likely.

"You don't have to like me, nor I you, but there is Rori to consider."

Cian wasn't sure if he wanted to laugh or punch the guy. "There's nothing for you to consider concerning my sister. Do everyone a favor—go back to Elvenwood and leave those of us who are truly concerned for Faerie alone."

"You think I don't care what happens to Faerie?"

They were of similar height and build, but Cian had no doubt he could best the thief in a fight. Verbal or physical. Still, he didn't have time to renew the familiar argument.

"I don't. Fortunately for you, I'm needed elsewhere." Cian shoved past the man, stopping when he'd crossed into the cramped hall. "If you want to convince me you care about our kingdom, you'll make sure nothing happens to Rori while she's at Midna's palace."

A slight tightening of the elf's jaw and flaring of his nostrils was the only sign Cian's words affected him. "What your sister does with the queen is of no concern to me."

Now it was Cian's turn to hide his feelings. This time, he was certain he wanted to punch the man. He looked Therron full in the face and dropped his voice low enough only the elf could hear. "We both know that's a lie."

The faint smell of perspiration reached Cian's nose. A rapid flutter at Therron's neck gave away the quickening of his heartbeat. His face remained unmoved, placid.

"I'm sure I don't understand."

Cian backed away, bowing as he did. The terror that crossed the elf's face was priceless.

"Does she know?" Therron challenged.

"Not that I've told her."

"I guess I should thank you for that." Therron stretched a hand toward Cian. "I'll keep Rori safe."

Cian grasped his hand in his own. "Yourself as well." He let go, but Therron tightened his grip.

"For what it's worth, I never bedded Midna nor any of her skivvies." A subtle challenge lingered in Therron's words.

"That's very honorable of you. Nor did I."

He turned away, chuckling to himself at the look of surprise on Therron's face. In truth, he was shocked the elf had been able to deny the Unseelie queen. She'd pursued him twice as hard as she had Cian. But then, Cian was merely a man with a long bloodline of spies and Therron was a prince. Still, Midna must be desperate for an heir if she was willing to risk the ire of the elf king to have a child.

Whatever the Unseelie queen's motives, Cian was happy his involvement with her would be delayed until he returned to Faerie. By then, he hoped the queen had moved on in her affections and found a suitable concubine. Her álainn obedience were much more than students, but few outside Midna's inner circle knew of the power generated from their lovemaking. Midna fed on the emotions evoked from her many lovers, and in return, her magic protected all of Faerie, including the kingdoms and villages that claimed no alliance with the fae. Cian called it sex magic, but it was so much more than that. And now Rori would be a part of Midna's ceremonies.

With each step he took toward Rowan's study, the further he forced thoughts of Midna, Eirlys, Therron, and even Rori far from his mind. His focus pinpointed to one thing—Edinburgh and finding Malcolm Dagniss.

As soon as the thought entered his mind, Cian remembered Rori's words about their father being alive. *Impossible.* Yet Meg had confirmed her belief, too. Rori didn't know that Cian had watched their father die. She'd been too young at the time to travel beyond Faerie and wasn't with Cian that day nearly fifteen years earlier.

His steps faltered. Rowan's study was a few more paces, but he couldn't bring himself to close the distance. Time slowed, then rewound to those last few precious moments when Cian was standing with his father atop the castle walls, looking out at the city that had utterly charmed him. The day was clear, with a crisp chill to the air Cian quite liked.

"I should like to live here one day," the teenaged Cian had told his dad. "Right there." He pointed to a Georgian building opposite the gardens. "So that every day I can look up and see the castle."

Hagan MacNair rested a hand upon his son's shoulder. "What? You've no desire to live at the castle?"

Cian shook his head and pointed to all the tourists. "There'd not be any privacy, I think."

It was then Cian saw the man. The one in shadow he could never fully make out, even in his nightmares. Hagan saw him, too.

"Son, go to the chapel and wait for me there. Go now. Don't argue."

Cian had wanted to stay by his father's side, but the look of calm in his eyes had falsely made Cian believe there was nothing to fear—despite his senses telling him the opposite. He obeyed and jogged up the slight incline to the chapel, but he didn't enter the small building. Instead, he turned to see the man in shadow raise his arms. A sharp cry from his father was the last he heard before a bright flash of orange burst from the shadows, knocking Hagan backward.

"No!" Cian cried out and ran down the stairs to his father.

Those standing nearest to the body shouted and total mayhem ensued. The shadow man disappeared into the crowd. Police with automatic weapons arrived and made a space between Hagen and the tourists. Cian ducked beneath their outstretched arms to kneel beside his dad.

The pall of death clung to his father. Someone tried to pry him away, but he told them to leave him alone, this was his father. A strong set of hands grabbed him and practically lifted him off Hagan. Cian watched in horror as men rushed to his father with their modern equipment of tubes and braces. Whoever had grabbed him kept them moving, up the little hill, toward the chapel. Cian fought against the progression. His father needed him.

The last he saw of Hagan MacNair was a blanket being pulled over his face. It wasn't until they were in the chapel that Cian turned to confront whoever had dragged him away.

"Forget something?"

Cian snapped his attention to the elf, to the hallway where they stood, to the present. Therron must've followed him.

"I, erm. No, I think I have all I need. You'll honor your promise?" He didn't need another assurance, but the elf's presence unnerved him.

"If I say I'll do something, I will. Don't try my patience, MacNair." Therron brushed past him toward the common room, where multiple conversations could be heard above the din of chair legs scraping the hardwood, dishes being washed, and life being lived.

Silently, Cian wished the man well. Knowing he hadn't slept with Midna raised his esteem greatly. For a solid month, he'd relegated the prince to something he wasn't and now—well, now he supposed he had no issues with Therron except for his connection to Rori. But that was something he could deal with another day.

A door opened just as the elf passed and Rowan glanced down the hall toward Cian. "Saying your farewells?"

"In a sense. Are you ready?"

Rowan waved him inside and closed the door behind them. A key turned in the lock and several bolts slid into place.

"One can never be too cautious." The sorcerer's genial smile barely hid the worry etched across his features. "Now then, where are we off to?" He clapped his hands and rubbed them together.

"Edinburgh."

The color faded from Rowan's rosy cheeks. "Are you sure, my boy?"

"I wish I wasn't, but yes. I need to start in Edinburgh."

Rowan blew out a long breath and nodded. "Of course, yes. Still," his whiskers vibrated with his trembling, "I never thought after I found you that day that I'd be the one facilitating your return."

Nor did Cian ever think after Rowan had taken him through the portal in the little chapel that he'd ever have need to go to Edinburgh. In fact, for fifteen years he'd avoided the entire city, making sure his assignments kept him far from Scotland.

"You never did tell me what you were doing there that day." A lump caught in Cian's throat. "The day my father was murdered."

Rowan indicated a small brass gong on his desk. Two leather straps held it suspended between a metal frame. "The queens aren't the only ones who keep watch over who comes and goes in Faerie. I knew your pa was taking you into the city and I kept watch over the pair of you, waiting for your return." He turned away from his desk and the gong. Tears shimmered in his old eyes. They had once been as blue as the night sky. Now they had the gauzy appearance of faded silk.

"Do they know? The queens?" Cian was curious how the

queens might feel about Rowan spying on those in the human realm.

"They know everything that happens in Faerie, don't you doubt that." Rowan tapped the bookcase where fifteen years earlier Cian had stumbled through with the sorcerer. "They allow me my hobbies as long as I remain neutral between the two courts." A wry smile lifted the lines of his face. The perpetual rosiness of his cheeks returned, a blush staining them several shades darker.

"I don't believe I ever thanked you. And I again owe you my gratitude." Cian clasped the man's hand in his own. Rowan hugged him with his free arm and patted his back. "Watch over my mum and sister, will you?"

"As I always do." His sigh was like a breeze through a meadow. "Alas, you and I both know neither of those ladies would appreciate being protected. Still, must needs and all that."

It was true. Labhruinn MacNair had once been Queen Eirlys's highest ranked officer. A warrior in a time of peace, but that hadn't stopped his mum from kicking ass in the training arena. Any man who thought Labhruinn weak because she was a woman soon learned different.

"I'll see you again soon, my friend." Cian turned to face the bookshelf and waited while Rowan said the mystical words that would turn the wall into a portal. This was one of the few doorways that Cian couldn't activate by himself. Three others existed that he knew about, with certainly more scattered throughout the universe. Someday, he vowed, he'd travel beyond Faerie and the human realm to another world, galaxies away.

But today he'd only go as far as his past.

❧ 4 ❧

The hairs on his arm stood on end as absolute blackness folded him into a claustrophobic embrace. Time didn't exist in this place. Nor, he feared, did life. No sound, no breeze, not even a whisper of existence could be found in the void of space. Cian kept his thoughts focused on the small chapel inside Edinburgh Castle's grounds. Some doorways led to a specific location on the other side, but Rowan's could be manipulated to anywhere. Lulled by the calm darkness, Cian cast back in his mind to that day long ago when his father was struck down by the shadow figure and immediately the void began to vibrate with his anxiety.

Never before had his mood affected the in-between and Cian jerked his thoughts to the present. To the little chapel. To his mission.

The shuddering stopped. The void was once more motionless. He had the distinct impression the void had wanted him to get lost in the memory. To drown in his sorrow, even. A listlessness settled upon him like a heavy cloak.

The tiniest of lights shone in front of him and he mentally grasped it. The brighter it became, the more his ennui departed.

By the time his shoes touched upon the rough stones of the chapel, he was left with a bitterness in his gut. In all his travels through the portals, he'd not once encountered anything—malevolent or otherwise. Yet this time, on his return to Edinburgh, he had the distinct impression that something had tried to stop him.

Never one to run in the face of adversity, he wouldn't let whatever force was working against him succeed—despite the fear creeping through the dark places of his heart.

Cian stood to his full height of two meters and stretched his shoulders, then cracked his neck. He needed precision thinking for this assignment, not willy-nilly concerns of the unseen. With a snap of his fingers, the velvet coat and black trousers he wore in Faerie disappeared, replaced by a sleek blue suit and crisp white shirt, a much better pairing to his black leather Oxford shoes. Just being in human clothes relieved some of the nerves swirling in his belly. If Earth had magic, he'd happily live among the humans full-time.

But magic was nearly dead on this planet. Which made it difficult to do his job, sometimes. As a rule, the use of magic was forbidden.

From the time Cian was a young lad, he'd heard horror stories of what happened to those unfortunate souls who had crossed the line in the human realm. Their fate wasn't just determined by the queens, but rumors swirled about humans who hunted magic in a vampiric way. Scyvers, they were called. Somehow, they were able to suck power from those who wielded magic. Cian believed in them with the ferocity of a witch her spells. That's why he kept magic use to as little as was needed—nothing more.

Having never met a scyver, and hoping he never would, Cian had no desire to become a target. The small amounts he used wouldn't alert Faerie's watchers—or the humans. He hoped.

He paused a moment to listen before taking the few steps to the chapel door. At this hour, there wouldn't be tourists lurking at the castle, but there would be armed guards. Rori had taught him the trick of using Glamour to confuse the cameras, which he was grateful for, but even fae magic couldn't prevent an attentive soldier from seeing a door open and close. He'd yet to learn how to float through something solid and until he sorted that trick, he'd have to use caution.

No untoward sounds came from the other side of the door. He cracked the ancient wooden panels enough to see into the small courtyard outside the chapel. A huge cannon sat perhaps three meters from where Cian was, its muzzle pointed at the city. At one time, that cannon and similar, smaller ones were used to defend Edinburgh Castle from invaders. Now they sat along the battlements as decoration of a time long past. This morning, the cannon known as Mons Meg was being used by a guard as a prop to keep him upright.

Cian stayed where he was, concealed by the chapel's shadows, and studied the man. He wiped his palms along his trousers and licked his lips. Stay calm. Stay cool. He could handle a single guard, as long as he didn't call for reinforcements.

After several minutes, he decided the guard was either sleeping or dead. He'd not moved at all. Cian flicked a finger at a spot just to the guard's left and the sound of a rock hitting the wall pinged in the quiet air. The guard remained motionless.

From his angle, Cian couldn't make out the man's features, only a partial glimpse of his chin and slack lips. The soldier stood in profile, half facing the city. His hat had slipped over his eyes, making it difficult to see if they were open or closed. A slight breeze lifted the edges of his kilt, but still no movement from the man. The browns and golds of the fabric blended into the dull greys of the castle walls. Mists shrouded the city beyond the battlements. Cian took in every detail surrounding the guard, from the lack of birdsong to the gloved hand resting atop the cannon, another at the man's waist where a heavy sword hung near to the ground. Thick socks stretched over his calves to well-worn leather shoes.

Warnings and red flags popped up in Cian's thoughts, urging more caution than usual.

He ran a hand through his hair and leaned against the cool stone of the chapel to process what he saw and what his intellect told him. Nothing good. The Seelie queen's guards were famed for being able to stand still for long periods of time, but this wasn't Faerie. Something wasn't right about the soldier. He couldn't pinpoint exactly what, but a nagging disquiet shadowed his thoughts.

His choices were clear—stay in the chapel until the guard left, leave the chapel and hope for the best, or use the doorway to go somewhere else.

Cian needed to find Malcolm Dagniss, and his last known address was located half a mile from where Cian stood. Using the doorway to travel elsewhere made little sense. As did waiting for the guard to leave. By his watch, he'd already wasted quarter of an hour and the sun was starting its ascent. If he wanted to best use the last vestiges of night, he needed to move now.

Cian pulled open the door and stepped into the bracing Scottish air. *Fucking Edinburgh.* It could be mind-numbingly cold year-round, but was especially so now, at the beginning of spring. Cian glanced at a nearby tree, at the tiny buds forming on otherwise naked branches. With a brief wave of his hand, a long wool coat covered his suit, with a thick scarf encircling his neck. Black leather gloves hugged his hands. Better.

Still, the guard didn't turn or acknowledge Cian.

Anxiety pooled in his gut as he took one, then another step toward the cannon, avoiding looking to his right, where fifteen years earlier he'd watched his father die. Instead, he ambled left, away from the guard and his memories.

The leather soles of his shoes made no sound on the cobblestones as he turned toward Foogs Gate. He kept one eye on the guard, alert to any movement he might make, and another on his surroundings. Sounds of soldiers waking and starting their day could be heard in the distance. He had to hurry or be caught where he ought not to be.

A movement at the peripheral of his vision halted his steps.

His heart rate increased; sounds became more acute. Cian turned his head to take in the guard who now stood facing him. He reached for a gun that wasn't there and spat a curse. This wasn't his usual entry point where he had weapons, ID, and money stashed. He'd have to make do with what he'd had in Faerie. He patted his inner pocket, relieved to feel the hard case of his mobile. As a rule, he didn't bring human possessions into Faerie, but his mobile, a passport, and a few quid were the exceptions. Unlike Rori, Cian never brought guns or knives into Faerie. Definitely not swords.

Cian stared harder at the man. Who the hell had a sword in the modern age?

It was then he noticed half the man's face was missing. A moment later, the ghostly image of complete facial features flickered into place, before disappearing once more.

Cian blinked like a fool, unsure what he'd just witnessed. The specter pointed to the stairs on his left, a stern glare in his dark, soulless eyes. Cian flicked a glance around him, at the shadows moving up the cobblestones, at the lights now visible in the guard's quarters. He dipped his head and touched his brow with two fingers in a thanks-filled salute to the ghost. The kilted guard did the same, a smile crooking up the damaged lips.

The eerie sight wormed its way into Cian's psyche with a nagging familiarity and he shook to rid himself of the image, yet it stayed. He sped down the road and turned left, away from Foogs Gate toward a set of stairs tucked into the hillside. Three steps before reaching them, a flash pulled his attention toward the spot where his father had been slain. Cian didn't want to look, tried to keep moving, but he couldn't *not* look.

The area was empty. Even the spirit of the guard had disappeared. Sounds softened into non-threatening morning noise. His body relaxed. His mind went fluid, with thoughts coming and going with no purpose. His heart rate lowered.

An image of a man rose from the cobblestones where his father had fallen.

Cian took a step forward. But the image was not of his dad. Instead, he faced the shadow man who had murdered Hagan MacNair.

A sword appeared in Cian's hand, its blade glowing orange, like the flames the shadow man had used fifteen years earlier. When he tried to release his grip on the sword, his fingers curled tighter around the hilt—someone was using magic to adhere the weapon to his hand and it wasn't Cian. Unable to lose the sword, he advanced on the man, ready to impale him with the fiery blade.

Cian's own heart had grown cold. In its icy depths, he knew he'd longed for this moment since that day his father had been slain. His thoughts echoed his heart, urging him to destroy the shadow man. Yet his training cautioned him from killing the man outright. He alone had answers to the questions Cian most wanted to ask. A battle raged within his mind whether he needed to know why or if he'd be better off ending the man's life.

With each step he took, the battle raged harder.

With each step he took, the shadow man faded.

The flames upon his sword licked his palm, singeing his skin. Pain was nothing new to Cian, but this was a curious stinging, as if he'd run his hand over nettles. He glanced at the blade, then to where the ghost guard had been standing. Emptiness surrounded him. There was no kilted guard, no shadow man, nothing. Just cobblestones and sky.

A slew of angry voices rose above the sound of his heart pumping.

"There he is! You there, drop the weapon." Footsteps followed the command.

Cian kept his back to the soldiers. The sword vanished, but the burns did not. Shouted orders came from behind and to his left. He was surrounded by a low wall, one of the castle's many fortifications. Beyond the wall was a road that semi-circled the whole of the area. Another wall, higher than this, was past the road. And beyond that were steep cliffs made of volcanic rock.

He was well and truly fucked. Unless he could get to the chapel and through the doorway. Cian chanced a quick glance at the small building, his heart dipping at the sight of ten soldiers, all with automatic weapons drawn, blocking the path.

Drawing a deep breath, Cian held his hands above his head in surrender and turned to his right. Several more soldiers held their guns targeted at his chest. Before he was fully facing them, he bolted over the low battlement.

$$\text{❋} \quad 5 \quad \text{❋}$$

The sound of gunfire rang out, followed closely by a sharp command to cease fire. Cian took the wall in an easy leap, hoping he hadn't misjudged what was on the other side. Fortunately, his memory hadn't failed him. Soft grass broke his fall and he scrambled down the sharp hill. More shouts, more commands, more footfalls came at him from all directions. He didn't like his choices, but being dragged into a cell wasn't on the agenda.

The next battlement was taller, but not unassailable. He used one of the many decorative cannons as a step and bounded to the top of the stone wall. Below him was a shallow road and another wall. Two more leaps and he'd be out of the castle grounds.

Cian felt the bullet before he heard the shot. A searing pain gripped his calf and he wobbled into a half tumble. He flailed mid-air, managing to land on his feet and tuck into a roll. He came to a sharp stop, his head hitting the cobblestones with a crack. Firecrackers and whizz sticks went off behind his closed eyes. Beyond the throbbing of his leg and objections of his body, the guards were still in pursuit. He thrust himself up from the ground and sprinted to the last wall, hoping there wasn't a fence on the other side.

Sharp crags that looked as though they'd make decent flesh shredders were a dozen feet below where he stood. The sound of soldiers clambering down the stairs and several car motors starting spurred him onward. He didn't have the luxury of time to sort out the best escape route. It would have to be the crags.

Sending a silent prayer of forgiveness to his queen, Cian surrounded himself with magic and sprang up to the top of the ancient stones. His injured leg thumped against the hard rock and, with a savage curse, Cian jerked his body over the wall. His magic kept him from slamming onto the crags, instead making the descent more of a slide than an outright plummet.

Gunfire sounded and a shot sizzled past his shoulder. He darted to his left and jumped an iron railing to scramble down a grassy slope covered with bright-yellow daffodils. The moment his feet hit the ground, he sprinted along a paved path to another slope. Losing his footing, he rolled through the blooms to the bottom of the hill. Chancing a quick glance above him, he saw several soldiers along the wall, waving others in Cian's direction.

The gunshot wound burned, but he had to keep moving. To his left, the pavement ended at the base of the castle rock. He knew that path, knew there was a secret passage halfway around, but also knew it would be difficult to reach with the guards chasing him. To his right stretched a long walkway through the gardens, but that was most likely where he'd get caught by the guards in vehicles.

With valuable seconds ticking by, he took off at a dead run straight ahead across the bridge and toward the West End, where a cemetery and church would provide him much-needed cover until the soldiers thought him gone. The gardens remained shadowed by the hulking castle, giving him even more camouflage. He ran as fast as his injured leg would allow, staying as close to the edge of the path as he could. The few people he came across paid him little attention. They were too absorbed in their own lives to care about a businessman jogging through the park.

At the church entrance, Cian slowed to a walk. He scanned the area for approaching policemen or soldiers and saw neither. The vault he needed was tucked into the corner just to his left, in an unkempt, ancient part of the churchyard often overlooked. He limped across several broken headstones to the structure he sought. A wooden door with scrolled iron workings popped open at his touch. Above the door, barely legible after so many centuries, was the family name of MacNair.

Cian closed the door behind him and took a deep breath of the musty air. The crypt hadn't been used in at least two hundred years, nor did Cian suppose anyone had entered the space in all that time. A thick layer of dust covered a marble sepulcher that held the bones of the human ancestors who shared more than their name with his family. He placed a hand upon the cool stone and said a fae prayer for their souls.

Outside the structure, voices rose and lowered as they searched the premises. Static sounds came across their radios, all easily heard by Cian where he hid. The search on Princes Street turned up nothing. Nor did the area next to the train tracks, where Cian had considered running. Blood was found on the pavement, but it was inconclusive whether the blood in question was his.

Cian glanced at his leg, where a rip in his trousers showed a glistening dark circle. Fae blood couldn't be traced through their sophisticated computers and labs. Because he'd only been in the human realm a short time, any drops he left behind would turn to nothing more than a shimmering of dust within minutes, but that didn't mean he could be careless. If he stayed too long with the humans, his blood would lose its evaporative quality.

He loosened his tie from around his neck and propped his leg upon the marble. The bullet had only grazed his flesh, leaving an inch-long divot mid-calf. Cian wound the tie around his leg, securing it with a tight knot. The binding eased some of the pain, making it more comfortable to stand. He tucked the tie into itself and pulled his pant leg over the temporary bandage.

He returned to the door and pressed his ear against the wood. His hearing went beyond the churchyard to the busy streets, where buses and cars mixed with the sounds of businesses opening and people going about their morning. The day had yet to wipe away the sleepiness of night and slowly came to life.

Of police or radios, he heard nothing.

For the moment he was safe, but he hadn't garnered the position of Queen Eirlys's number-one spy by being hasty. Cian slid down the wall and settled against the cold stone, his chin resting against his chest. The cramped space didn't allow for much movement, nor could he stretch out his injured leg. At some point he'd need to get proper supplies—but first he had to get past the guards looking for him.

A male voice caught his attention and he straightened, his ear against the oak.

"Mornin', Officer. Seems a lot of activity around here today. Are we expectin' a visit from the queen?"

"Thankfully, no. Just a spot of trouble up at the castle."

"Anyone in particular I should keep watch for?"

The hairs on Cian's arm rose and his senses went on full alert.

"Be aware of who you pass and if you see anything suspicious, let us know."

"Will do, sir. You have a good day now."

The sound of footsteps faded in the direction of the castle. After several moments, Cian heard the shuffle of someone walking across the uneven churchyard. They approached the crypt where he hid, paused for a long moment—during which Cian didn't breathe—then moved off in the opposite direction. His chest lowered with the exhale of air.

A scyver. He'd hoped the magic he had to use to escape from the castle would've slipped under the radar, but he'd bet all of

Queen Eirlys's treasure room the man was one of the humans who hunted magical creatures. If so, it also meant he'd probably alerted those in Faerie who kept track of such things. Bollocks.

His morning was off to a brilliant start.

He'd have to be more careful going forward. If one scyver was looking for him, there would be others.

For the next ten minutes, he stayed in the cold box, listening, waiting. When the only sounds he heard were of hurried footsteps and joggers, he slowly opened the crypt door and peered through the shadows to the corners of the cemetery. Seeing nothing to alarm him, he sidled between the wood and stone, using the structure as much as he could to conceal himself. From where he stood, he had two exits from the churchyard, both leading to busy streets.

The left provided slightly more cover with trees on either side of the path. Instead of ducking behind headstones and using the wall to hide him, he stepped out into full view and strolled toward the walkway, keeping his gaze roving to either side. Several people passed him, most dressed as if on their way to work. A few were tourists. What Cian needed now was to find a crowded area where he could lose the traces of magic clinging to him.

At the top of the pathway, he pivoted right to cross a busy intersection. Buses and cars sped past, oblivious of the wounded fae. More people were on the sidewalks here, but not enough for his purposes. Across the road, he spotted a coffee shop with several people crammed inside. Perfect.

Constantly checking his surroundings, he strolled across the street and casually entered the shop, where immediately he was hit with smells of coffee beans, sweat, and perfume. Fae weren't as keen as elves at sight or hearing, but their olfactory senses matched, if not topped, the elves' ability. It was a blessing and a curse. This morning, Cian put the gift squarely in the curse category.

A young woman, wrapped up as though she were in the Antarctic, bounced on the balls of her feet, gum snapping in her mouth. Every few seconds, she would glance at the man behind the counter, then to the door. A tall gentleman, wrapped up much the same as the woman, wandered in and joined her. Cian eavesdropped on their conversation to pass the time. He removed his coat and surreptitiously rubbed it against the young couple's jackets. Like a lion marking his territory, he tried to put as much of his scent on the pair as he could.

Another man entered the shop behind Cian, and he resisted the urge to turn around and get a look at him. Without hearing his voice, Cian had no idea if this was the scyver from the graveyard. He shifted the coat to his left arm and checked his inner pocket for cash. Twenty pounds. It wasn't much, but it would do for now. He scanned the other customers waiting in line. Two businessmen chatted about a deal they needed to make that morning. A teenager tapped on her phone, white earbuds poking out of her ears.

"Nikala, coffee black."

Cian glanced at the woman who retrieved a large cup from the counter. Long, pale fingers grasped the paper. A white cuff protruded from the sleeve of her dark coat. His gaze traveled up her arm to a slender neck, elongated by her blonde hair pulled into a ponytail. She turned then, and startling blue eyes met his. Not light or deep blue, more cerulean, like an evening sky just past sunset.

A slight narrowing of those gorgeous orbs was his warning that he should pull his stare from her, but her eyes mesmerized him. He offered a weak smile as a consolation, which was met with lips thinned to a dangerous line. A final swish of her ponytail was the last he saw of the woman. The temptation to turn after her was great, but he refrained and stepped forward with the group waiting to order.

For several minutes, his heart beat a rapid staccato in his

chest. Something about the woman intrigued him, and it was more than her eyes. Perhaps it was the way she walked with authority, or the dare he saw hidden in her features. She was definitely a woman to be reckoned with, and that more than anything excited Cian.

The woman was a distraction he didn't need. Difficult as it was, he shuttled her from his thoughts and focused on why he was in the coffee shop. Not for coffee, and not for a hookup, that was damn sure.

A phone rang and the man behind him answered, his voice low and gruff. Not the same as the scyver. Cian breathed a short sigh of relief, but didn't let his cautiousness fully relax. As the man spoke, he gesticulated several times, nudging Cian in the back. After the third jab, he turned around and froze at the sight of a policeman's hat. His bright-yellow hi-vis safety vest was in sharp contrast to the black uniform he wore.

The man nodded to Cian without any sign of recognition. He smiled and nodded in return before turning his back on the officer. Leaving now would look suspicious, so he remained in line until it was his turn to order. As he'd expected, the coffee and muffin took up almost half of his twenty pounds. He'd need cash sooner rather than later.

As he waited for his order, he ran through a list of known safe houses in Edinburgh. One he recalled was a few blocks from the coffee shop; another, several miles to the south. He hadn't been in the city for years, but if memory served, SIRE's offices weren't far from where he was. He mentally blocked the distance from the coffee shop to the flat on Rose Street and back to the West End.

That would take half an hour, at least. He didn't have time or the patience to track down the safe house. He'd have to improvise.

The clerk handed him his coffee and a bag containing his muffin. The policeman ambled over, phone in hand, attention diverted. A businessman about the same height and build as Cian headed toward them, eyes also on his phone. Cian calculated his risk, set the coffee and muffin on an empty table, and made his move.

He swerved slightly toward the businessman, who overcompensated by veering into the policeman. Looking as though he were reaching to help the first man, Cian reached inside his coat pocket to pluck out his wallet. The pair wobbled, muttering apologies and straightening themselves while Cian pocketed the wallet, grabbed his coffee and muffin, then casually circled around to exit the coffee shop.

In all, it took less than a few seconds and he was out the door with the men none the wiser.

On the street, he made a sharp right and strode down Princes Street toward the busy intersection, losing himself in the crowd. He walked quickly for the next several blocks, but not fast enough to draw attention to himself. Crowds of people now filled the sidewalks on either side of the street, a mix of tourists and city dwellers making their way to work. He ate the muffin in two bites, followed by a long swig of coffee before he tossed the remnants in a bin. As much as he appreciated coffee, he didn't need his nerves frayed now that he was this close to Malcolm Dagniss.

The headquarters for SIRE Unlimited were in a posh Georgian townhouse located in one of the wealthier areas of Edinburgh. No sign on the door indicated which floor housed the company, nor was there a directory to help him find the exact office. From his research, however, he knew Malcolm was on the top floor, near the northeast corner. An elderly lady was exiting when Cian approached and he held the door open for her. She trundled down the steps, thanking him along the way. When she was safely on the walkway, he pushed open the door and headed for the lift.

On a good day, he'd take the stairs, but today his leg required a bit of care. The lift pinged his arrival at the fifth floor and Cian slipped his tie from around his leg and dusted it off before inspecting the damage he'd done to the fabric. Deciding it wasn't up to snuff, he shoved it in his pocket and took out the mobile phone, switched it off, and returned it to his pocket. The empty hallway was quiet as he padded down the narrow patch of carpet. Doors on either side bore the names of workers and companies Cian cared nothing for—his focus was on the last door to the left. There, he had business.

As he approached, his steps slowed. The door was ajar, and a female spoke within. Cian paused—his free hand rested on the doorknob, ready.

"I don't care, Malcolm. Look, if it's that important to you, why don't you come up here and hunt her down? I've waited two days and she hasn't shown. I'm not your fucking babysitter."

Silence, followed by the sound of drawers banging.

"Yes, I understand how important this shipment is. I get it, all right?" A long pause, then, "Fine. Yes, I'll take the next train to London. What? No, I didn't buy a plane ticket because I thought I'd have the shipment and you know how fragile it is. I couldn't trust the airlines not to break anything."

Cian listened, a curious smile touching his lips. Whoever this woman was, she definitely didn't fear Malcolm.

"Yeah, okay. I said okay. Geez, take a pill, Malcolm. You'll give yourself a coronary. Yeah, will do. Bye."

Cian couldn't help himself from peeking inside, where he saw her toss the phone on the desk. Her hands went to her face and a long, heavy sigh came from delightfully pink lips.

"Motherfucker. He's going to blame me for this."

A slight tremble entered her voice and Cian wondered if perhaps he'd misjudged her. Maybe she did fear Malcolm.

"This is not good." Her hands pushed back over her blonde ponytail and Cian was left staring at the most remarkable set of cerulean blue eyes.

The urge to hold her in his arms and protect her from whatever it was that upset her overwhelmed him. Dormant passion, something he prided himself on controlling, woke and flared through his veins. His hand trembled on the doorknob and he tucked it into his pocket. Something terrible wrapped itself around his heart. Not fear; that would've been a blessing. Something far more dangerous—clarity that this woman, this stranger, was someone he could love.

He was so screwed.

❧   6   ❧

Nikala St. James stared at the man in the doorway. Something about him tugged at her memory. That ridiculous blue suit and that smug smile—of course, it was the man from the coffee shop. She glanced at his empty hand, the only one she could see; the other was tucked into his pocket, where she hoped he didn't hold a pistol. Guns weren't her thing. Never had been, and in truth, terrified the snot out of her.

"Can I help you?" She didn't need this right now. She was in Edinburgh to meet a dealer, but she hadn't shown. Nikala gave the man a once-over with renewed interest. Perhaps he was the seller's proxy. Usually Malcolm made the buys, but he was tied up in London at the moment and had sent her to complete the deal. The last she'd heard, the dealer was a woman and this man clearly didn't fit the description. Plus, Malcolm hadn't said there would be a proxy.

"I have an appointment with Mr. Dagniss. We were to meet in," the man checked his watch, "five minutes."

An obvious lie, but Nikala would let it slide. "I'm sorry, but Mr. Dagniss is out of town on business. His receptionist should've called to reschedule."

He was handsome, this interloper to Malcolm's offices, but she'd long ago stopped letting pretty men intimidate her. He wore his dark hair not too short, nor too long, but styled away from his face. The suit, of a color that was neither light nor dark, but shy of denim, did not wear him—he definitely wore it. Her gaze roved over his body, noting not just the suspiciously bulging pocket, but the ripped pant leg and, she squinted to make sure she wasn't mistaken, gold flecks. Sort of glittery dust. What a strange man.

The way he leaned to his left slightly made her think he might have an injury where the trousers were torn. Definitely an intriguing, unusual man. And possibly her contact. Malcolm wasn't always as detail-oriented as he should be. It wasn't a stretch to think he might've gotten some specifics about the dealer and/or proxy wrong. Yet, mistaking a handsome man for a woman was quite a leap, even for Malcolm. Never mind the fact she'd just gotten off the phone with him and he hadn't mentioned someone else showing up with the product.

Several curse words tumbled through her thoughts. The dealer might be stalling to get a better price. It didn't happen often—especially not to Malcolm—but it did happen. She softened her face to appear more inviting. Contact or not, she needed him to feel comfortable in her presence.

"To be honest, I could have the wrong day. My phone died and," he tapped his temple, "I'm relying on memory, which isn't always a good idea."

"Perhaps it's not. Who shall I tell Mr. Dagniss came to see him?"

The man's eyes narrowed and he took in her appearance, the same as she'd done to him. Idly, she wondered what he thought of her, but not enough to give it any further concern. What he thought, or didn't think, wasn't important. Getting him out of Malcolm's office was. Unless he was the seller. Although, the longer he stood there, the firmer her belief became that he wasn't.

Not only didn't he fit the brief description Malcolm had given her, he didn't have the merchandise.

"Cian MacNair."

Lord, but the way he said his name, pronounced "Keeyun" with a delectable accent—Highlands, maybe?—made her want to lick every syllable. She bit the inside of her cheek to keep from letting the thought amble where it ought never trespass.

"I'm down from Aberdeen for a few days and would appreciate a reschedule."

Aberdeen. Fuck. It might be a coincidence, but she didn't believe in happenstance. "Assuming you had the date wrong." Nikala raised an eyebrow for emphasis, which he ignored.

"Of course."

He finished his roving of her face and body, a smirk firmly planted on those oh-so-kissable lips. That was it. She'd had enough of the stranger distracting her.

"Well." She stepped out from behind the desk and crossed her arms, then uncrossed them. "It was a pleasure to meet you, Mr. MacNair. I'll let Mr. Dagniss know you're available. Can I tell him the purpose of your visit?"

"I wish to discuss Acelyne."

If she wasn't mistaken, he'd said the name with a certain inflection. To test her, perhaps, but the name meant nothing to her.

"I'll let him know. Good day, Mr. MacNair." She held the door for him with a soft smile. The kind she used to get men to do what she wanted.

Cian MacNair was having none of it. The smile he returned was equally as fake.

"Good day, Miss…?"

"St. James."

This time his smile was genuine, and full of cockiness. Fuck. By omitting her first name, he probably took it as a silent challenge.

"Nikala St. James." Better to just give it to him than play all the games.

His hand gripped hers and, swear to the gods above, an electric current ran the length of her arm straight to the apex of her legs. She snapped her hand away, desperately wanting to wipe it on her pants, but refused to give him the satisfaction.

The smirk was gone from his smile, replaced with a look of confusion. A moment later, it disappeared and his confidence returned.

"I hope we meet again. Soon." He left the office and she was tempted to make certain he wasn't lingering outside. When the lift pinged, she waited to the count of five before popping her head through the doorway. At the sight of the empty hallway, she exhaled the breath she'd been holding.

Whoever Cian MacFuckingNair was, he was Dangerous. With a capital *D*. And what Nikala didn't need right now was more danger.

She closed the door behind her and made sure she locked both locks before she returned to her search of Malcolm's files. Thus far, after two days of searching, she'd found nothing on the Dawn Project and was beginning to think she'd misheard. To be fair, she *had* been eavesdropping at the time, and there *was* a wall between her and Malcolm, but she'd been so certain he'd been discussing something called the Dawn Project.

Whatever it was, Malcolm was keeping it secret from her, and Nikala hated secrets. Especially when they were meant to keep her in the dark. No matter. This was simply a new challenge she would conquer.

But not in Edinburgh. She slammed the final cabinet drawer closed and huffed several choice words. She'd been sure the files would be in this office. The fact that they weren't—and Malcolm's mysterious trips to London, not to mention all the time he'd been spending down south—added up to a sum Nikala didn't like.

Malcolm was moving the entire operation to London. Which meant she was fucked.

He was in London.

Despite herself, a shiver tracked its way from the base of her skull to the divot above her ass.

Hunter Pearson.

The one man in all the world she'd gladly kill, but the only person Malcolm strictly forbade her from harming. It was all kinds of fucked up. But then, when had her life been anything but?

With controlled force, she punched a hand into the desktop, enjoying the snap of flesh hitting wood. Another blow and she let the anger recede. Her fist glowed an angry red and showed several cuts where splinters tore her flesh. She smoothed her good hand over the damage and watched, fascinated, as the skin knit back together, the redness paled. In a matter of minutes, broken bones would be healed, all evidence of injury vanished. Damaging the desk was her only regret.

She blew out a long breath and arched, smoothing her hair away from her face as she did. Hunter was a part of her life, always had been. She'd have to make peace with that at some point. It didn't matter that she'd spent the better part of the last two years traveling anywhere, especially the grimiest, loneliest places, just to avoid him. She resisted the memories of faceless men she bedded to excise demons of her own making. The days and nights spent in a haze of pity and rage. Nothing—not drugs or alcohol or mindless fucking—could erase what she'd endured. She'd sworn off drugs and sex, replacing those addictions with a cruel focus on her skills as an assassin.

As long as Malcolm continued to do business with the sadist, Nikala had to tolerate his presence.

She straightened and another shiver raced across her skin. Unconsciously, she gripped the amulet she wore, her thumb stroking over the smooth glass.

"You lived through his hell. He can't ever touch you again." The words, spoken out loud, did nothing to reassure her nerves. Malcolm had no idea what she'd been through. Even if she told him, she doubted he'd believe her. Fucking men and their code of honor.

Or maybe Malcolm knew and that's why he'd given her to Hunter when she was eight years old. Although, Malcolm preferred to see it as he'd placed her in Hunter's care to be raised as a respectable lady while he built his empire.

A quiver started low, down where she'd avowed no man would ever touch her again. Not that Hunter had ever touched her sexually, oh no. That was all her own fucked-up fantasizing and wrong on so many levels she couldn't keep count. It was desire and fear and guilt and hatred knotted together and she was helpless to stop it. Just thinking about Hunter brought about feelings she'd tried to bury for most of her life.

If not for Malcolm— She stopped the thought. Hunter Pearson would be a burr she'd have to deal with forever. No matter how many times she imagined his death.

Her phone beeped and she pushed the bubbling emotions to the far corners of her mind. Some day. One day. But not today.

Surprised to see the pendant clasped in her palm, she tucked it between her breasts, where it had been since she'd stolen it from Malcolm two months ago. A wry smile spread across her face. Not even the pretty little amulet could lift her spirits. With a sigh, she collected her coat and bag, the one she'd had packed and ready, but now was half empty because her contact never showed. Whatever. Let Malcolm sort it out. She had other business to attend to, and it didn't involve being his personal mule.

Gods, but she wanted to change out of the starched white shirt and dress pants she wore, but she'd play—and look—the part of being a good SIRE employee for a little while. This farce as a businesswoman didn't suit her personal tastes, and the clothes were a little too confining. Once she arrived in London and pacified Malcolm, she could slip back into her jeans and T-shirt. Maybe seeing her dressed up might keep him from totally losing his shit. Doubtful though she was, one could always hope.

After making certain the office was secure, she hurried out of the building. The train station was only a mile away, less than a twenty-minute walk, which gave her ten minutes to buy her ticket. Plenty of time. It was one of the things she loved most about Edinburgh—the village feel of a big city. Nothing was entirely too far away and on a nice day, she could walk a good part of the city. By habit, she swept her surroundings with a quick surveillance. That man, Cian, lounged against a building across the street. She'd half expected to see him, but it was another gentleman, several meters from where Cian stood, who made her senses sparkle and snap.

She'd seen him before, this oddly dressed fellow. The long brown oil coat he wore didn't fit with his tweed jacket and trousers. He looked like two different people had dressed him—a professor and a sheep herder. Her glance took in his shoes. Neither work boots nor Oxfords, but hybrid hiking trainers. She shook her head with a giggle. If he was trying to blend in, he needed a refresher course on spying.

But why would someone be spying on her? Her right hand went to her cleavage. If Malcolm knew she'd stolen the amulet, he might be cross with her, and rightly so. And it might give him the impression she wasn't to be trusted. Again, rightly so. But to send an oaf to take her out? That didn't sound like Malcolm. No, if he wanted her watched or eliminated, he'd send someone slicker. She hurried up the street and caught her reflection in the window of a shop.

He'd send someone like Cian MacNair.

She quickened her pace and strode past the gardens, with the castle watching over her to the right. As castles went, it was hunched and ugly, but Nikala loved everything about her castle.

Especially the little chapel on the hill. Something about the place gave her comfort and she often retreated there to find solace.

As much as she could use the peace, a visit was not in the cards for today. She was headed to London, where she'd have to console the irate head of SIRE. Seriously, if the shipment was that important to him, he damn well should've been the one to meet the seller.

It didn't matter. She knew somehow Malcolm would blame her for the buyer not showing. Why she stayed at the company, she had no idea.

Loyalty. A sense of family. Love. All those misguided ideals she'd been instilled with—and desperately believed in—long before Malcolm had traded her to Hunter. Had traded *her*, for SIRE. Whatever. She was a grown woman who could do whatever she wanted. She didn't need SIRE or Hunter or Malcolm. She could make it on her own.

How many times had she had the same conversation with herself? How many times had she promised the woman in the mirror that she'd leave? She'd live somewhere remote, where neither man's spies could find her. She'd tried that and yet, here she was, hurrying to catch a train with not one, but two strange men tracking her every move.

All this fuss over a pendant. Why? Why had she taken it? "Because it spoke to her" was about as naïve a reason as she could think of. Yet that's what had happened. As soon as she spied it in Malcolm's safe, she needed to have it. Needed to possess it. Needed to wear it against her skin and feel its soothing warmth. In a very real way, it *had* spoken to her soul.

Yeah, that was going to go over well with Malcolm. Hopefully he wouldn't confront her about the amulet, but if he did, she'd have to improvise and hope he didn't shoot her on the spot. Above all else, Malcolm demanded loyalty—the same blessing and curse that kept her tethered to a man who should've protected her, not sold her out.

Nikala swung right at the stairs leading to the train station and cast a glance over her shoulder. Yep, there they were—Cian MacFuckingNair and the odd fellow. It was hard to tell, but she thought he might be following Cian, and not her. Or, most likely, they worked together. Malcolm had probably sent both men. When the odd fellow had failed, he sent backup—a cleaner. She grimaced at how much that would've cost him.

Fine. If that's the way they wanted to play, she would beat them at their own game.

Cian kept the swinging blonde ponytail in his vision as best he could as he ducked and weaved around the tourists along Princes Street. He knew where she was headed but had to make certain he boarded the same train. If she was meeting Malcolm, he needed to know where the man was and London was a big city.

He pivoted to avoid a pram and jogged around a cluster of teens waiting for their bus. The scyver kept pace with him, staying a respectable thirty feet behind. Cian had hoped he'd lost the man in the coffee shop, and when he'd left SIRE's building, the damned man was nowhere to be seen. However, his false hope was dashed as soon as Nikala emerged from the front doors and skipped down the steps.

Cian spotted the scyver sniffing around the street and when the pretty woman headed toward Waverley Station, the scyver gave her a long once-over that made Cian's insides turn. It was like watching a serial killer choose his next victim. Nikala had no idea she'd been marked, and it was his fault. When they shook hands, he must've transferred some of his magic to her.

As she rounded a corner, the scyver wavered a moment before

following. Cian hurried across the street to put himself between the woman and the magic hunter. If the scyver wanted a fight— he'd make sure she wasn't involved.

He took the stairs two at a time, dodging suitcases and sleepy travelers along the way. As he passed the board listing train times, he noted which one left next for London King's Cross. Nikala was already at the kiosk purchasing her ticket when he reached the ground floor.

Cian casually strolled past where she stood with her back to him and went inside the booking office to buy his ticket. During his wait for her to leave SIRE's office, he'd rummaged through the wallet he'd stolen from the businessman in the coffee shop and found £400, several credit cards, bank cards for two different banks, and an unused condom. No family photos, no store loyalty cards. A fact he found most curious. Cian had taken the cash and bank cards, then dropped the wallet into a post box. It eased his conscience to think of himself as an assassin and spy, not a completely heartless thief.

The next available train was leaving in approximately six minutes, which didn't give him a lot of time to debate between standard fare or first class. Cian glanced toward the trains, imagining a woman like Nikala St. James didn't often travel less than first class. The persona he'd created in his mind for her involved a lot of expensive things, but he had the sense she didn't need them as status symbols. She wore nice clothes and the only jewelry he noticed was a diamond solitaire on her right ring finger. But did the persona he created fit the actual woman?

She was a mystery, he had to admit. Her manner spoke of confidence, but there had been several moments when they'd talked that he detected an unbalancing within her.

He pressed the screen for a first-class ticket and entered the required payment amount. He'd find out soon enough if his suspicions about the woman were unfounded. On his way to the platform, he saw the scyver pacing near the kiosks. When he spotted Cian, his entire body shifted. A veil of fanaticism covered his features and Cian quickened his step. The man would need to be dealt with, but not in a crowded train station with only minutes remaining before his train departed.

With any luck, the man would be stranded in Edinburgh without his prize.

Luck, it seemed, was not on Cian's side this day. His train sat on a platform that didn't require a ticket for entry. As he stepped up into his coach, he saw the scyver board several carriages down. His mind spun into action, formulating several viable options for dealing with the menace. As a rule, he tended to only kill people when absolutely necessary, and not in broad daylight with witnesses. Definitely not on a train where the body would be found before the end of the trip. This would take planning and forethought.

At the other end of the nearly empty carriage, he spotted a familiar blonde ponytail. He found a seat several behind Nikala and stretched his aching leg. From where he sat, he could see her slim fingers wrapped around a mobile phone. Her thumb lazily scrolled up as she checked messages or email or something he couldn't quite see.

An attendant stopped by his seat and asked if he'd like breakfast. The growl his stomach gave indicated his desire and she gave him a knowing smile.

"You businessmen are all the same. Too rushed in the morning to get a proper meal. We'll get you sorted." She left to ask the seat behind him about breakfast.

Nikala turned to look his way, her eyes hardening when she saw him reclining into his seat. A mix of emotions crossed her face and she snapped her attention to the window, where Edinburgh slowly passed by.

The train attendant swished past, her ass making a jaunty tilt in his direction. At the carriage separator, Cian saw the scyver approach, with a mean glint to his eye. Cian straightened, all senses on alert. His magic coursed through his body in a tempest, waiting to be unleashed. With as much calm as he could muster, he tamped his desire to smother this man with magic. Kill him with the very thing he hunted.

Before Cian could stand, the scyver bellowed at the attendant to get out of his way. Without warning, he lashed out, his fist striking the pretty lady across her temple.

Cian was on his feet and rushing to the woman even before her cry had finished its agonizing crescendo. Nikala sprang forward, too. They pushed through the cramped space to the glass door separating the carriages. The scyver wavered, as if unsure what to do with the injured woman who blocked his path. Cian took advantage of his confusion and leapt past Nikala to tackle the man. Others arrived, train employees as well as two passengers.

The scyver's face bled where Cian had smashed his nose on the floor, and he fought against Cian's grip on his wrists. One of the passengers held the man's legs while one of the train attendants took Cian's place of holding the man face-down while another attendant attached plastic zip ties to the scyver's wrists. As they lifted him up, Nikala, who had been seeing to the battered attendant, reached out toward his leg. It was done quick, without anyone but Cian noticing. A moment later, she was crouched beside the stricken woman.

It happened so fast, Cian might've doubted what he saw, but he'd been trained to notice the smallest details. Nikala St. James became even more curious and he was determined to find out everything he could about the mysterious, complicated woman.

The male attendants took the scyver to the other end of the carriage and sat him in a seat facing away from them. They helped the attendant to stand and Cian spied a small gash at her temple that trickled blood to her cheek.

"Do you have a first-aid kit?" Nikala studied the cut while visually inspecting the rest of the attendant's face.

"In there." The woman motioned to a cupboard.

Cian retrieved the little bag and handed it to Nikala.

"I can do this on my own, thanks." The attendant's once rosy cheeks looked like chalk.

"Shush. You take care of others all day. Just relax and let me see to your injuries." Nikala rummaged through the kit and made tsking sounds.

Once again Nikala surprised Cian. He'd not slotted her for a mum or even nurturing, yet here she was, comforting the attendant and assessing her wounds.

"You hit the cabinet pretty hard. Are you sore anywhere else?" Cian asked, genuinely concerned.

Nikala glanced at him with a cheeky grin. "Are you trying to steal my patient?"

"Oh, you're doctors." The attendant breathed a grateful sigh.

Neither Nikala nor Cian contradicted the woman. Instead, they shared a conspiratorial look while Nikala cleaned the woman's cut and dressed it with several Steri-Strips.

"You'll have a whopper of a headache, but soon you'll be right as rain."

"Thank you. Both of you." The attendant gingerly touched the plasters on her temple.

Another employee arrived and asked after the injured woman. She graciously thanked Nikala and Cian again before retreating to the bathroom.

"Crazy morning. Must be the weather's changing. But why would he attack Lucy like that?" The train attendant scratched at his beard, a confounded expression on his face.

"Drugs, most likely," Cian suggested. "They do things to a person's mind. Makes them not right, if you know what I mean."

"Yeah, must be." The fellow rapped on the bathroom door. "You take your time, Luce. I'll cover your carriage."

A muffled thanks came through the partition.

Cian headed back to his seat, his mind spinning. He didn't

think the scyver would admit to hunting a magical being, but if he did, Cian would need a ready excuse. Drugs would work for that, too, but unless they actually found drugs in the man's system, the authorities might ask uncomfortable questions.

"Join me, please." Nikala stood by her seat, her hand outstretched in greeting. "I feel I owe you a debt of gratitude."

She owed *him* a debt? This day was getting more interesting by the moment.

"I'd love to." He grabbed his coat and placed it alongside her belongings on the rack above their seats. She slid across the leather to settle beside the window and he sat opposite. A table kept them at a respectable distance, and for a moment Cian wished there was no table, no space between them. He watched her fingers toy with a strand of hair that had escaped the bound ponytail. The scent of sweat drifted to him. Deodorant, shampoo, and soap mingled with the smell, but couldn't disguise her nervousness.

"Here. See to your leg." She pushed the first-aid kit across the table.

"My—?" Then he remembered the gunshot wound from that morning. "Oh, right. A dog bit me. Annoying little blighter."

Her smile said she knew he was lying but would let it stand. He grabbed the kit and rose from his seat. With a cocky look over his shoulder, he asked, "Are you sure you wouldn't like to treat me, Doctor?"

Her laugh was as unexpected as anything else she'd done that day. "I'm sure you can handle this one on your own."

"Pity."

The flush that spread across her cheeks was more than just a girlish blush. Beneath her skin, he saw a faint glimmering. He stared hard, but the luster faded to nothing and he shook his head. In the bathroom, he took stock of the wound on his leg, happy to see that it had begun to heal. He and Rori had the remarkable ability to heal quickly, something she always said was their own kind of magic and he'd laughed because he loved her and her innocent way of looking at life. But now, he wasn't laughing. He was grateful for whatever genetic gift they had that allowed them speedy recoveries.

As he cleaned and dressed his wound, his mind drifted to his sister. He hoped she was taking it easy and allowing her body to repair itself. Knowing Rori, she was already stomping around Rowan's cottage, anxious to be doing something besides waiting. He'd find a way to send her a message after he met with Malcolm. It was time he let his baby sister in on what he'd been working on for the past few years.

He washed his hands, noting their pale plainness. The burning sword had singed his skin, he was certain of it, but now his flesh was unmarked. He turned his hands over and flexed his fingers. Even with expedited healing capabilities, this was odd. Unless he'd imagined the ghost and the blade and the shadow man. *Get a grip, MacNair. You're letting Meg's warning about Dad interfere. Dad is dead. End of story.*

Cian blew out a breath and took stock of his appearance in the little mirror. Not bad. Hair slightly disheveled, small bags beneath his eyes, the shadow of scruff on his jaw. In all, he looked like he always looked. Ruggedly handsome, if he did say so himself. He dusted remnants of his blood from the tie and secured it around his neck, fiddling until it sat just right. With a few swipes down his coat, he dislodged the few remaining twigs and was set. No one would know he'd escaped an armed pursuit by sliding down an ancient volcano.

At the table, a cup of coffee, along with a steaming plate of food, waited for him. Nikala was tucking in to her meal when she saw him and indicated his breakfast. "I wasn't sure if you wanted coffee or tea. I'm sure Lucy would be happy to bring you another cup."

"Coffee's fine, thanks." He left the first-aid kit at the edge of the table where Lucy could retrieve it.

His stomach growled again and he shrugged with a sloppy grin. He couldn't remember the last time he'd eaten anything of substance. Did he have breakfast at Rowan's? Or was it dinner? In Faerie, it would be nighttime. The time difference always did his head in. Whenever he'd last had a proper meal, it was too long ago to be of much good. The muffin he'd had an hour earlier barely counted as food. He started eating, making sure he didn't shovel his food like Rori might. As hungry as he was, there was no need to eat like a troll.

Lucy stopped by their table with fresh coffee and pastries. She saw Cian's empty tray and scurried away.

"I think she has a crush on you. Same with that guy." Nikala motioned to the car attendant who'd asked after Lucy. "He practically swoons every time he looks over at you."

"I think she's grateful that man didn't kill her and can show that gratitude by filling our coffee cups. As for that attendant," Cian waved to the young man who simpered and blushed, "can you blame him?"

Nikala rolled her eyes with an exaggerated sigh and her lips quirked to the side. "Did you know the guy?" Her tone lowered and became serious.

"Who? The druggie?" Cian shook his head. "Never met him before. You?"

The tightening of her lips warned him she might lie. "I've seen him around the offices a few times, but didn't think anything of it until this morning."

Surprised she'd admitted seeing him, and even more surprised the scyver was interested in Nikala, Cian leaned forward. "Why do you think he was following you?"

"I have no idea."

But Cian suspected she did. Her hand raised toward her blouse, then dropped to her lap.

"Tickets please." Another crew member, not Lucy or the male car attendant, stood in the narrow walkway. They gave him their tickets and waited until he'd moved down the coach before speaking.

"You were telling me why that guy, the crazed druggie, was following you."

"No, I was saying I don't know why. I've seen him a few times outside SIRE. As far as I know, he's never followed me before today. Could be he's upset with Malcolm over a deal. I really couldn't say."

The male train attendant moved into view, his face full of apology. "If you don't mind, the police have asked that we get names and phone numbers for anyone who witnessed the incident. They can't stop the train to question you, but would appreciate if you could make an appointment to speak with them at your earliest convenience."

Cian withdrew an ID card from his breast pocket and handed it to the gentleman. He used a small amount of magic to blur the name and face so that the man would see what he wished him to see and not what was printed on the card.

"Viggo McCabe, thank you. And your phone number?" He handed the ID back to Cian.

Cian gave him a number, not to his personal mobile, but to an answering service he used in London.

Nikala handed him her ID, a little smile making a dimple in her cheek.

"Thank you, Miss…" He peered at the ID, then at Nikala. "Virginia Pemberley. And a phone number?"

Nikala took the proffered ID and gave him a number. Probably a service like his. When the attendant left, he looked at her with the same little smile she wore.

"Virginia?"

"Viggo?"

Then she leaned forward and whispered, "I saw your ID. It was for a man, balding, with a triple chin whose name is not

Viggo McCabe. Who are you, really? And why was that man following you?"

Cian relaxed into the seat, letting his body sink into the leather. Her elbows rested on the table, giving him a glimpse of her cleavage, where a piece of silver glinted in the sunlight streaming through the window. He stared at her breasts, drawn not to their lovely curves, but to the tiny fraction of jewelry he could see. Magic encased it, he was certain.

"See something you like?" Her tart tone a warning. Still, she didn't move or try to close the gap of her blouse.

She'd not been fooled by his use of magic on the ID and now, she wore something no one in the human realm should have.

"Actually," Cian drawled, his gaze traveling from the silver between her breasts to her face. "I do." He pointed to her cleavage. "That doesn't belong to you. How did you come into possession of it?"

Her hands went to her blouse. Two fingers shook slightly as she tucked the piece of jewelry deeper into the crevice of her breasts. The color drained from her face, leaving her almost as white as the blouse she buttoned near to her neck.

"Have you come to kill me?" The words, spoken barely above a whisper, were edged with sadness. Not fear. Not anger. Sadness.

The simple question stole Cian's breath. Who *was* this woman? And why did she think he'd kill her for a pendant?

$$\text{\textsection} \quad 8 \quad \text{\textsection}$$

From far away, Rori heard chopping. As if someone were cutting down a tree. Or knocking on a wooden door. She shoved a pillow over her head and groaned. It wasn't morning. Couldn't be. Shortly after Cian left, she'd trudged upstairs, hoping for a night of dreamless oblivion. Meg's horrid sleeping potion still coated her tongue.

Another knock, followed by muffled voices.

"Go away! I'm sleeping."

"Then you must be talking in your sleep." Therron's words broke through the pillow and she sat up.

"What do you want? It's the middle of the night."

"It's not yet midnight, darling. We're leaving immediately and unless you wish to skip questioning Acelyne, I suggest you get dressed." The teasing note in Midna's voice didn't fool Rori.

She sprang from the bed and hopped from foot to foot, jerking her pants up with her good hand. Rivulets of pain flowed through her leg and she winced. The wound on her thigh didn't look as angry and the skin had begun knitting back together. All the same, she gave a little more care to sliding her jeans over the stitches. Rori paused to inspect her pants. They were freshly laundered, without a single tear. These weren't the jeans she'd been wearing earlier.

Her gaze roved over the sleeping chamber and settled on the open door to the room Cian had used the night before. Soft snores came from inside and her heart jittered with expectation. She jostled her boots over her feet and shrugged into her leather jacket before stepping lightly to the doorway.

A peek inside melted the anxiety she'd been storing in the pit of her stomach. Curled into the blankets of the small bed was her mum.

Rori tiptoed to kneel before the sleeping woman and brushed a strand of hair off her face in the same way Labhruinn used to do to her.

"Hey."

Labhruinn's eyes opened and a smile creased her face. "Hey yourself. Feeling better?" Her mum stretched and yawned as she sat up, her eyes cloudy with sleep.

"Much. Midna says it's time to go. How long will you be here?"

Labhruinn shook her head. "Not long. I can't leave the animals. I had to make sure you were sorted." Her mum stroked the side of Rori's face, a wistfulness to her voice.

"I'm good, Mum." Meg's words bounced through her thoughts, but she couldn't bring herself to say them. Cian was right—if their dad was alive, it would only bring their mum pain. Instead, she said, "Thanks for coming."

"I heard you're going to Midna's court for training." A slight pink crossed her mum's cheeks. "I was there once, long ago. Did you know that?"

Rori shook her head. She'd never heard so much as a whisper about it. She should've been mortified, but somehow, knowing her mum had studied at Midna's made the whole enterprise less overwhelming.

"Guard your heart, dearest. You're there to learn, not fall in love. Sometimes Midna forgets that little detail." Again, the faint blush to her cheeks. Labhruinn's glance went to the door. "She's impatient. Go now." Her mum kissed her forehead and breathed deeply. "I've missed you."

"And I you." Tears stung the backs of Rori's eyes. Why had she been so reluctant to see her own mother? It was ridiculous, really. She'd been afraid. Afraid Labhruinn would insist she stay at the palace and guard Eirlys, even though it wasn't what Rori wanted, but her mum did.

"Are you happy?" Labhruinn's sapphire eyes sought hers and Rori nodded.

"This is all I've ever wanted. I know you wish I'd stay with Eirlys, but this," Rori's glance went to her bandaged hand and wounded thigh, "is the life I choose."

"Then make it a life worth remembering." Her mum folded her into a hug and Rori sensed her apprehension.

Labhruinn was afraid she and Cian would disappear like their dad had. Rori knew that fear, but used it to keep her wits sharp.

"I'll come see you when I get a chance. I promise."

She left her mum and joined the others in the hall. Therron cast a concerned glance toward the room, but Rori ignored it. She was fine. Everything would be fine.

"Let's go." She didn't wait for an answer.

The three of them walked quietly down the stairs to Rowan's study. The old mage waited for them by a bookshelf, his hands folded in front of his robe. At a nod from Midna, he waved his hands in the air and muttered a few words. The air shifted and a doorway appeared out of nothing.

Beside her, Therron sucked in a breath. Her own lodged somewhere between her lungs and her throat. She had no idea it was possible to make a portal without an actual doorway.

Midna thanked the mage and beckoned Rori and Therron to follow. Rori reached out to squeeze Rowan's hand before stepping into the undulating air.

A familiar darkness enveloped her and she waited for the air to thicken, but it didn't. Instead, she smelled orange and mint. A faint light started at the end of her vision, elongating with each passing second. By the time Rori counted to ten, she was standing in a dank cellar.

She blinked against the glare of several torches. At least three burned on each wall, giving warmth to the room as well as light. On a stone slab in the center of the space, Acelyne rested in her clear coffin. Beside the dead witch, a slight fellow with sallow skin and watery eyes stood watching them. A feeling of worms crawling through her skin made her shudder. The necromancer smiled at her movement. Black and yellow teeth protruded from his soft lips.

Therron placed a hand at the base of her spine. That small thing, the touch of his skin, even through her clothing, brought calm to her racing heart.

"Everything's ready, Your Majesty." The necromancer indicated they should stand on the other side of Acelyne's body. When they were in position, he began chanting.

Rori caught wisps of words and phrases, but tried not to hear more than brief snatches. Not being a necromancer herself, she wouldn't risk raising a demon by accidentally reciting a phrase wrong. Given her luck the past week, it was totally possible.

The more he spoke, the more Acelyne's corpse jostled and shook. His words reached a crescendo and a shriek came from the dead witch's lips.

"She's ready. Ask your questions. Keep them simple. The dead don't like to be interrogated."

Rori almost laughed. In her experience, neither did the living.

"Where's Mairead?" Midna wasted no time getting to the heart of her questions.

A gurgling laugh preceded a hissing. Then Acelyne said, "Somewhere you'll never reach her."

"Tell me where she is, you miserable hag."

"Or what? You'll kill me?" Again the disgusting laugh.

"Who ordered you to kidnap fae?" Rori ignored the glare Midna shot her.

"Oh, yesssss." Acelyne's head swiveled toward Rori, her closed eyes as penetrating as any living person's glare. "The perfect sssssspecimen. What he could accomplish with you." She smacked her lips before licking them with a blackened, swollen tongue.

"Who is he?" Rori pressed.

"A shadow, a hunter, a myth. No one knows who he is. No one sees him coming. No one sssssusspectsss him. Ssssssshadow man."

"How did you get the fae to the human realm?" Midna crossed her arms over her chest, then shook them out and balled her hands into fists.

"Courier."

"Who?"

Acelyne twisted from side to side. Her mouth worked, but only black oil oozed from between her lips.

Midna motioned to the necromancer, who said several words quickly and with surprising emotion.

"Maxxxxxxx," Acelyne blurted with a horrified gasp.

Midna looked to Rori, but she shook her head. She didn't know a Max. She expected Midna to question Acelyne further, but she remained silent, eyes full of fury.

"Why didn't Arianna return to normal size when I broke out?" The question continued to plague her thoughts.

Acelyne's head jerked from side to side, her ghastly tongue flicking out. "Poisssson feeds, poissson bleedsss."

"How do you free the fae from their glass prisons?" Therron shifted where he stood, his fingertips stroking along his clenched jaw.

His question calmed the thrashing witch. "Magic wordsssss. Dark magic. *Arcadae dialoma.*" Acelyne chuckled low and deep and full of hateful spite. "No more help. You have to earn it." Her finger rose and pointed at Rori. "You know where to find the ssssssspell."

Rori's eyes widened and she looked at Midna. "I don't know any dark spells."

"I didn't say you know it; I ssssssaid you know where to find it." Acelyne's horrible cackling echoed against the stone walls. "Sssssupposed to be sssso ssssssmart."

Rori felt the sting of her words. A dead witch was mocking her. Great.

"Where is Mairead? Tell me now, you miserable cow, or I'll banish you to the realm of fire, where you'll know the intimate points of torture to infinity."

Acelyne's head tilted to Midna. "She's with her beloved. No more answers. The dead call for me."

Cracks formed in the casket and Rori was reminded of the amulet Acelyne had trapped her inside.

"Why?" Rori asked the witch. "Why kidnap fae?"

Acelyne's skin began to crumble, but her lips moved in answer. "War."

Rori cast a worried glance to Midna.

"War? With Faerie? Is the shadow man human?" the Unseelie queen asked.

"Not. Human," Acelyne choked out.

Bile rose up the back of Rori's throat. "The man doing this, is he fae?"

Acelyne no longer had a face and the cracks in her coffin split to form gaping holes.

"Please," Rori shouted, "is he fae?"

"No. More." Acelyne's coffin and corpse turned to dust.

Therron punched the stone slab, scattering Acelyne's ashes to the floor. Rori stared at the ceiling, her mind whirling with the information they'd been given. Midna stood with a fingertip tapping against her lips, her other arm folded across her chest. The white gown she wore was a stark contrast to her raven hair. Her skin vibrated in a rainbow of color. Rori's fingers flexed in an unconscious need to touch the queen. To comfort her.

"There's nothing more for us here. Come, let us ponder this in better suited accommodations."

Rori took several steps then paused. "Why didn't Eirlys come with us?"

Midna's gaze flicked to the necromancer and back to Rori. The queen nodded in the direction of the stairs and Rori followed, with Therron a step behind. Once clear of the crypt, Midna shook out her arms and transformed her gown into a floaty pink thing, with hair to match. She looked like candy floss as she drifted across the marble floor toward the main part of the palace.

"I do not, as a rule, trust necromancers," Midna said by way of explanation. "Nor does Eirlys. With Arianna still affected by Acelyne's spell or potion or whatever has caused her to remain sleeping, Eirlys couldn't risk being too close to the enchantress. She took that traitorous guard with her in the hopes he might give answers Acelyne would not."

Rori nodded in understanding. She'd not been entirely comfortable in the crypt, either. Therron walked to her side and his fingertips brushed against hers. She reflexively sought his touch, but shoved her hand into her jacket pocket. He was getting much too familiar.

They strolled through the palace without haste. None of them spoke, nor did their footsteps make much sound on the thick carpets. Midna led with confidence and for the moment, Rori was happy to let her. They traversed stairs and corridors without encountering any servants or courtiers. The lack of activity unnerved Rori, but she couldn't say why.

Finally, they came to an expansive balcony and Rori recognized it as the one she'd stood on in her dream. She rubbed her forehead and searched for the marble column that she'd bumped into. It had been so real, but surely it was only a dream?

There was one way to be certain. She could look over the banister separating the balcony from the room below. If she saw a divan placed in the center, then she'd know it had been real. But did she wish to know?

"I am vexed with Acelyne's answers and need a release. You two shall stay with me tonight."

Therron stiffened and his jaw clenched. Her own nerves pinched with the command.

"Your Majesty, I must decline." Therron's bow was more a folding at the waist than a fluid movement. "As I have previously stated, I am not here for carnal pleasure."

Rori's full attention snapped to the elf. "You haven't—? I mean, you and her—?" She fumbled for words, too shocked to form a coherent sentence.

Midna's chuckle did little to ease her confusion and discomfort. "Despite my desire, we have not. Therron and your brother are quite skilled at evading my bed." A spark of challenge lit the queen's eyes. "But that doesn't mean I shall stop trying."

Midna loved a challenge, it was true. Therron had denied her on many occasions? Rori processed this new information, unsure what to do with it.

"People come here for answers. Sometimes those are found through pleasure, and other times through denial. I am simply the instrument by which they come to know themselves."

Therron shifted and Rori caught the faint scent of perspiration. Being near Midna made him uncomfortable and now she understood why. It would take a strong will to deny the Unseelie queen if she had her sights set on him. A flicker of elation tickled Rori's heart.

"I told you, everyone who comes here does so of their own accord. I do not force anyone to participate in my entertainments." Midna waved a hand to indicate the palace. "What happens here is sacred to me. But," she focused her gaze on Rori, "why are you here? Truly?"

Rori swallowed hard and fought for the right words. She forced her eyes to stay locked on Midna. If she glanced to the left and saw Therron, she might lose her nerve. "I thought perhaps it would serve me well to hone my skills in all ways. I've been accused of being too impassioned. Directing those emotions would serve me well." Rori took a deep breath and continued, "My body is as much a weapon as any sword and if I could sharpen my abilities, I could learn to control myself with as much precision as my daggers."

It was true, partly. She did wish to learn the ways of seduction, but there was another reason she couldn't yet admit. Not even to herself.

Midna nodded, as if she knew all along why Rori was there. "And learn what you must, you will. Be careful, young Aurora, for a weapon cuts both ways."

The queen drifted from them to the balcony and stood with her hands spread wide, resting on the marble.

Rori blinked several times, trying to make sense of the warning. She glanced at Therron, at the unreadable expression he wore, then followed the queen. She gazed at the room below, at the divan situated in the center of the room, at the courtiers who reclined on sofas or stood in small groups, chatting.

All clothed. None wore masks.

A soft sigh escaped Midna's lips. "Everyone has a reason for coming to my palace. Only the fortunate discover their purpose. Unless you wish to participate tonight, I suggest you find your rooms. Therron, I assume you know the way?"

Before the elf could answer, Midna's wings unfurled and fluttered, lifting her into the air and over the balcony ledge. Rori watched in awe as the Unseelie queen drifted to the room below. The air shifted with her arrival. An almost palpable sense of passion crackled between the gasps and heartbeats of the courtiers. Several swooned in Midna's direction and Rori smelled the slightly musky odor of arousal.

Midna's bare toes touched the divan and a lone male approached. He was the man from her dream. The one who she'd feared was Cian. As he stepped closer, he began unbuttoning his shirt, a look of pure devotion on his face. Rori was struck by the love this man had for his queen.

At the same moment, she realized the crushing despair of Midna's loneliness. She was a queen who gave of herself fully to her subjects, feeding them with her love through sex, but longed for someone to replenish her with more than a release.

Despite being in a crowded room, the queen was alone. A crashing realization came over Rori and she saw herself in that moment—surrounded by people, yet utterly and despairingly alone. Whether in Faerie or the human realm, she'd built a life of solitude and had convinced herself there was no other option. Her heart went out to the queen. To the long nights of giving, of depleting herself for the good of her people. How many times had Rori worked past exhaustion for the same cause—for the good of Faerie?

She felt the queen's despair as if it were her own. Rori's gaze flicked to the now half-naked faerie. Why couldn't Midna see how much he adored his queen? Or did she see it, but mistook it for nothing more than the adoration every queen commands?

"If you wish to stay and observe, I can find a steward to escort you to your room. I have seen enough of Midna's orgies to haunt all my days."

"You don't approve?" Rori was surprised by Therron's admission and embarrassed that she did want to stay, but only to see how Midna and the male fae interacted.

"I have no issue with copulation. And I have no issue with Midna's entertainments, but these trysts bring me sorrow."

"You're a romantic." It wasn't a question, but a statement and

Rori hid a smile. Who knew the gruff, scarred, mysterious thief would have a soft spot in his heart for love?

"Hardly. Come, your room is this way." He took her elbow and a little thrill shivered up her spine.

"Then what? Why do Midna's actions bother you? Do you object so much to love?"

Moans and cries of excitement followed them as they left the balcony and walked along a wide corridor.

"Love? Is that what you see?" Therron skipped up the stairs and Rori struggled to keep up.

The gash in her wound objected violently. He turned, a grimace set firmly on his face. Upon seeing her limp one step at a time, his face softened and he hastened to her side, wrapping an arm around her waist and gently lifting her with each stair.

"I do see love. Not in the traditional sense, but there's more than just rutting going on here." Rori blew out a breath, irritated that it took so much energy to climb a set of stupid stairs.

He grunted and heaved her up to the landing. "It must be a fae thing because I see only orgies and decadence."

"I'll admit, when I first heard about Midna's álainn obedience, I thought it mad that anyone would willingly submit themselves to random sex. But now, I don't know. I feel like maybe there's more to it than I'm understanding."

"And you wish to be part of it," the blue of his eyes darkened and his scar turned a violent shade of red, "to understand?"

The emphasis on the last word caught Rori by surprise. He didn't approve of her being there, at least, not for the purposes of learning. She leaned against him for support and liked the feel of his sturdy torso against her. Liked the way his arm snugged around her back. Liked the way he cared what she thought.

"I want to be the best spy I can be." She didn't speak the rest of her thought: that if it meant becoming one of Midna's álainn obedience, she would. What silenced the words was her own uncertainty. She'd assumed Therron was a part of that and would be there with her, but she'd never thought beyond the two of them. Nor had she considered what it would do to her to see him with others. Being with him now, she was torn.

Therron stopped outside an ornate door. White with gold filigree scrollwork, this room was an improvement from the one she'd stayed in a few days earlier. Rori could guess at the reason for an upgrade in accommodation, but she was too tired to care. As long as it had a bed, bathtub, and fireplace, she was happy.

"May I escort you inside?" Therron's lips twitched with a nervous tic.

"If you promise to be a gentleman," Rori teased, but regretted her words at the scowl that covered his features. Just when she was beginning to understand the man, he confounded her again.

He opened the door and waited while she limped into the room. All the walking had taken its toll and she felt every movement, every scrape of fabric over the stitches. She stopped in the center of the huge space and blinked at the opulence of the furnishings. Satins and silks adorned every surface. Draperies hung from the tall ceilings to the floor, and a four-poster bed big enough for an entire family of eight sat prominently against a wall. Overstuffed chairs begged for long hours of tea and conversation. To her right, a wardrobe overflowed with garments in soft pastels.

Despite the lushness of the room, her attention was drawn back to the bed. She could sleep for a month.

"I'll get a fire going for you."

Therron set about making a fire while she stood still, her hands empty but her thoughts full. What had Midna meant when she said a weapon cut both ways? Did she mean Rori would find heartbreak in the palace?

Her gaze went first to the wardrobe, then to Therron. He knelt in front of the blossoming flames, his face intent on the task. The scar on his left cheek flickered in the wavering light like a dragon's wing and Rori swallowed a gasp.

The room spun with terrifying speed and Rori leaned into it —leaned into the maelstrom of her emotions. Clear as a medieval church bell ringing across an English countryside, she understood what Midna had been asking when she challenged Rori's reasons for coming to the Unseelie Court.

It had very little to do with the álainn obedience and everything to do with the fear and desire swirling around her heart. To let go, to submit to another without regard to what you received in return—that was what truly terrified her. Her body wasn't a weapon, far from it. Yet what she saw in that split second was more deadly than any poison she might ingest, more terrifying than any illusion Acelyne might conjure.

She knew exactly why she'd come to Midna's palace and it had everything to do with Therron.

❧ 9 ❧

The man, Cian or Viggo, or whatever his name was, didn't answer Nikala's simple question. Had he come to kill her? Instead, he slouched into his seat, shifting until he was comfortable, his steady gaze never leaving her face.

If he had been sent to take her out, she wished he'd do it already. The tension, the unknowing, was the worst part. Although, if she wasn't mistaken, the question had startled him. He probably thought her a paranoid lunatic after admitting the man who attacked the train worker had been following her. Why had she told him? Then, to just simply ask if he'd been sent to kill her—yeah, the man with two names most likely thought her bonkers. That suited her just fine. Let him think her a bit mad. That might keep him off-balance. If he'd been hired by Malcolm, then he'd understand being tailed. But to be asked straight up? No one she knew would expect that.

She kept her hands in her lap, despite wanting to clasp her blouse firmly closed. He knew the pendant wasn't hers, which would suggest Malcolm had sent him. Then why the ruse of pretending to have a meeting with him? Another thought buzzed through her mind—*Cian worked for Hunter.*

It would make sense if he truly came from Aberdeenshire, where Hunter's mansion was. But then, how would he know about the pendant? As far as she knew, Hunter wasn't aware of what, exactly, Malcolm bought and sold. The questions kept pinging through her brain. Was Cian a spy for another company? If so, which one? SIRE had many competitors. Any one of them might've sent him to seduce her into telling SIRE's secrets.

"You intrigue me," Cian drawled in a lazy way that she was certain meant to ease her nerves. "Why would I want to kill you? For a trinket? Surely you're worth more than that."

The tone of his words, the implication of their meaning, sat awkwardly in her gut. "And how would you know my worth, Mr. …?"

"MacNair." His grin wound its way to her unease and loosened her anxiety. "Cian MacNair is the real me."

She chuckled and took a sip of her coffee. "I have a feeling no one knows the real you, Mr. MacNair. Not even yourself." The words were more solemn than she meant and his smile dipped to a frown.

"I have a feeling you might be correct." He leaned forward and placed his forearms on the table. She returned the intensity of his stare without blinking. "But wouldn't it be fun finding out?"

She narrowed her eyes with a smirk and sat back. "I think I'd rather have that drug addict stalking me." His offended look was comical. "Seriously, if I had a snaggletooth and spots with frizzy hair out to here," she put her hands a foot to either side of her head, "you wouldn't give me a second glance. You know nothing about me. Please don't pretend you do."

"Interesting choice of words, coming from someone who only minutes ago seemed to have strong opinions about me." Cian relaxed his posture and downed the rest of his coffee.

The male car attendant, the one who couldn't stop staring at

Cian as if he were the second coming of Christ, brought them more coffee, and another breakfast tray for Cian.

When he left, Cian eyed her steadily. A strudel hovered near his face and she hated how tantalizing the pastry was that close to his lips. His mouth opened and his white teeth sunk into the sugary goodness. Such a simple act, something people did over and over again on a daily basis, but seeing Cian bite into the danish did things to her body she'd sworn never to allow.

"See something you like?" His words mocked her.

"Yeah, that pastry. I wonder who I need to save to get another one?"

He held the strudel out to her, his look playful. "Have mine."

Oh gods, she wanted it. Wanted that flaky goodness. But she declined.

A man dressed in plain clothes, but with the look of a policeman, approached and identified himself as an officer of the British Transport Police. He took Viggo and Virginia's statements and thanked them for their assistance.

"In the future," he said with a thick Midlands accent, "it's best if you don't get involved. While we appreciate your concern, your safety is our highest priority."

Nikala affected her best conciliatory pout and agreed to let the train staff handle any further incidents. When he left, she met Cian's eyes and her blood warmed. Lingering in their depths, she didn't see a murderer or one of Malcolm's thugs, but a man who was as intrigued with her as she was with him. They were playing a dangerous game. At the moment, she didn't know who might win.

At Berwick, uniformed police boarded the train and took the deranged attacker away. Nikala didn't look in his direction, but could feel his glare burning into her. Cian hadn't moved or even opened an eye to see the policemen escort the quiet man away. The only words the druggie had spoken were just before he attacked Lucy.

Soon enough, he wouldn't be able to speak, or breathe. She absently toyed with the ring she wore, the one she'd had custom-made with an ultra-thin needle hidden in one of the prongs. With just the right touch, it would inject poison into an unsuspecting annoyance. This morning, it was the odd fellow who'd taken a lethal fancy to her.

Once the train resumed its journey, she slipped into the bathroom and removed the necklace from her décolletage and tucked it into a small pocket in her trousers. Immediately, she missed the feel of glass against her skin. Knowing the amulet was safe was enough for now.

She returned to her seat and opened her laptop. Work wouldn't cease just because someone had tried to attack her on the train. She opened her email and began a note to Malcolm, then trashed the message. He didn't need to know about the attack. Or about Cian MacNair. Not yet. She still wasn't sure whether he was the contact's proxy, and until Malcolm confirmed it, she'd let the man sleep.

The train rocked a steady rhythm as it barreled down the east coast of England. She glanced out the window and took a moment to appreciate the view. Hers was a life of speed. Everything had to be done yesterday and now was a moment too late. For a few minutes, she allowed herself to be at peace.

When she looked away, Cian was watching her. Instead of being frustrated or angry or nervous, she felt calm. In fact, he radiated a serenity she found lacking in her life.

The man was trouble. For so many reasons.

She returned her attention to the laptop and didn't look up again until they reached London.

The conductor announced King's Cross over the speaker and she rose to gather her belongings. Cian or Viggo—or whatever he called himself—was already dressed and standing in the breezeway by the time she'd jerked her leather bag off the metal rack. She shrugged into her coat and smoothed a few stray wisps of hair off her face. If Malcolm had sent him to kill her, she'd find out soon enough.

"I suppose you're going to follow me now?" She beamed up at him, doing her best not to notice the cockiness lurking in his eyes. *Ugh.* He probably thought she was interested in him sexually. Hell, didn't all men think a woman who showed the slightest fraction of interest were sexually attracted to them? She supposed this Cian/Viggo wasn't any different. Although, part of her wanted him to be and she didn't know why.

"If you allow me to walk with you, it might be more expedient."

"You assume I can't lose you."

"Oh, I have every expectation that you will try. And a brief understanding that you might succeed."

She held his gaze, her smile widening. "Sounds like you'd enjoy that."

His head tilted a little, revealing a small scar on the underside of his jaw. She was tempted to kiss it.

"I would. Immensely."

Gods, but this man was bad for her. "If I allow you to walk with me, then I need to know your name. Your real, real name." In her profession, everyone had a dozen names. It became not just important, but critical that she knew his true identity. She had no idea why she craved knowing who he was behind the façade. Equally upsetting—she wanted him to know the real her, as well.

His chuckle was rich and deeply layered, like a good Highland whisky. "I like your cynicism. On my honor, Cian MacNair is my given name."

"And Nikala St. James is mine." She held out her hand to shake his. His skin was warm against hers—soothing, and disturbingly comforting. "I hope we can continue to be this civil."

Cian leaned in close to whisper in her ear, "Only if you behave."

A dark thrill thumped its way from her heart to between her legs and back up to lodge itself in her throat.

Definitely dangerous with a capital *D*.

The brakes squealed as they slowed and arrived into the station. Nikala shifted with the movement, her body brushing against Cian's. He was like a brick wall, sturdy and solid. Not for the first time that morning, she asked, *Who is this man?* Bugger it, she had no clue at all. Not even a fragment where to begin. He intrigued the hell out of her, that was for certain. If he had been sent to kill her, she'd give him one hell of a chase.

"We're this way." She stepped down from the carriage to the platform. The tilt of her head indicated they walk out of King's Cross toward St. Pancras. She could've taken a taxi, but the Underground would be much more fun. Seeing this well-dressed man scuttled between people gave her a perverse thrill. She doubted it would make him uncomfortable, but it would be jolly entertaining for her. And, more importantly, it would delay their arriving at Malcolm's.

They jogged across the street against the light and headed into the busy, well-lit shopping area. She scanned the shops, not sure what she was looking for, and continued on. What she really wanted was time. Time to sort out what to say to Malcolm. If he knew she'd taken the pendant, how could she defend stealing from him? It was a trifle, but perhaps to him, the amulet meant something more? She didn't know. The possible assassin striding at her side gave a clue, though. Except, Malcolm wasn't petty. He didn't eliminate people without good reason. Why the hell was she so paranoid today? It wasn't a good look on her.

She pressed her Oyster card against the gate and shoved herself through the plastic doors, her bag's strap catching at the last moment. With a grumbled swear word or five, she shook the bag to loosen the strap and clutched it against her body.

From the corner of her eye, she caught Cian waving his hand over the card reader, but there was nothing in his palm. The doors opened and he glided through. Like a goddamned god across water. Who the bloody fucking spawn was he?

"Down here." She spun and jogged down the steps to the Northern line. A rush of hot air blew up from the tunnels fifty feet away. They'd just missed a train. Hopefully, it wouldn't be too long a wait for the next.

Cian kept pace with her, his face set in that annoying half grin, half sneer that seemed to be its natural state. On the ride south, she'd studied him while he read the paper or dozed. He didn't once check his phone for messages or scroll through emails. In fact, she couldn't be certain he had a phone. He'd given a number to the attendant, but it could've been fake, just like hers.

She took a step into the short tunnel that led to their train and was suddenly jerked sideways. "What the—?"

Cian pulled her into him with a dire warning in his dark eyes. His head dipped low to hers. "Kiss me."

"What?" It was more of a hiss than question.

"It makes people uncomfortable. Kiss me."

She tilted her head up to argue, but he captured her lips in his. The cheeky bastard. The walls vibrated with the passing of a train and bells dinged from far off. For a split second, she thought about the knife up her sleeve and how easily it would slide between his ribs. Then his lips widened and all her sensibilities evaporated.

❧ 10 ❧

Cian's warm breath tickled the soft spot beneath her nose. His arms wrapped around her, all-encompassing and not horrible at all. For one mad moment, Nikala let herself imagine what it would feel like to truly be kissed by this man, to let herself melt into his embrace and return the kiss. The heat of his breath spread to her core and farther, down low. Her thoughts spun with dizzying ferocity as her mouth opened to taste him. Coffee and danish. Bittersweet.

Fuck. She'd let the fantasy go too far.

Nikala struggled to escape his grip. Who the hell did he think he was to grab her like that? And in the middle of a Tube station. Gross.

His commanding lips and the strength of his hold were not lost on her. The need in the far reaches of her psyche wanted her to soften, to return the kiss—to trust. No way was that happening. She slipped the dagger from its sheath hidden in her sleeve and twisted it until the point was against his midsection.

"I suggest you release me, unless you secretly crave a public disembowelment." The words came between clenched teeth, her lips still touching his.

"Scyver."

She'd had enough. She jerked out of his embrace, sheathing the dagger as she did. He wasn't watching her. Instead, his gaze followed a young man in his mid-twenties, longish hair, jeans worn low on his nonexistent ass. His leather jacket swayed with his gait. When he'd reached the escalator and was nearly out of sight, Cian breathed out and his entire body relaxed. Well, it softened. She doubted the man was ever truly at ease. Even on the train, she'd been tempted to rifle through his pockets while he dozed, but had the sense that, like a puma, he only napped enough to rest his body, but his mind stayed alert to danger.

"Who's Scyver?"

"Not a who, a what. That fellow there is a scyver. Magic hunters."

Her snort turned into a full-bellied laugh. "You're having me on, surely." Deliberately, she wiped her lips with the back of her hand, making certain he saw. To think, her lips had been against his—a mad fool. She was losing her touch—had to be. Magic hunter. That was a new one. And would next he see unicorns farting fairy dust?

Cian tracked her hand as it crossed her lips, his eyes a mystery. What color were they? At times deep brown, but then they lightened to amber, as if they had a flame behind them. She could lose herself in those eyes. If she let herself, which she wouldn't because he was a lunatic. Like the man on the train. It was her day to collect the crazies.

"Ours?" He motioned to the train pulling into the station.

"Bugger. Come on." She pivoted and jogged to the first car, jumping inside before the doors closed, Cian right behind her. So close, in fact, he pressed his very hard, very unrelaxed body into hers. She could only imagine the discipline it took to maintain abs like his. Although, she recalled him eating all kinds of crap food on the train down to London. Every chance he had, he'd grab a muffin or bread. When the car attendant offered him lunch, he gladly accepted even though he'd already had at least a pot of coffee, two full breakfasts, several pastries, crisps, and two bottles of water. He was a human garbage bin, yet his muscles were those of a gym rat.

Such a conundrum, this Cian MacNair or Viggo McCabe or whoever he truly was. Batty as a loon, but damn fine to look at. Just her stupid luck.

As the Tube jostled and lurched, she kept her thoughts away from his body, and the fact her breasts continually bumped against the front of his suit. She toyed with the dagger up her sleeve, seeking reassurance from the cool metal. What if he hadn't been taking the mick? But seriously—magic hunters? The fuck? Like, magicians with a cape and pull rabbits out of a hat? The hairs on her arms stood on end and she flexed her shoulders, taking her a half step away from Cian. Magic. Like witches and shit, that's what he meant. Someone hunted them—to what end?

She let her gaze rove over the passengers. Was that woman a scyver? Or this one with the holes in his ears the size of a fifty pence piece? What about this one with the baby? Could babies be scyvers?

Great, now she was letting Cian's asinine idea seep into her brain.

She shimmied between the crush of people and faced Cian. "Assuming you're not batshit crazy, which I'm not totally convinced yet you're not, what did you mean by 'magic hunter'?"

The train pulled into a station and stopped to let passengers on and off. Cian didn't take his gaze from her. Several emotions flickered in the depths of his eyes, confusion one of them. Instead of answering, he raised his hand and pressed it to her cheek. She forced herself not to flinch, even though his touch was gentle. He'd already taken too many liberties with her. One more and she might have to do more than knife him.

She kept her eyes locked to his, ignoring the other passengers and his hand on her face. New emotions crossed his features.

Curiosity mingled with questions. She could almost hear his brain working hard to make sense of something, but what? Then, without warning, a wall came over his features, shutting out everything. It was like an eclipse, where the sun is blocked by the moon and for a moment the world is dark. But the sun didn't return to his face. There was no light in his eyes.

"Are you quite finished fondling me?"

Cian removed his hand and looked above her head to the train's route. "What stop are we?"

"Seriously, are you this familiar with every woman you meet? I'm starting to feel like you intentionally like to make people uncomfortable and unbalanced."

His eyes softened when he looked back to her. "Darling, that's exactly what I aim to do. And by the blush on your cheeks, I'd say I exceeded even my own expectations."

"You're insufferable." She fidgeted with the dagger up her sleeve. In this crowd, it would be difficult for anyone to know exactly where the blow came from, but she'd been seen with him on CCTV entering the station and the Tube, so there would be questions. Too many for her comfort level.

She cocked her head and glanced at the station lines. "A few more stops. I'll let you know when we're close."

He shifted his stance, widening his legs for balance as they took a curve. She gripped the bar tighter, willing herself not to fling into him lest he think she enjoyed the touch of his body. *Pompous jerk.*

"Are you going to answer my question?"

"Yes, but not here."

She started to press for a real answer, but decided to trust his word.

They remained silent as people entered and departed at the next station. A young couple squeezed between them and Nikala was grateful for the break in Cian's constant presence. He really was like a puma—always alert, ready to pounce. It was exhausting just being around him. She couldn't imagine what it was like to actually *be* him.

The trip lasted just over fifteen minutes, but felt as long as the journey down the eastern coast. The entire Tube ride, Cian kept watch over her, but she also sensed he mentally prowled the rest of the car, scrutinizing every passenger, sizing them up based on threat level or snackiness. She couldn't be sure.

"This is us."

Cian waited until she breezed past him and stepped down from the train, minding the gap like the constant droning speakers reminded her to do. He alighted from the carriage and maneuvered to her side, his gaze scanning, always scanning. For magic hunters, probably. Poor deluded soul. By his scowl, he believed in fairy tales.

She pivoted to her right, bumping him a little, and continued on without an apology. He stayed within one step of her the entire way. If she'd wished, she could've lost him several times, but a part of her wanted to take him to Malcolm's, to see the look on his face when she presented him with the assassin who had failed. It would be a cruel reminder to him that if he wanted her dead, he'd have to do the job himself. She'd told him so on numerous occasions, but today would be special. She had actual proof he'd hired not one, but two men to take her out and she'd survived them both.

And by her reckoning, only one had survived her. Point to Nikala.

By the time they reached the pavement and fresh air of London, she was ready to be done with tubes, trains, and traveling. It had been a long day and it wasn't over yet.

"This way." She angled away from the river and Cian kept pace with her, head bowed, hands in his pocket.

They strode in silence to the massive glass building where Malcolm Dagniss waited. Nikala hated everything about the place—the design, the colored tiles, the shape. All of it screamed "Look at me!" It was everything about Malcolm she detested rolled up into an architectural nightmare. The building belonged to a faceless corporation, but Malcolm had loved it so much he rented two entire floors. One for his suite of offices near the top floor, and another for Hunter's lab. For most of her life, Malcolm had based his business out of Edinburgh, but being a global entity, necessity dictated he be available anywhere in the world, hence the move to London. Still, she hated it.

Not necessarily London, but the hugeness of the city. The gaudy glass skyscrapers and tourists. At least in Edinburgh, she could escape the noise and people. In London, that was nigh impossible. The worst thing about the move to London was Hunter leaving Scotland and setting up in Malcolm's building. She'd spent two years putting as much distance as she could between her and the madman. Now they'd be practically neighbors. Unless she could convince Malcolm to let her stay in Edinburgh. Then all her problems would be solved. Or, she could quit. As if. As much as she'd love to, she wasn't there yet. Soon, maybe, but not today.

Nikala swung open the door, ignoring the security guard who rushed to hold it for her. "Good afternoon, Miss St. James. I didn't know Mr. Dagniss is expecting you."

He bloody well should've known. "This is Mr. McCabe. Malcolm knows he's coming." The lie slid over her tongue with ease.

"Certainly, miss. If you wouldn't mind, Mr. McCabe needs to sign in."

Cian strolled to the desk and scrawled his name across a line. A second security guard handed Cian a visitor's pass to clip to his jacket. Nikala thanked both men and led Cian to the private lift tucked into the back corner. She held her hand to the screen and waited while a computer somewhere verified it was her.

"High tech. Very posh."

"Or paranoid." She hadn't meant to say the words aloud, but whatever. Malcolm was totally paranoid. And for good reason.

Soft music played as they rode to the top of the building. The entire trip lasted maybe thirty seconds, but it felt like a decade to Nikala. Blistering pricks irritated the back of her neck and her palms were moist by the time they exited the lift. Cian, insufferable jerk that he was, looked as calm as a man on holiday sitting beside a pool, drink in hand.

She ignored the receptionist and stashed her luggage in a small office to the right of Malcolm's then walked straight into his more opulent space. The woman scurried around her to announce Malcolm had visitors. Poor lamb. Nikala hadn't made her day any easier by sidestepping protocol. It was ridiculous—Malcolm already knew she was in the building. Not only had she texted him while Cian signed in, she was certain the guards had let him know. And more than likely, they'd told him she had someone with her.

She gazed around the room, at the treasures Malcolm had collected over the years. Her cameras were hidden among the memorabilia. He probably had his own cameras and microphones all over the place. For all she knew, he had surveillance screens in the toilets.

"Nikala, a pleasure to see you." Malcolm rose from his oversized chair and came toward her, arms outstretched.

She prepared herself for the greeting by keeping her body pliant, by not letting the urge to dick punch him overpower her. His lips grazed her cheek, his goatee scratching against her skin. His arms enfolded her in an embrace, squeezing a little too tight, but not enough she could protest. He knew exactly how much affection to show, how far to push her limits.

"Good to see you, too." Another lie, easily spoken.

He stood back, his gaze going from her to Cian. There was no sign of recognition in his dark, almost black eyes. "And who is your friend?"

She almost laughed at that. "We're not friends. He came to the Edinburgh office to see you. He said he had an appointment. Introduced himself as Viggo McCabe and said he needed to speak to you about something having to do with"—she turned to Cian—"what was it you said? Ace-a-line?"

Cian held himself back, surveying the situation as surely as Malcolm was sizing him up.

"Acelyne."

"Right. Ace-lynn, not line." Nikala watched Malcolm, noting the tightening of his jaw, the flexing of his fists. Whatever Acelyne was, Malcolm wanted no part of it.

"Nikala, wait for us outside, please."

Now it was her jaw that tightened, her fists that clenched. "Are you sure? You don't know this man."

"No, but he traveled down here with you, and you appear unscathed. I think I'll be safe. If I need you, I'll call."

Summarily excused, she exited through the same door she and Cian had used a few minutes before. Instead of planting herself on one of the decorative yet uncomfortable chairs in the reception area, she hurried to the much less opulent office.

Without bothering to remove her coat, she slid into the leather chair and opened her laptop. She entered her password and tapped several keys. The screen lit up, showing four scenes from the cameras in Malcolm's office.

Malcolm was speaking, but his voice was too low, or the sound muffled on her computer. She clicked several more keys, but the sound cut out completely. Frustration singed her veins and she snatched a pair of headphones from her bag. Just as she was pushing them into her ears, Malcolm looked straight into one of the cameras. A moment later, it blinked off. Then the others followed. Whatever Malcolm had to say to Cian MacNair, he didn't want her to know.

She leaned back in the chair and worried a nail. Two could play that game. She inserted a memory card into the laptop and typed in several long strings of code. A moment later, the screen blinked with a display of several camera angles. A few more lines of code, and she was done. She shut the laptop and locked the office on her way out.

If Malcolm didn't want her to know what he and Cian discussed, he'd have to do a lot better than finding the cameras she'd hidden in plain sight. She hadn't spent more than two-thirds of her life with Hunter and not learned to always have backups of your backups. That included plans and cameras. She'd come back later and retrieve the disk, which at that moment was happily recording everything in his office.

She strolled to one of the chairs and sat facing the receptionist, with Malcolm's office to her left. The girl kept glancing from Nikala to her boss's door. After a few seconds, she shrugged and began typing on her computer. Nikala grinned and opened a game on her phone. While the video streamed to a small window on the screen, she appeared to be playing a silly game of matching candies.

Malcolm's voice crackled in the headphones and Nikala tensed at the tone of his blatant lies. Whatever Acelyne was, she would have to tread carefully to uncover the truth.

❧ 11 ❧

It would've been impossible to miss the tension between Malcolm and Nikala. There was history there, and not all of it good. It might be a thread worth pulling. Although, Cian owed her one for introducing him as Viggo to her boss. He didn't turn to see her leave. Instead, he kept his attention squarely on the man standing two feet in front of him. Not imposing in a large stature kind of way, Malcolm Dagniss held a quiet kind of lethalness that intrigued the spy. This was a man Cian didn't want as an enemy.

And yet here he was, about to make himself the least welcome man in the building.

"As Ms. St. James pointed out, I'm here about a mutual sodality of ours. I believe you've had dealings with Acelyne in the past."

Malcolm smiled breezily, his manner one of welcoming, friends chatting over coffee. He did a funny thing then—he looked just beyond Cian's left shoulder and scratched his nose. If Cian wasn't mistaken, Malcolm Dagniss used a spark of magic and disguised it as a simple itch. He did it three more times, each with a tiny glow coming from his fingertip. A human wouldn't have noticed, but Cian wasn't human. A fact Malcolm didn't know.

Cian adjusted mentally. Until that moment, he'd suspected Malcolm of being fae, but couldn't corroborate his findings with fact. The use of magic, discreet as it was, confirmed his worst fears. A fae kidnapping fae. Rage simmered through his veins and he shoved his hands in his pockets to keep from reaching forward and strangling the man. Caution was needed until he verified Malcolm was responsible for the kidnappings. At the moment, all he knew was that Malcolm had magical abilities.

Malcolm's smile turned smug, less friendly. "I'm afraid you're mistaken, Mr. ah, McCabe, is it?"

"Call me Viggo."

"Of course. Mr. McCabe, I've never heard of this Acelyne. Is it a company or product I might've sold in the past? You know, the import business can be quite taxing. But I do my best."

He was good at playing the part of overwhelmed executive who tried to stay in touch with the millions of dealings his company had, but just couldn't keep up. He actually wiped his brow before indicating a chair for them to sit.

"Shall I have tea brought in? I'm sure you're tired from your journey. I just wish I had better news for you about this, erm, Acelyne." He rubbed his chin, his eyes cast far off into some fabricated memory or hard thought. "Sounds Malaysian, or perhaps Turkish?" He shook his head for dramatic effect. "No, I can't place it." Then, he leaned forward, hands on his knees, his dark eyes soft, innocent. "What could be so important you had to travel all the way from Edinburgh to London? Especially when I haven't a clue what it is?"

Cian mimicked his movement, meeting Malcolm's approachable look with one of his own. Innocent, malleable. "I'm so sorry, Mr. Dagniss. I had it on good authority you were the man to speak to about Acelyne, but now I see I've been misled." He sighed and let his head fall forward, defeated. "I've been working on this for months. I was so sure I had it right this time."

"It's understandable to be disappointed, but don't let it dissuade you from working even harder. If this Acelyne is meant to be, you'll find a way to make it happen." Malcolm leaned back, his forefinger stroking his upper lip like a mad megalomaniac cliché. His gaze traveled the length of Cian, who also reclined into the chair, his fingers tapping a rhythm on the armrests. "You seem to have torn your trousers."

Cian looked at his pants, a surprised expression covering his irritation. "Well, look at that. Must've got caught on something, like a fence post, or a rose bush." He reached down to fiddle with the hole. "Or perhaps when armed guards were shooting at me this morning. Not really sure." He stood and reached a hand out to Malcolm. "Thank you for your time, Mr. Dagniss."

A flicker of annoyance crossed Malcolm's eyes before he, too, stood. "Mr. McCabe."

They shook hands, two warriors calling the battle a draw.

"If I should get any information on this Acelyne, do you have a card with contact details?"

Cian shrugged and sauntered to the door. "Not really. I'll give Ms. St. James my number." His sneer was meant to be cocky, but at the thought of Nikala, his rage simmered into lustful desire.

Malcolm watched him like a hunter tracking his prey. "Please do. She can relay any messages you might have. I am curious, however, why this Acelyne is so important to you."

"I never said Acelyne was important. I just wanted to discuss some matters I thought would be of interest to you."

Cian didn't give him a chance to reply. He opened the door and breezed through the reception area, ignoring Nikala and the receptionist tucked behind a huge desk. At the lift, he pressed the ground floor button and slipped his hands into his trouser pockets. While he waited, intimately aware of the two women who watched his every move, he hummed a tune and rocked back and forth on his loafers.

The lift binged and he stepped in, catching a reflection of Nikala in the mirrored doors. Like Malcolm, she looked ready to pounce. Yet he didn't think he was the prey this time, but rather Mr. Dagniss. By her expression and gait, she'd been none too happy when her boss kicked her out of the office. Cian was certain words would be shared. Harsh words. What he'd give to be able to eavesdrop on that conversation.

As the doors closed, Cian met Nikala's gaze and winked. Her lips quirked into a smile. With a shake of her head, she lifted her hand and waved. Cian raised a brow, a silent invitation in that one movement. If she caught it, he'd see her soon. If not, well, he'd see her soon regardless. He suspected she wasn't about to let him get too far out of her sights. He'd been targeted, as was his plan.

No guards tried to stop him on his way out of the massive glass building, nor did anyone give him undue attention. Most likely, Malcolm was letting Cian believe he didn't care about some random stranger asking after someone or something he was unfamiliar with. It was what Cian would've done. As soon as he stepped onto the sidewalk and the brisk spring air caught his coat, he tightened his arms into his pockets and hunched against the wind. A lone figure eased away from where he'd been smoking a cigarette, and another man finished his coffee, folded a paper, and rose from his chair to leave the outdoor café where he'd been, ostensibly, enjoying his afternoon.

All told, Cian counted six people following him. Four men, two women. They cycled in and out, like a perfectly choreographed dance. Cian walked aimlessly, turning in to a store here, an alleyway there. At the Tower of London, he paused long enough to check his phone for any messages, pretending to answer an email or two. It gave him the time he needed to pinpoint each of his retinue.

At the ticket booth, he paid with his stolen cash and thanked the woman behind the glass window. A group of tourists ambled in front of him, their cameras at the ready, headphones stuck to their ears. He wove in between the crowd as they entered the Tower grounds. Once inside, he zigzagged from one group to the next, using the tallest of the men as cover when possible. At the Traitor's Gate, he swerved left and jogged up the stairs toward the Beauchamp Tower. Cian didn't want to lose his followers as much as he wanted to see how committed they were to their job.

Only two of them entered the Tower grounds, leaving four to watch the exits. One of the women, a shortish thing with cropped brown hair and wearing military issue boots, turned up the path behind him. He ducked into the first open door, a room that had once housed Elizabeth I before she was queen. Down a corridor and through another dwelling brought him to a set of doors: one locked, one leading to yet another part of the building. Cian checked to make sure the room was empty before he tapped the locked door, using a tiny spark of magic to unlock it, and slipped through the slight opening.

His magic wove through the wooden boards to the iron lock on the other side of the door and secured it closed. When his watchdog entered the room, she wouldn't see anything out of the ordinary, nor would she know he'd escaped through a passageway built over a thousand years earlier by a paranoid monarch. A trait he shared with the dead queen. Even if the lass following him had magic herself, which he doubted, she couldn't sense the small amount he'd used. Years of practice had taught him how much magic could be used without notice. Getting snared in someone else's spell wasn't pleasant and was to be avoided at all costs.

Stairs led to a foul-smelling cellar, where the door to the secret passageway was hidden behind a pile of rubbish. He used the flashlight app on his phone to light his way. Cobwebs, some older than himself, dangled from corners, their frayed ends catching his hair and tickling his face. At the center of the cellar, Cian stood for a moment and listened.

Footsteps shuffled against the old pine boards above him. Muffled voices came between the cracks, but no one had followed him down here, to this forsaken area. After the sounds quieted, he removed the rubbish and slipped through the ancient door to a series of tunnels he doubted anyone in the current century knew existed.

A perk to being fae meant his memories went further back than any human's. Actual time, as in the number of hours in a day or week or year were the same, but the experience of years lived in Faerie were equivalent to a moment for those in the human realm. And today, he used that information to escape the thugs following him. Having sussed out their commitment, which was admirable, he could do without an entourage following him any further.

A globe of drossfire lit his way as he traversed the myriad pathways beneath London's streets. He made a mental list of what he'd need to do once at his flat. First item on the agenda was to find out all he could about Malcolm Dagniss and Nikala St. James.

Malcolm was obviously lying about Acelyne, but did Nikala know anything? He hadn't gotten a sense that she did but she might be lying, like her boss. And the pendant she wore was definitely similar enough to the pendant Rori had given to Midna to cause concern. It might be possible Nikala didn't know what was in the amulet, and it was the source of magic the scyver hunted. Or Nikala was in on the kidnappings. Either way, she was part of his mission, nothing more.

The way his veins warmed and heart thundered just thinking about the woman proved otherwise. Cian didn't have time for infatuations. His focus was finding the missing fae, not getting tangled up in a romance that would end badly. He shoved aside images of her smile and the way her nose scrunched when he said something she disagreed with. Dammit, but she intrigued him.

Eirlys had given explicit instructions to kill anyone associated with the kidnappings. That included Nikala. He'd do well to remember she was the enemy until proved otherwise. Sometimes his job sucked. It would bring him no pleasure to end her life, but if necessary, he would. A momentary flicker of grief wedged in his heart, then flitted away like it always had. He was an assassin. Emotions were messy and best avoided, no matter how much he might wish otherwise.

Cian paused to get his bearings and turned down a short tunnel to a set of steps. He emerged from the side door of a utility room on a quiet lane. Cars rumbled past farther down toward the main road, but where he stood was empty of people. He strolled toward Monument, aware that Malcolm's building hovered over his right shoulder. His flat was a thirty-minute walk west, near Temple Church. Taking the Tube would be quicker, but Cian had no doubt the Underground was being watched. He'd take his chances with walking and hope the thugs wouldn't think to look two blocks from their own building.

In this part of the city, most of the structures were modern, but a few older pubs and tenements interrupted the glass and steel landscape. As he hustled down the busy walk, a strange nagging sense settled in his thoughts. As if he were forgetting something important, but couldn't grasp what. He paused to regard an old pub. The plaque stated it had been established in 1873, but many of these freehouses had been there since Roman times. Names changed with new owners, and buildings were updated, but the foundations could be thousands of years old.

Nothing about the exterior of the pub caught his attention. His gaze roved over the bay windows to the flats above. On the top floor, a pair of darkened windows drew his attention. The other windows were brightly lit from the inside. It was the vacant flat that tugged at him. He sensed magic and something more, something ephemeral he couldn't explain.

Without giving himself time to debate his choices, he went inside the pub. Tourists crowded the tables, and in the back, a raucous group of men cheered for their footie team. Cian avoided them and headed toward the kitchens, hoping to find a stairway leading to the upper flats. Instead, he found a door that led down to the basement. The nagging increased and he slowly made his way down the creaky steps into a cellar. Wooden barrels and broken chairs littered the cramped hallway. Lamps from the First World War flickered and gave enough light by which to see, but not much more. He couldn't risk using drossfire here, so he squinted into the dimness and counted three closed doors—two on the left and one on the right.

It was the door to his right that made his heart rate ratchet up and his fingers twitch in anticipation. The closer he stepped to the innocent-looking wood, the deeper a thrumming sounded in his ears. This was no ordinary door.

He reached out and touched his fingertips to the smooth surface. Despite the steadiness of his hand, his nerves pinched tight. Beneath his light touch, he sensed ancient power. A hiccup of excitement caught in his throat.

This door was a portal.

Not one he knew about, which made him wonder whether the queens of Faerie knew it existed. The magic ingrained in the wood wasn't any kind he was familiar with.

Several thoughts ricocheted through his mind, only one standing apart from the others—if there were portals and doorways unknown to Faerie, then who used them?

"Can I help you?"

Cian turned around and smiled to the young woman who stood halfway up the stairs, a basket of linens in her arms. "I was looking for the toilets and it appears I got rather lost."

Her chuckle was soft and welcoming. "They're upstairs. Ground floor, toward the back and to the left."

"Thank you." He waited for her to descend the stairs, then asked, "Do you happen to know if any of the flats above are available?"

Her shrug was noncommittal. "No idea. But you can ask Donyatella. She's at the bar and knows all about that sort of stuff."

Cian thanked her again and shuffled up the stairs. At the bar, he asked for Donyatella and was directed to an older woman who looked as if she'd been working there for as long as the pub had been established. She sat at a table, reading the paper while her fingers tapped a glass of water. When he approached, her piercing gaze roved his entire body, missing nothing. When he inquired about a vacant flat, her lips tightened to a single white line. Cian had the distinct impression she knew what he was and didn't approve.

"No flats for let. Try a service. They can help." Donyatella's gravelly voice managed to invoke dismissiveness and distaste wrapped in indifference.

"I will, thanks." As much as he longed to know who lived in the top floor flat, and where the doorway in the cellar led, he'd already wasted too much time. He'd come back another day when he wasn't being pursued.

Cian strolled at a casual, yet brisk pace in the direction of Temple Church while keeping a watch for Malcolm's thugs. He made sudden turns and ducked in and out of shops several times until he was certain no one followed him. The closeness of the pub and Malcolm's building wasn't lost on Cian. He added Donyatella to his list of names to research when he reached his flat.

Something about the woman, and that pub, set off alarms in his mind. He needed answers. And he knew who he wanted to interrogate first.

Tickling the back of his mind was the notion that Nikala was the key to everything, but getting her to talk wouldn't be easy. Cian smiled to himself. Easy wasn't his style. He'd get his answers, hopefully with Nikala's help. Sex it out of her, as Rori would say. That was his preferred form of interrogation—and much more enjoyable than the alternatives. But if Nikala proved uncooperative, well, he'd hate to have to kill her. If she got in his way, that's exactly what he'd do.

❧ 12 ❧

Therron watched Rori as she slept, his focus on the rapid movement behind her closed lids. When she'd passed out as he was lighting the fire, he'd put her in the enormous bed. That had been five hours ago. Now, he sat in one of the comfortable chairs, waiting for a sign, anything to signal she would be well.

He sat with his hands pressed together, his forefingers against his lips. The past few days had been harrowing for Rori. Meg had told him the injury to her leg should've killed her, yet she walked with barely a limp. Only when they entered this room had he witnessed any sign of weakness from her. He was surprised she let him help her up the stairs. To be sure, Rori MacNair was a fighter.

He just hoped whatever it was she fought in her dream didn't follow her into Faerie.

She kicked out and cried against an unseen foe. Therron's heart pounded in his chest and his fists clenched. He half stood, sat down, then stood fully to pace along the bed. Another whimper and he was undone.

Rori might resent him come morning, but he couldn't listen

to her wails any longer. He slid beneath the covers and cradled her body next to his. She stiffened at his touch, but he shushed her and draped a protective arm over her hip.

"I'm here, Rori. I won't let anything happen to you." His whispered words were a promise, an oath, but she couldn't know they were spoken out of fear.

"Therron?" Her sleepy drawl tugged at his heartstrings.

"You had a nightmare."

"Someone killed you. Not someone. Some *thing*." She rolled over and put a hand to his cheek. He instinctively flinched, but she kept her fingertips lightly upon his scar. "Tell me how you got this."

He resisted the urge to brush her hand away and cover the deformity. It was his curse. His reason for living.

As she looked up at him, eyes wide with questioning, blue hair fanned around her face, his breath caught. Every nerve ending felt alive with fire. Without thinking, he bent his head and brushed her lips with his. The moment their skin touched, the scar turned to ice, then molten. His body vibrated with suppressed desire.

Rori's soft mouth opened, inviting him deeper. A moan came from deep in her throat and he swiped his tongue against hers. Her scent teased him and he breathed in through his nose to imprint her smell on his memory. Tomorrow—well, today, actually, considering it was nearly dawn—she'd begin her education with Midna. Until then, he'd hold her as long as she let him.

Rori pulled away to gaze into his eyes. A wildness had entered her blue orbs and a cheeky grin lifted the corners of her lips. Her pelvis shifted against him and his erection pushed painfully against his trousers. He dipped his head and ran the tip of his nose from her collarbone up her neck to behind her ear. Her scent intoxicated him.

Without a word, she tugged at the court jacket he wore, not even flinching when she ripped the expensive velvet. It was one of

Midna's many gifts to him and truth be told, he preferred his traveling clothes to the fancy attire he wore at the palace. Yet Midna insisted those in the palace wear appropriate court apparel. With a few quick jerks of his shoulders, he was rid of the thing and wasted no time adding the cotton shirt he wore to the pile.

Rori's hands were on him, exploring, tripping over his scars, scraping through the hairs on his chest. A look of wonder replaced the wildness of her eyes and she rolled her lower lip between her teeth. A growl came from his solar plexus and Therron took her lip between his own teeth. Her yelp excited him further and he sucked hard until her mouth was once more claimed by his.

Slowly, he removed her clothing. When she tried to help, he batted her hands away. With each layer removed, he delighted in the feel of her skin. His gaze skirted past the scars that told of a life lived with danger. She was his equal in all things. As it was meant to be.

Her breasts teased him with their pert nipples and he spent several minutes purling his tongue over them. She arched and moaned, but she did not tell him to stop. Her words to Midna echoed in his mind and he doubted their sincerity. This was not a woman who used making love as a weapon. At least, he chose not to believe her. Chose to think he might mean more to her than a mission.

His heart rammed against his ribs. It was too much to think it was him alone who brought her pleasure. Therron jerked his mind from that line of thinking. It would only end in disaster if he convinced himself she had feelings for him that didn't exist. The gods knew he was lost to her. Curse or no, he could love this woman for all his years.

The way Rori's Glamour shone beneath her skin and the delirious smile she wore would suggest she might return his affections. He couldn't let himself get carried away with hope, though.

She'd come to Midna's court to be an álainn obedience, not his lover. Whatever transpired between them now, he cautioned himself to not hope for more.

Therron removed his lips from her breasts to a mournful whine. He kissed his way to her hips and unfastened the unusual trousers she wore. He dragged the fabric over her buttocks and thighs, being careful not to catch the stitches Meg laboriously applied. Pink edged the wound, but not from infection. He paused to place kisses along her thigh, then continued to remove the rest of her garments.

As he knelt at her feet, he gazed at the loveliness laying before him. A lump caught in his throat and traitorous tears stung the backs of his eyes. There was no turning back for him. As for Rori, he couldn't make that decision for her. He would love her. Would make love to her. But couldn't force her to love him. He would give her everything and ask for nothing in return. Whatever time the gods had given them, he'd be grateful for. If she was the instrument of his death, he welcomed his demise.

He stripped off his trousers and leaned forward to kiss his way up her legs. At the apex of her thighs, he nudged her bud with his nose and breathed in while flicking his tongue to lick her most intimate parts.

Rori's gasp went straight to his cock. She opened her legs and he made one long, sensuous stroke with his tongue up her outer folds. As tempted as he was to remain there the rest of the night, he eased his body up until his face was level with hers. A shiver of fear raced down his back, followed by brutal desire.

Apprehension flickered in Rori's eyes. Therron lowered his lips to hers as he entered her. She sucked in a breath, bringing cool to the warmth of their mouths. His tongue sought hers and he rocked slowly, wanting their lovemaking to last. Her hips lifted to meet his rhythm again and again. The heat of her channel, the slick embrace, almost undid him. He groaned against her mouth, his need building.

Her gentle lifts turned to thrusts and they became a manic movement. Hands grasped hair; fingers pinched skin. Their tongues danced to a tribal beat that matched his heart.

They came undone together. Sparks lit behind his eyes, narrowing his vision to Rori's face. The sheer power of emotion he felt in that moment could shift stars in the sky. His mind swelled with possibility and every fiber of his body thrummed with joy. It was a feeling he'd never had. For a moment, he feared it would consume him. Then he feared he'd never experience this sort of pure bliss ever again.

Tears streamed from Rori's eyes to disappear in her hair. Therron cocked his head, concern spiking through his happiness.

"Did I hurt you?" He stroked her hair and started to move off her body, but she put her hands on his hips to stop him.

A little chuckle came from her throat and she hiccupped. "You didn't hurt me. I just, I mean, I never—" She looked away. A sweet blush stained her cheeks. "I didn't know it could be this good."

Therron turned her face to him and kissed her lips. They trembled beneath his. "Maybe you just had the wrong partners."

He as well. He'd known other women, certainly, but none had ever brought his emotions from the depth of his being like Rori had.

"I'm a spy, Therron. This can't happen." She motioned from him to herself. "No personal entanglements." But her words lacked conviction.

"Your father was a spy and loved your mother, yes?"

"Yes." Sorrow shadowed her features and he immediately regretted asking the question. "But my father disappeared and in a cruel way, I lost my mum, too. She mourns him to this day."

"I'm sorry. It was unkind of me to remind you." He stroked her hair and kissed her temple. "Being a spy doesn't mean you can't love."

He nuzzled his way down her body and distracted her with

his tongue. She didn't complain or argue or tell him it shouldn't happen. She did, however, make the most wonderful cries of delight as he brought her to the brink of release time and again, then finally took her bud between his lips and sent her over the edge with thrashing and shrieks that could wake the dead.

Later, as they lay curled in each other's arms, Rori said quietly, "If you won't tell me about the scar, will you at least tell me why fae and elves hate each other? I know what I learned at the Academy, but suspect you have an alternate history."

Little did she know the reasons were one and the same. Therron took a deep breath, kissed her shoulder and began a tale he'd heard his entire life.

"Long ago, there was a beautiful faerie princess named Ishnara. She wanted to see the elven kingdom and traveled there with her maids and several guards. On the way to the palace, she stopped in a town for refreshments. There, Ishnara saw the most handsome man. He was a cobbler, and poor, with nothing to offer a princess, but Ishnara fell instantly in love with him."

Rori snorted. "That's such bullshit. I mean, falling in love after just one look? What if he was a creeper? Or had the pox?"

Therron ignored her questions. He knew it was possible to fall in love after seeing a person for only a moment.

"To continue, this lad, Heracul, he did not return Ishnara's affections. Even when she insisted he come to the palace with her, he denied her. Ishnara left the man in his town and traveled to the elf king, where she told him of her trouble with the man, Heracul. The king, being wise and just, told her he couldn't make a man love her, but that he would see about bringing the cobbler to the palace."

Rori's fingertips scratched along his chest and Therron adjusted himself lest she feel his burgeoning erection.

"Are you intentionally trying to distract me?" he asked, more than happy to end the story and make love to her again.

"Not at all. Please, continue."

Therron adjusted himself with reluctance. He would much rather make love to her again than recite the story. With a sigh, he continued.

"Heracul came to the palace as commanded by his king, but no amount of begging from the princess could make him love her. She tried many times to seduce him, each ending with Ishnara in tears. Heracul would not return her affection. He wasn't promised to another, nor did he think she was unworthy. He simply didn't love her.

"Humiliated, Ishnara returned to her kingdom and summoned her most powerful dark mages. She ordered them to place a curse on the elven kingdom. Once every century, a prince would be born who would fall in love with a faerie. Not a princess or queen, but a faerie with no title, no wealth, and no heart to return his love."

Rori snickered. "She was irritated with Heracul and cursed the future generations out of spite. Kind of a bitch thing to do. I mean, you can't force someone to love you. Can the spell be broken?"

Therron's heart quickened and his breathing became shallow. "It can."

"Are you going to tell me how?" She plucked at a hair on his chest.

"Ouch. Yes, I'll tell you as long as you don't pull any more hairs." He kissed her forehead and let his lips linger against her skin a moment before he said, "The cursed prince will know his mate the moment he sees her. If she returns his affections, the spell is broken. If not, he'll perish within three moonturns of their meeting and the curse will continue."

What he didn't tell her—couldn't tell her without giving himself away—was that each prince born to the curse was marked. Every marking was different—it could be an irregular birthmark, an extra toe, perhaps a missing finger, or a scar upon one's cheek. Therron's hand went instinctively to his face. Rori reached his scar first and his hand covered hers.

"That's a sad tale indeed. But surely, it's been long enough elves and fae could forgive and forget?"

Therron hitched her leg over his hip and nudged his cock against her womanly folds. A flash of surprise lit across her face.

"Again?"

"What can I say? You excite me, Aurora MacNair." Like no woman ever had, and no woman ever would again.

The countdown to his three moonturns had begun.

❧ 13 ❧

Nikala scraped at a cuticle and waited for Malcolm to finish a phone call. She'd been in his office for half an hour without him saying a word about Cian MacNair/Viggo McCabe. Fortunately, she was used to his moody silences and could wait him out. The receptionist had been in twice to refresh their tea and bring more biscuits. Nikala turned her attention from the errant cuticle to the cup sitting on the tray in front of her—untouched. If Malcolm wasn't going to drink it, she needed the caffeine. In one gulp, she emptied the cup and set it down with a smack to her lips.

From where he sat across the desk from her, Malcolm scowled and shook his head in warning. She'd already eaten his biscuits. Nikala grinned and gave a sheepish shrug. She was hungry. The least he could do was take her to dinner after the horrible past few days. First waiting in Edinburgh for a contact who didn't show, then traveling with that madman who thought he saw—what did he call them? Magic hunters, but something else—*scyvers*. Yes, scyvers. What kind of fool did Cian MacNair think she was?

Malcolm swore into the phone and slammed it down.

Nikala glanced at the handset and then to Malcolm. "Trouble in paradise?"

"Your friend slipped past the detail sent to follow him."

Nikala couldn't stop herself from laughing. "You mean those idiots Yasheda and Jude you hired when I advised against it?" In truth, she liked the pair, had even trained them herself and considered them friends, but she knew Malcolm, knew he got nervous if she showed any kind of sentiment toward his employees.

Malcolm ran a hand over his face and sighed. "They're ex-special forces. They're good." He swiveled his chair to look out over the London skyline. "Do you have any idea where Viggo McCabe might go next?"

"None. All he said was he wanted to meet with you. Did he have anything interesting to say?"

Malcolm waved a hand, as if what they discussed was unimportant. "I really have no idea what he was rambling on about. I want you to find him, Nikki. Find him and trail him for a few days. I want to know what his motivation is. Why seek me out?"

Nikala studied Malcolm as he spoke. A light flutter at his throat showed his pulse raced and a sheen to his forehead indicated raised anxiety levels. She rose and Malcolm followed suit. He stepped around the huge desk to stand in front of her.

"I know you will not fail me, my love." His breath singed against her skin.

"I never have."

He reached forward and unbuttoned the top few buttons of her blouse. With each opening, she had to force herself to remain calm, to give nothing away. She kept her heart rate low, her breathing even.

Malcolm pushed the collar of her blouse to the side and frowned. There was nothing sexual in his actions—he'd been searching for something and was disappointed not to find it. Immediately, she thought of the pendant and just as quickly shuttled the thought from her mind. Malcolm had the uncanny ability to know what she was thinking.

"See anything you like?" Bitterness edged her tone.

His eyes narrowed and lips thinned. "It's a shame, really. Such a pretty girl like you should adorn yourself with jewels." He held her right hand up to his lips and kissed her fingertips. "Yet all I ever see you wear is this ring. And you've yet to tell me who gave it to you."

Nikala's shrug hid a sigh. "I told you, I bought it for myself. I'm never getting married, so why not?" She forced a laugh and placed her hand over his cheek. "As much as you'd like otherwise, it won't happen. No grandchildren for you, I'm afraid. As for jewelry, I have no need unless a mission calls for it. You know the life I live. Do you really think I should be weighed down by baubles and nonsense?"

His dark eyes flickered with merriment for a brief moment and Nikala snatched the memory before it was gone. Malcolm wasn't a man who laughed often. She savored those moments when he wasn't foreboding and fierce. When he was almost paternal.

"I suppose not. Go now, my precious, and find our lost friend."

Nikala was at the door before Malcolm stopped her. "By the way, I seem to be missing an amulet from my safe. Either that, or I miscounted the number of pendants from our last shipment. Do you happen to know what happened to it?"

The urge to cover her pocket burned through her veins. Instead, she gave a look of pure innocence mixed with shock. "Your safe is impenetrable. Even I don't know how to get inside. The only thing I trust more than the security of your vault is the proficiency of your mind." Nikala scrunched her face in thought. "It's a conundrum, to be sure. But you are getting older," she added playfully, "and they say forgetfulness is inevitable."

She knew the jab at his age would rattle him and he took the bait. "I'm not so old yet. You can stop planning my funeral." A smile lit up his face and he waved her to the door. "Just one more thing before you go."

Nikala's heart beat in her throat. She hated it when Malcolm did this. A fake smile plastered to her face, she replied, "Just one." It was a tired game they played. She started to take a step toward him for the requisite kiss to his cheek.

"Entertain our new friend—do whatever it takes to find out what he really wants—then let him go. Permanently." The smile Malcolm wore was as fake as her own.

Relief trickled in cool pinpricks over her skin. She didn't have to give the perfunctory kiss. Then a pit dropped in her gut. What Malcolm meant was—fuck Cian to get answers, then kill him. Shit. The former would be no problem; he was easy enough on the eyes she wouldn't mind the interrogation. The latter? Well, that might be more difficult. But it would be fun nonetheless and Nikala loved a challenge.

"Of course." She bowed her head and stepped away from Malcolm to exit the office. Once in the reception area, she swallowed the lump lodged in her throat. She'd long ago given up the fantasy of having a normal dad, but every now and again, that simple wish—to have her father be proud of her for doing stupid shit like coloring a bad drawing—nagged at her confidence. She was his spy, his tool, his assassin. Some days, she wished she could just be his little girl.

That wish, and those days, were long past. Her focus now was Cian MacNair. Nikala had a feeling the usual methods wouldn't work with him. He was slick and would see through her attempts at flattery. A twisted grin pulled her cheeks higher. Oh, yes. Interrogating Cian MacNair wouldn't suck. It just might be the most enjoyable thing she did this week.

With a bounce to her step, she made her way to the lift, ignoring the wide-eyed stare of the receptionist. She ran a search for Cian MacNair and Viggo McCabe on her phone, unsurprised when neither name got a hit.

Molly, her friend at MI6, could help, but she didn't want to involve her if possible. Molly had already put her career on the line too many times for Nikala and she didn't like owing favors. Although, she always said it was no big deal to help out and never asked for anything in return. Still, Nikala had a nagging feeling that someday Molly would call in her chips.

She worried a cuticle on the ride to the ground floor. Even when her nail started bleeding, she kept gnawing on the loose skin.

Who was Cian MacNair?

Why was he in Edinburgh at the same time she was to meet with Malcolm's contact?

A ringing started in her ears. The vibrations echoed out to pound against her skull and upset the rhythm of her heart.

Malcolm hadn't asked about the contact or the product.

Nikala paused in the foyer of the ridiculous glass building and debated her options. She could go back up to Malcolm's office and ask him about the missing contact, or she could consider it a stroke of luck that he'd not bothered to reprimand her.

She didn't believe in luck, but she didn't want to court Malcolm's ire, either. If he chose not to question her about Edinburgh, then he probably already knew what happened to the contact and would arrange for someone else to pick up the delivery. Which was fine with her. She hated being Malcolm's errand girl almost as much as she hated having to kiss his cheek.

The fact that he genuinely didn't seem to know Cian set her mind at ease on one thing—at least she no longer thought Malcolm had sent someone to take her out.

Nikala breathed in the crisp London air and turned her face to the sky. A ray of sunshine warmed her cheeks and she grinned. Cian MacNair would be a tough nut to crack, but she relished the challenge. How long had it been since anyone gave her even the slightest thrill? Forever, really. Yes, she'd enjoy questioning her mysterious assignment. First, she had to find him.

She tapped the screen of her phone and brought up an app she'd created specifically for her own use. When Cian had gone to the toilet on the train, she'd slipped a tiny chip into the collar of his coat that would allow her to track his movements. The situation wasn't ideal and she'd have to find an opportunity to make the tracker permanent. Until then, she hoped he still wore the coat. The app showed several blinking icons and she tapped the one associated with Cian. The rest she ignored.

A tiny orange dot tormented her and she doubled her focus on Cian's blue marker.

Hunter Pearson was in London. That stupid orange dot confirmed her suspicions. Why hadn't he contacted her? He must think she was still in Edinburgh and until Malcolm told him otherwise, Nikala was happy to let Hunter think she was unavailable. A shudder wormed its way down her spine and settled in her gut. The longer she could avoid seeing Hunter, the better. It had been two years since their last meeting and that hadn't been near long enough.

With a deep, cleansing breath, she set off in the direction of Temple Church and cleared her mind of the man who, for almost twenty years, had used her as a human lab rat. A hand reflexively smoothed over the arm where he'd inserted hundreds of needles during her stay with him. He'd made her what she was—a freak. An enhanced human, he'd called it. A gunshot would heal within hours; she was stronger and faster than anyone she'd encountered, and as far as she knew, couldn't be killed.

Hell, if the vile liquids and potions he'd made her drink hadn't knocked her off, nothing could. She swiped a hand over her lips as if to remove the taint of the drinks. A thrumming of her heart reminded her of the gentler moments she'd shared with Hunter. He was as much a father to her as her own dad. He was the one who taught her how to fight. It was Hunter who gave her the skills necessary to become an elite spy. She had him to thank for her life, such as it was.

And yet—if given the chance, she'd kill him.

Except, she couldn't. God knew she'd fantasized about it enough, but something always kept her from going through with it.

A car honked and brought her out of her misty remembrances. Yes, she owed much to Hunter, but she couldn't forget he was also the man who tortured her. Embarrassment burned against her ribs at the memory of her clumsy attempt to seduce him when she was still a teen and raging with hormones. Whether out of some naïve belief that he might end the torture if they were lovers, or some unconscious form of Stockholm syndrome, she couldn't be certain.

He'd been kind, but stern in his rejection. He wasn't interested in her in that way, he'd explained. The denial had stung and she'd buried her hurt deep, along with every other emotion she didn't know how to deal with.

Even though he'd claimed he wasn't interested in her sexually, much of what he did to her was far more intimate and invasive than sexual intercourse. He abused her in ways no one should have to suffer and in her messed-up pubescent mind, that equated love. Love that he wouldn't return.

She supposed he did love her, in his own way, but to Hunter, Nikala wasn't a woman—she was a weapon that he honed and adjusted. Even after all of his experiments and tests, he was never satisfied with his work. Never satisfied with her. She'd left Hunter, humiliated and confused. He wanted perfection and Nikala would never measure up to his standards.

A flash to her right caught her attention and she tucked the phone in her jacket pocket. She checked her reflection in a shop window and adjusted her ponytail. One of Malcolm's security operatives trailed her by about fifty feet. She slid her glance across the street and there was Yasheda, trying to look casual, as if she were nipping to the shops. That Malcolm had sent backup to follow Nikala sent fury blazing through her blood. The man was insufferable. He knew she was capable of handling Cian.

Unless he thought she'd been compromised. Or he'd lost trust in her. *Shit.* She'd miscalculated his response to Cian's presence. She'd pushed too far this time. It would be an easy thing to regain his trust—it always was. Malcolm needed her for the same reasons she needed him—they were all the family they had.

Whatever Malcolm's reasons for sending the agents, Nikala would make certain he understood she would handle Cian on her own terms. Alone.

❧ 14 ❧

Nikala strolled along the street at a decent pace, keeping an eye on her pursuers, Yasheda and Jude. They were Malcolm's current favorites and two of his agents she'd had the pleasure of training herself. At one time, she would've even called them friends. Seeing them trailing her now, she wasn't sure they felt the same.

They hung back far enough to not lose her, but close enough to catch her if she bolted. At the corner, Nikala turned sharply and entered a grocery store. Before Jude entered, she hurried to the rear and kicked open the back door. An alarm blared, startling a woman nearby. Nikala ducked into a corner of the store and waited until Jude rushed past and out the door before she went to the front of the store. As expected, Yasheda darted through traffic across the street. She glanced at the entrance of the grocers, then ran to the back alley.

Nikala counted to ten, then left the shop and jogged to the next corner. Sirens sounded and she slowed to a walk. Her racing heart kept pace with the speeding police cars. With any luck, both Yasheda and Jude would be caught in the alley and off her tail. She brushed a few stray hairs that had come loose from her ponytail off her face and grinned. She could just imagine the hulking Jude behind bars. It would be like putting a bear in a dog crate.

"Nice try, princess." Jude's velvety voice sounded behind her and Nikala's grin drooped.

She turned and faced all six feet five inches of him. "It was a fifty-fifty shot and looks like it worked fifty percent."

A tic at the corner of his eye showed his irritation. "One of these days, your luck will run out."

"Really? I thought it already had. Or is there another reason you're following me?" When his eye twitched again, the grin returned to her lips. "Malcolm didn't send you, did he? You're just pissed that you lost your target and had to squelch off me. Good plan, but I don't share."

Neither did he, which was why she knew using their friendship wouldn't work. This was business, not personal.

She slammed her fist into his solar plexus and darted down a narrow lane. His big feet slapped against the cobblestones, echoing off the windows of nearby buildings. She kept her pace fast enough to evade, but not lose him. A parking garage opened to her right and she pivoted to enter. Jude followed, a few steps behind.

She ducked behind a Mini and waited. Adrenaline ripped through her bloodstream and her hair follicles turned electric. She loved this. The chase, the confrontation: this was her thing. Leave boring meetings to Malcolm—this was where Nikala excelled. This was what Hunter had modified her for.

Jude's footsteps halted and she listened harder. His labored breathing came from two cars over. She eased around the Mini and rushed him from behind, her enhanced speed making her little more than a blur. Her attack startled him, but not for long. His big paws formed into fists and one connected with her side. The air whooshed from her lungs, and she stumbled backward. Jude took her action for weakness and a sly grin curled his lips.

"Not so badass, after all. What does Malcolm see in you?"

So, this was about pride. Nikala made a show of holding her side and breathing heavy. She shook her head and watched him from the corner of her eye. No one knew her connection to Malcolm and she wouldn't give him the satisfaction of knowing who she really was. Best to let him stew and rage, burn through his energy because he couldn't believe Malcolm might prefer her over him. Pride got you killed.

When his fists relaxed, she kicked out, landing a boot under his ribs. He swore and puffed, then lumbered toward her. She was ready.

Another kick, this time to his stomach, followed by an uppercut to his chin. Jude struck out and she defended herself with blocks to his moves. He'd been trained in martial arts, same as her—hell, *by* her—but his size worked against him. She didn't take anything for granted, though. She knew his record. Knew what he was capable of—something she doubted he knew about her.

Their fists whipped through the air, making contact more often than missing their mark. With each hit, she resolved to hit him harder. With each kick, she absorbed his energy and returned it two-fold, using just enough of her modifications to beat him, but not so much he became suspicious. The goal wasn't to kill him. Oh, hell no. She wanted him to return to Malcolm, tail between his legs.

Sweat rolled down his face and his movements became slower. Her heart pumped harder with each passing minute, but not from exhaustion. With practiced control, she held herself back from giving him everything she had. Why waste precious resources? When his eyes were wild and a sneer pulled his lips over his teeth, she knew the fight was over. She'd unleashed his rage and he'd either try to kill her or subdue her, and neither option would suffice.

Jude growled and rushed her, but she was ready. At least, she thought she was. Jude's movements were too quick, too precise for a normal human. The speed of his whirling fists were met with deflections from her. She lost the upper hand and went on the defensive, confusion and dread streaming through her adrenaline, upsetting her rhythm. Jude was enhanced, too. Fucking Hunter and his experiments. She should've known it was a matter of time before he ventured into other areas—super spies. Bollocks.

Nikala took a kick to her middle and shuffled backward, more to gain a moment to think than to recover. If Jude was modified, most likely Yash was as well. She glanced around the car park, but didn't see the woman. Jude advanced, his big paws held up like a boxer. Nikala made a show of breathing hard and even let spittle drip from her mouth. The agent's chuckle ignited the fury buried beneath her dread. Once more Jude rushed in, and this time she *was* ready.

A second before striking, she slipped to the side and kicked his feet out from under him. All of his pent-up energy went into his fall and he hit the ground hard. Nikala jumped onto his back and wrapped her arm around his neck. He struggled against her hold, grasping at her clothes and kicking against the concrete. She held firm until his movements slowed, then ceased.

She rose up from the unconscious man and wiped her brow with the back of her hand.

From somewhere behind her, clapping sounded.

Nikala turned to see Yasheda walking toward her, the same stupid sneer on her lips that Jude wore.

"Well done. Jude always underestimated you, but I didn't. I knew there had to be more to you than just a pretty face."

"Walk away, Yash." Nikala tilted her head toward Jude. "You don't want that."

"No," Yasheda withdrew a knife from inside her jacket, "I don't. But I can't go back to Malcolm and tell him I lost you as well."

Motherfucker. Malcolm *had* sent them. Asshole.

Nikala cracked her neck and rolled her shoulders. She shook out her wrists, then beckoned Yasheda closer. If the foolish woman wouldn't take Nikala's good advice, then she'd have to teach her a lesson.

Smaller and faster than Jude, Yasheda zipped around Nikala like an annoying gnat. Too fast for a normal human. She'd been right—Yash was enhanced as well. The flash of her blade caught the yellowish glare of the overhead lights. Nikala kept an eye on the knife while fending off Yasheda's kicks and quick jabs. The woman's determination startled Nikala. So much for being friends. The way Yash went for her throat with the sharp blade proved her loyalties had shifted entirely to Malcolm.

Anger flooded her thoughts, blurring the line between rational thinking and murderous intent. Her focus narrowed to Yasheda's face and Nikala struck hard. One, two, three quick jabs and blood gushed from the woman's nose. A roundhouse kick to her side and she went sprawling across the floor. The knife clanged when it hit the ground and disappeared beneath a car.

The urge to kick the stupid woman until she no longer took a breath overwhelmed Nikala, but she held back. There was no honor in defeating a fallen opponent. She heard Hunter's stern voice berating her, telling her that she was weak to let the woman live. He'd have her slay them both and discard the bodies where no one would ever find them.

Nikala shook her head hard to silence the menacing taunts of her youth. Even if Yash had forgotten their nights out drinking to ease the stress of their job, Nikala hadn't. She wouldn't kill a friend. Instead, she kneeled on Yasheda's back and ripped her shirt to make strips for tying her hands together. Yash struggled, her arms flailing, nails ready to scratch Nikala. She grabbed a handful of hair and slammed her head against the concrete.

"Move again and I will kill you."

Yasheda quit fighting. Nikala tore another strip of Yash's shirt and bound the woman's ankles and then secured them to her wrists. She looked like a hog ready to roast. When Nikala finished with Yasheda, she did the same to Jude.

As she left the parking garage, she glanced at her one-time friend. Fear lingered in the woman's eyes. Nikala staggered out the door and rested her hands on her knees. What did Yash fear? Certainly not Nikala. She could've killed her, but didn't.

If not Nikala, then Malcolm. But why? Had he sent the pair to take out Nikala or find Cian or let Nikala find Cian then kill one or both of them? They were good agents—skilled at deception, same as her. In her absence, she'd lost the ability to know when they were lying. But then, in her absence, they'd undergone modifications from Hunter. Their new strength wasn't as honed or as battled hardened as Nikala's, giving her the advantage—but for how long?

Question after question tumbled through her brain. Behind them all, Hunter's face tormented her thoughts. It could've been a test. She wouldn't put it past Hunter to override Malcolm's orders and bribe Yash and Jude. Even after two years of living on her own, Hunter still tried to control her.

Malcolm or Hunter: it didn't matter who had sent the pair. She wouldn't let them get the better of her. Anger fueled her need to find Cian and prove those assholes wrong. She was more than capable of getting answers from him. The final question rummaging through her mind was—would she give the men the truth? After their failure with Yasheda and Jude, Nikala once again wondered why they deserved her loyalty. She knew the answer and refused to allow it space in her mind. Shoved it to the depths of her soul and forbade it from entering her heart.

One question she didn't evade: why had Hunter enhanced Yasheda and Jude? Then, a second, more terrifying question turned her blood to ice—how many more people had he destroyed with his tests and modifications? It unnerved her to believe she wasn't alone, while at the same time she found solace in the fact that there were others like her. A macabre family, of sorts.

She rose and stared at the rust spot on her trousers. She turned her hand over and winced at the gash across her palm. Yasheda's blade had cut her and she'd not even felt it. Nikala tore a strip from her blouse and wrapped it around her hand. That was three shirts she'd ruined in less than five minutes. Not her best record time, but close.

With a shrug and shake of her shoulders, she took out her phone and set off in the direction of the blinking blue dot. At the corner of where her app said Cian was, she slipped into a shadowy doorway to observe the property. A five-story sandstone and brick Georgian building with one main entrance. She scanned the windows, noting those with closed drapes, but lit from within, and those that were dark. The top floor flats all had balconies and as Nikala's gaze roved over the darkened windows, she stopped at the last on the right. A light flicked on and a moment later, Cian drew back the drapes. Her heart pounded as she watched him step from the flat to the balcony, looking for all the world like a king surveying his domain.

She slouched deeper into the doorway to avoid being seen. His gaze swept over the street, pausing to stare at something to his left, Nikala's right. She desperately wanted to know what caught his attention, but stayed pressed against the wall. After several moments, he continued his surveillance without even a blink when his gaze passed over her hiding place. Another sweep of the area and then he ducked into the flat.

Nikala let out the breath she'd been holding. It was showtime.

With a last glance at the empty balcony, she jogged across the street to the front door. She scanned the names on the registry, not seeing either McCabe or MacNair. Mentally, she worked out which might be Cian's flat and buzzed. When no one answered, she moved to the next guess.

A woman answered. "Hello?"

"Delivery for flat six. Can you let me in?"

A moment later, the door clicked and Nikala slipped through the opening. She carefully closed it behind her, checking the street for Malcolm's thugs. Not seeing anyone of interest, she turned toward the staircase and jogged to the top floor. At Cian's door, she paused, taking a moment to make certain she looked suitably mussed. As she raised her hand to knock, the door opened and Cian stood before her, tall, handsome, and imposing. He'd taken off his coat and suit jacket, and loosened his tie, leaving his tailored white shirt unbuttoned, allowing a peek of chest hair.

"Miss St. James." His features twisted into a look of, *I should be surprised you're here, but somehow, I'm not.* His smile, however, did its best to disarm her, and dammit, it worked. Her knees shuddered at the way his upper lip curled to reveal pearly teeth.

For a second, she imagined those teeth sunk into her skin and another shudder raced from her heart to between her legs. She squeezed her thighs together with a silent reprimand.

"I was hoping you'd have a first-aid kit." She held up her cut hand with a sheepish grin.

"Come in." Cian stepped backward to allow her entrance and her gaze swept over the immaculate, sparsely yet fashionably decorated flat. His tastes, if they were his, ran to casual comfortable with a traditional flair.

He checked the outside hallway before closing the door and locking it.

Nikala affected a wounded doe demeanor and simpered up at him. She might've even batted her lashes. "Clumsy me. I slipped on a cobblestone and landed on a piece of glass."

He took her hand in his own and unwrapped the scrap of her blouse. His gaze flicked to the torn remnant peeking from her trousers. A small whistle came from between his lips and he nodded to a door opposite the large windows.

"Wash up. I'll be right back." Cian disappeared into another room and she did as told.

Nikala removed her coat and placed it over the back of a sofa. She took her time in the bathroom, using a soft washcloth and soap to cleanse the wound, and also to freshen up after a long day. When she returned to the lounge, Cian was waiting with plasters, antiseptic, and two tumblers of what she hoped was whisky. After the day she'd had, she wouldn't be picky, though. Any alcohol was appreciated.

He held out his hand and she placed hers palm up. Warmth spread across her arm up to her chest. A strange tingling followed. Once it reached her rapidly beating heart, the tingling spiraled to her extremities. After the tingling came a pinch. Not unpleasant, but unknown.

Nikala watched Cian's face as he swiped an antiseptic-soaked cotton ball across her skin. What should've burned didn't. She braced for the sting, but felt only the cotton's pressure. Cian blew against her palm and her thighs trembled as if he'd blasted her with a turbine engine.

"How did you find me?" His casual tone didn't fool her. He'd probably been expecting her.

He concentrated on cleaning her wound and dressing it with several Steri-Strips. If he knew the sensations his touch caused, he didn't show it.

"I, erm." She swallowed the desire to stroke his dark hair. "I saw you on the balcony. A few minutes ago." Her shrug upset his grip and his fingertips wrapped around hers, holding her hand firmly in place.

"Good fortune, that." Once the plasters were applied, he wrapped her hand in a gauze bandage.

Then he raised her palm to his lips and kissed it.

Nikala fought the urge to jerk her hand away and slap him.

She also fought the urge to melt into a simpering mass of goo.

Damn him and his irritating way of confusing her emotions until she wasn't sure which way was up. Fuck questioning him. She needed to kill him and get out of his flat as soon as possible. She was certain CCTV saw her enter his building, but doubted anyone had seen her enter this flat specifically. Her mind raced with ways to make it look like an accident all the while he held her palm in his big, warm hand.

"Try to be more careful in the future. That glass infected your skin. You could've had a nasty reaction and had to get a tetanus jab." His thumb traced over the bandage, sending fresh spirals of whatever the fuck it was through her body.

"I should go. It was wrong to impose on you. Thank you, but I should go." Her stammered words held little conviction and she didn't try to take her hand from his grip.

"Of course. But first, something to help with your recovery." He handed her a glass and took one for himself.

She hesitated and he chuckled. The deep vibrato did things to her already overworked heart.

His glance went from her glass to the diamond solitaire she wore on her right ring finger. "If whisky isn't your poison, I have wine."

She curled her fingers against her trousers. It might've been a cute saying, but Nikala had the distinct impression Cian knew exactly what she'd done to that man on the train. She'd made it look like she simply reached out to touch his leg. How could Cian guess she'd poisoned the man? He couldn't. That would be ridiculous. It was just a saying, nothing more.

"Whisky's fine." With a brazen swipe, she claimed the tumbler and took a healthy swig. Notes of honey tickled her tongue and she swirled the liquid in her mouth before she swallowed. A satisfying burn coated her throat and stomach. One more gulp and she emptied the tumbler.

"Damn." Cian chuckled again and she swooned. "I like a woman who enjoys her whisky."

"And I like a man who can treat a wound." *Fuck it.* She set the glass on the table and grabbed him by the tie, pulling him close. Surprise lit in his eyes, followed by a devilish grin.

His mouth claimed hers and she tugged at his tie, almost ripping it to get it undone. She worked to unbutton his shirt as his fingers worked on hers.

"No, my shirt stays on." Nikala moved his hands lower, to her pants.

They were a flurry of motion, each stripping the other while keeping their lips locked in a battle to stay connected. His belt jangled open and she hurried with his trousers, desperate to feel him inside her.

Frenzied sex she knew well. No thought, just passion and release. No emotion, just down and dirty, get the job done. This was how she liked sex. Detached.

Cian growled into her mouth, the sound coming from low in his sternum. The corners of her lips quirked in a smile. They kicked off their shoes and, both still wearing socks, Cian lifted her to his eagerly waiting cock. As she slid onto his erection, he pushed her against the wall. Her head hit with a satisfying *thunk* and she sighed into his mouth.

His fevered pace matched her own need. Harder, faster.

Sweat glistened on his forehead. Beneath the sheen, a curious iridescence shone through. Like pearlescent nail varnish swirling across his skin. Fascinated, Nikala stared for a moment until she remembered herself and turned away from his handsome features. Don't make eye contact. Don't let it be personal.

She repeated her mantras until she was rocking against him, taking every thrust deeper and deeper. Her orgasm crested and she panted with her coming release. Veins protruded on Cian's neck, snaking their way to his forehead.

Fuck, but he was damn sexy.

Naked, on the cusp of coming, teeth gritted against the

effort, he wasn't a god, but right then she would've prayed at his altar.

Look away, Nikala.

She cast her glance down, to his chest that heaved close to hers. Her nipples raked against the hairs on his pecs and she arched to keep contact. Just one pinch and she'd be over the edge. Just one touch of his hand to her throat and she'd release. Silently, she willed him to do something, anything, that might cause a fissure of pain, but she kept her mouth closed. Maintained silence.

Her traitorous gaze went to his face and she sucked in a breath at the intensity in his eyes. He was fucking her, yes, but there was something lurking in the brown depths that unsettled her. She tried to look away, but couldn't. The confusion and fear she saw in his expression tore through her psyche.

Why would he fear her?

His head bent and a moment later, his lips were on her neck, sucking with such force she knew he'd leave a mark and for once, didn't care. The delightful pain went straight to her core. A mumbled, "Oh God," escaped her clenched lips and she felt herself tumbling into her orgasm.

Cian's lips returned to her mouth and she opened for him, hungrily sucking on his tongue, milking it with her mouth. His groan rose to the ceiling and, she imagined, out through the roof to cover all of London. Her own cries came as shuddering gasps as she pulsed around his cock.

Instead of pushing away from her and gathering his discarded clothes, he gazed at her with a look of wonder in those gorgeous brown eyes. His fingertips swiped errant hairs from her face, only to return a moment later and trace over her skin. His lips made featherlight landings upon her chin, her cheeks, her eyelids.

She let him. Gods help her, but she let him.

Her legs wrapped around his waist and she leaned against the wall for stability. She moaned when his hands cupped her breasts, and whimpered when his hot tongue sucked on her earlobe.

Gods help her, she wanted more.

"I'm going to shower, and would love your company. Then I'll make us dinner." Cian's words drifted to her through a dreamy fog.

"Mmmm hmmm." She lowered her legs and regretted losing contact with his skin.

She watched him walk bare assed to his bedroom. At the door, he gave a cheeky grin with a nod toward the shower, then went inside.

Nikala pressed her hands to her face, enjoying the scratch of bandage on her sensitive skin. Bollocks. The water turned on and Cian called out to her, but she wasn't joining him any time soon. She grabbed at her panties and yanked them up while cramming her legs through her trousers. In less than a minute, she was dressed and out the door.

Fucking Cian MacNair. She should've killed him. But why had he looked at her that way? And for fuck's sake, why did he offer to make her dinner? This wasn't a fucking date. Why had he been so sweet?

Therron stroked the cheek of his cursed love. Her whimpers had faded and she curled, relaxed, into the blankets. She no longer needed him. As much as he wished to remain, she hadn't asked him to stay and he didn't wish to overstep. With a muffled sigh of regret, he left her sleeping in the gigantic bed. All of the beds in Midna's palace were made to sleep at least three, preferably more. She might pretend she didn't encourage couplings, but Therron knew Rori had guessed the truth—the Unseelie queen delighted in love. It was she who was a romantic, not him like Rori had assumed. He smiled to himself as he left Rori's chamber and hurried down the quiet hallway.

At the balcony, he leaned over to see Midna reclined on her divan, several fae suckling various body parts. Dammit.

He jogged down the stairs to the ground floor and approached with caution. When the queen was in one of her moods, it made negotiating with her more difficult. He hoped the fae snuggled against her gossamer-covered ebony skin had satisfied her enough he could make a single request.

"Therron," Midna slurred and he relaxed. That was the sound he'd hoped to hear—contentment.

"Your Majesty." He knelt to whisper in her ear and she turned to catch his cheek with her lips.

"Why must you deny me?" Her nose angled toward his lips and she sniffed like a dog caught on a scent. "Ah." Laughter bubbled in the single word. "I see."

A hand snaked its way up his arm and she gripped his sleeve with hands like iron. The fae sleeping to her right lifted his head, his long hair covering most of his face. A snarl made his handsome features ugly. Not just the sneer, but a look of venom in his eyes.

"Easy, mate. I just need to ask her a question." The calm in Therron's voice belied the anger the young fae's possessiveness brought out in him.

Hangers-on, moochers—all of them. They took and took and took from the queen, but how often did any of them give something in return?

"I envy her," Midna was saying, close to his ear, but loud enough the fae also heard. "Does she know?"

"Not from me," Therron answered. He couldn't tell Rori his fate, or that he'd loved her the moment he saw her. She'd never believe him. "I wish to use your doorway to the Seelie Court."

"You're leaving us so soon? What will she think if you desert her now?"

He'd asked himself the same thing a dozen times and didn't like the answer. She came to the Unseelie Court for a reason and would be hard-pressed to pursue that education with him around. That was part of it, but he knew if he stayed, he'd lose himself to madness seeing Rori with even one of the handsome fae waiting on Midna. Jealousy, raw and primal, tore through his heart. He'd rather die than watch her lose her heart to another. After all, he was only a thief. At least he could leave knowing one thing for sure—Rori had stolen much more than his heart.

Midna sat up, dislodging the young fae and several others. The sneer the man wore turned to a hiss and Midna waved him off. "Go see to the others. Go now, that's a good boy." When she returned to Therron, a darkness had entered her eyes. "The young are so tedious."

Another fae approached, this one tall and muscular and handsome. His short hair caught the scant sunlight that shone from the covered windows, giving him a haloed appearance.

"My queen." He knelt opposite Therron. In contrast to the young fae, this man's eyes shone of devotion and, Therron admitted, love. He'd always thought the álainn obedience selfish in their wants, but this man sought to care for his queen, not take from her. "You should be in your chambers, resting. Let me accompany you."

"Yes, it was a taxing night." Midna held her hand to the fae and rose. "What do you seek in Eirlys's kingdom?"

Therron rose as well, his hand at Midna's elbow. "The guard, Dorchmeir. I'm hoping he can give us answers. And I'd like to know if there are others in her employ who wish Faerie harm."

"Smart man." She stroked his unmarked cheek. "I shall have to investigate here, as well." A sly grin lifted her lips. "Interrogations can be so much fun." A devilish glint lit the depths of her charcoal-colored eyes. A moment later, they turned a shocking shade of green and her skin gleamed like porcelain. "Fabian, see Therron to the Room of Mirrors, then come to my quarters. We must discuss how to find those who wish not to be found."

"Yes, my queen." Fabian released Midna's hand, reluctance clear on his features. He turned and strolled in the opposite direction. The short skirt he wore swung with his strides.

"Thank you." Therron leaned in to kiss Midna's cheek and whisper, "Let Rori discover her purpose on her own. She doesn't need to be confused with any sense of loyalty to me."

Midna nodded, a look of resignation in her eyes.

Despite the rumors, Therron knew Midna wouldn't force Rori to do anything she wasn't comfortable with. It was the question of how far Rori would push herself that haunted his thoughts. Of all the trapped fae, she was the only one to break out of Acelyne's glass prison and in the short time they'd spent together, he saw her ferocious need to succeed. Not win, but to do a task to her best ability, no matter the cost. Her confrontation with Acelyne was proof of that. He could only hope she wouldn't take her training too far at Midna's court.

Therron jogged to catch up to the pretty fae named Fabian and they walked in silence to the Room of Mirrors. Once there, Fabian bowed low to Therron.

"My queen is vexed of late. If there is anything I can do to help ease her burdens, please don't hesitate to ask."

Convince her to stop letting others use her. Tell her she doesn't need to be her kingdom's life-giving source. Love her with as much care and devotion as you've shown and earn her love in return.

All of these thoughts and more coursed through Therron's mind, but he simply said, "I will. And in return, I would appreciate Rori having a friend here in the palace. There are many who are not fond of the MacNairs, but would smile to Rori's face for their own betterment."

"It shall be done." Fabian gripped Therron's forearm and he did the same.

With nothing more to be said, Therron entered the room and took a deep breath. The last time he was here, it had been with Rori, and the strange little girl had shown up. He glanced from mirror to mirror, but saw only his own reflection.

Satisfied no one else was in the room, or watching from one of the many mirrors, he chose the frame that would take him to the Seelie palace and said the words required to open the portal. A wavering of glass beckoned and he stepped inside. The expected soundless blackness enveloped him. Therron kept his eyes open, aware that the portals were never safe, and ready for an attack at the other end. He couldn't be certain what he walked into. Eirlys had brought Dorchmeir with her to the vale. If others were involved, they might have overrun the palace in the queen's absence.

A dot of light came into focus and Therron stiffened with apprehension. The closer he came, the harder he listened, but only silence answered him.

He stepped from the mirror into the Seelie queen's Room of Mirrors and shook out the tension in his arms. In the few times he'd used a fae portal, he hadn't grown accustomed to the paralyzing emptiness within. Theirs had a different feel to them than elven doorways.

It had been several millennia since the same fae who cursed his family had brought portal knowledge to Faerie. In the centuries since, the fae believed they were the only ones who understood the magic of doorways between one place and another. The elves were happy to let them believe the fallacy and encouraged the lie.

If the fae didn't remember where the knowledge had come from, they wouldn't try to steal from the elves ever again. At least, that's what the elders believed, but Therron was of another mind —share information. Remove the mystique and stop the childish contention of who can best the other.

All of the problems happening around them stemmed from pride. From mistakes made in haste and grudges borne from lack of understanding. It did no good to fear the unknown. His hand went to his cheek and he flinched at the heat coming off his scar. Such a hypocrite. He, more than anyone, feared the past. Feared the darkness that spread over the land. He'd lied when he told Rori he didn't bother with fae politics. They were all connected— the faeries, goblins, trolls, brownies, imps, ogres: all the living creatures of this world created a precious balance. Even the mortal realm, or human realm as Rori called it, affected what happened in Faerie.

The relationship between these two worlds were intertwined in a way that made him uncomfortable. Humans were unpredictable and savage. They thrived on disruption and war, something he couldn't understand. Nor did he wish to. Yet, if he were to help Elvenwood and Faerie, understanding was just the beginning. How could they ever hope to survive a war with the mortal realm? They had war machines that could exterminate Elvenwood within moments. The elves had magic, but would it be enough? He shook himself to rid the awful images from his mind. It would be best to focus on the here and now, not worry about what-ifs that might never happen.

Therron scanned the mirrors, trying to recall which one was the exit.

A flurry of air to his left set his senses on high alert and he reached for his sword. A moment later, Eirlys stepped through the mirror and into the room. With one quick glance, she took in the entirety of the room. Her steely gaze settled on Therron.

"Why are you here?" Her accusing tone set him on edge. She brushed invisible lint from her velvet gown. "I could have you killed for trespassing, thief."

Therron placed a hand over his heart and bowed low. "I come with Midna's blessing to seek answers from your guard, Dorchmeir. Acelyne didn't provide us with much insight and it occurred to me that he might fill in some gaps."

Eirlys nodded, her lips pursed. "Is Rori with you?"

"I left her with Midna." His stomach pinched and his palms slicked. Thinking about what she would soon be doing at the Unseelie Court would do him no good. He had to concentrate on the task at hand.

"I see. Follow me." Eirlys swept past him and he moved in step with the queen. "I, too, seek answers. We shall question Dorchmeir together and hopefully be more successful than you were with the enchantress. Time is of the essence. Step quickly."

"Pardon me, ma'am, but I thought you were averse to being near the necromancer?"

"Not the necromancers. Acelyne." Eirlys turned a door

handle cleverly hidden in the design of a mirror's frame. "I couldn't risk her using one last trick to capture Arianna again."

They rushed down the hallway, with courtiers and servants scurrying out of their way. Once outside the palace proper, Eirlys turned in the direction of the gardens and strode across a vast lawn to outbuildings on the edge of a forest. At the door to the second stone structure, she paused.

"What you hear in here must be kept between us. No sharing with Rori or her brother. Am I understood?" Therron nodded, a lump caught in his throat. "Good," Eirlys continued, "because what I'm about to do is against every doctrine and protocol upholding my reign as the Seelie queen."

She yanked on the door handle and ushered him inside the musty-smelling space. Eirlys indicated a door to his left and he held it open for her. A whiff of roses struck his senses as she passed to descend the staircase. Neither spoke as they circled lower and lower beneath the ground. After several minutes, and protestations from his thighs, the stairwell opened to a large room. Like in Midna's crypt, several torches hung from iron clamps attached to the walls.

Three marble slabs occupied the room, but only one was in use. Dorchmeir's corpse lay as if sleeping, with his hands crossed at his chest, his legs splayed slightly. Eirlys grunted and approached. A man emerged from a side chamber, his bald head shining in the firelight.

"My queen." His bow was low, full of reverence.

"Is he ready?" Eirlys didn't look at the newcomer, but kept her focus firmly on Dorchmeir.

"He is. Shall I begin?"

Eirlys nodded and the man chanted similar words to what Midna's necromancer had spoken not more than a few hours past. A chill swept down Therron's back, same as it had in the Unseelie dungeons. This kind of magic was forbidden in the elven kingdom. The dead should stay dead, his father always said.

In theory, Therron agreed, but they needed precious answers that only the dead could provide.

A plume of black smoke rose from Dorchmeir's lips and Eirlys hissed.

"Ask your questions, but be quick. This one does not wish to depart. He has unfinished business and will attach himself to one of you if you linger overlong." The necromancer bowed again and slipped into the antechamber.

When the door clicked shut, Eirlys put her fingertips to the gash at Dorchmeir's throat. An audible whine came from the dead man's lips.

"How do you wake the kidnapped fae?"

"Don't. Know." Dorchmeir wheezed an answer.

Even then, Therron could feel the man insinuating himself into Therron's thoughts. An oily slickness crept up his arms with Dorchmeir's attempt to grab hold of the elf's living body.

"Who is Max?" Therron stood on the opposite side of Eirlys. Her sharp intake of breath and quick glare told him she knew who the courier was.

Gurgled chuckling was followed by a sneer. "She's not worthy—"

Eirlys pressed her finger into the wound Rori's dagger made and Dorchmeir screamed. "Who is kidnapping fae and why?"

The dead guard's head twisted from side to side. "Don't know and don't care. As long as she is destroyed."

Therron didn't need to ask who he meant. "Why did you hate Rori so much? Was this about revenge for you?"

"Yesssssss. She's not worthy."

"Why did you help Acelyne?" Eirlys pushed her whole hand against his throat and Therron felt her magic fill the room.

Eirlys was pumping her magic into Dorchmeir to steal his thoughts. Not only was what the queen doing forbidden, it was punishable by death. Therron met her questioning glance and dipped his chin in a nod that acknowledged he would keep her secrets.

But Eirlys didn't just steal Dorchmeir's thoughts—she somehow displayed them in the air for Therron to see, too.

There, dancing like images in the picture books his mother used to read him and his brothers, were people and places Therron recognized as the Seelie Court. Faces whizzed in and out of focus until they came to Rori. Dorchmeir's thoughts settled on her face and a strangled cry came from the dead man.

A sequence of events followed. Their time at the Academy, where Rori bested him at everything. Even her popularity was seen as a competition. Then his time at the palace, where Eirlys gave him a job as a guard despite his less than stellar record at the Academy. Several images of Esme came and went, mostly with Dorchmeir manipulating the woman to learn Rori's secrets, but Esme wasn't much help. Either the girl truly didn't know, or she was as skilled as Rori at keeping information hidden. A newfound respect blossomed for the girl.

Finally, Dorchmeir's thoughts roamed to Acelyne and their meetings. Eirlys and Therron watched as Acelyne convinced Dorchmeir he would be rewarded for his bravery. He truly didn't know who wanted the amulets, or even what was in them. At first, he thought they were trinkets, but in time he began to suspect they were much more.

Dorchmeir's usefulness to Acelyne had been in his knowledge of the Seelie palace. It was through his information that the enchantress had been able to enter unseen and kidnap the princess. When Eirlys saw the memory, tears tracked down her cheeks. Therron reached out a comforting hand and placed it on her forearm.

"We'll find a way to wake her, Your Majesty. I promise." Acelyne's cryptic message to Rori stuck in his mind. *Dark magic.*

"Thank you." Eirlys patted his hand, a wan smile on her face. "I fear our time is running short. Even now, I can feel Dorchmeir's desperation to redeem himself. He failed Acelyne, yes, but he also failed himself. His part in this was nothing more than a wish to see Rori dead. Pitiful, really."

For a man to spend half his life plotting to kill someone simply because they were better at something was not just pitiful, but an utter waste of potential. Dorchmeir never saw his own promise, just his rage.

Eirlys withdrew a glass vial from a pocket in her gown and uncorked it. She whispered several words, most of which Therron caught and made the hairs on his arms stand on end. Dorchmeir's memories swirled into a funnel and whirled into the glass like a maelstrom. When the last of the images faded, Eirlys replaced the stopper and tucked the vial into the unseen pocket.

"I suggest you look away," Eirlys warned and Therron tilted his head.

"Why, Your Majesty?"

"Because what I'm about to do is unkind, but necessary."

Therron didn't look away. He gave his consent by remaining where he was. Whatever the queen was to do, he would be complicit. This man had hunted Rori and sought to kill the only woman Therron would ever love. He deserved no less than what Eirlys was about to do.

The queen pushed her sleeves to past her elbows and stretched her hands over the dead body. Dorchmeir's body thrashed against the touch of her magic. She placed one hand on his forehead, and another above his heart. Black ooze dripped from his gaping mouth and also from the wound Rori's dagger had made. The smell of burning flesh tore at his nostrils and Therron gagged.

Dorchmeir flailed and lashed out with his arms. His legs kicked violently against the marble. Therron reached across to hold the man's arms at his side. The dead man's strength surprised him and he redoubled his grip. Beneath his fingertips, Dorchmeir's veins rumbled and his skin warmed.

The oily slickness slid off Therron's arms and Dorchmeir's tenuous hold on his mind snapped away. The dead man's body calmed and his skin turned cold.

Sweat ran down Eirlys's brow to her cheeks and her lips moved in a fervent whisper.

"Go now to the kingdom of the dead, where you shall pay penance for your crimes until the end of time." Eirlys lifted her face to the ceiling. *"Eiricanae vitrum desoloae."* The queen plunged her fist through Dorchmeir's chest and jerked upward. His dead heart pulsed once in her hand, then she crushed it until there was only a rotted mess dripping from her fingers.

Sourness swirled in Therron's gut and bile inched toward his tongue. He understood her need to be certain the guard could never cause heartache again, but indeed, her actions were cruel. Perhaps not to the fae, but elves believed in a different fate for the deceased. For an elf, being resurrected as a strong elvenwood tree was the ultimate honor. Those who were damned at best could hope to avoid an eternity trapped in the oily blackness of the runyon tree. Having no heart was worse than any condemnation Dorchmeir might've received while living.

It occurred to him that, as the queen's only witness, should she suspect him of treachery, she wouldn't hesitate to end him as easily as she ended the guard. For a mad moment, he wished he'd stayed above in the small antechamber. But he'd needed answers that only Dorchmeir could provide.

Dorchmeir's body caved in on itself and Eirlys released her hold over his corpse. She called out to the necromancer and a moment later, the door opened. He peered at the body, then at his queen, sadness in his eyes. It appeared even the man who dwelled with the dead understood the horrors Dorchmeir would encounter for all eternity.

"I will see to his remains. Is there anyone to claim him?"

Eirlys shook her head and wiped her hands on Dorchmeir's

trousers. "None. Bury him far from the palace, in an unmarked grave."

"A pauper's burial, Your Majesty?"

"He was a traitor to our throne. It's the least he deserves."

The gaping hole in his chest would suggest he got what he deserved, but Therron held his tongue.

They left the crypt and made their way up the endless stairs to the little room at ground level. Once there, Eirlys let out a breath and held her chest with both hands. For several minutes, she breathed in and out, her nostrils flaring with each inhale.

Finally, she smoothed flyaway strands of hair and met Therron's concerned gaze. "Speak of this to no one. Not even Rori."

"I promise, ma'am. No one will know of this from my lips."

"Good. Now, I need you to tell me all you learned from Acelyne."

They strolled across the grounds, two nobles taking in the fine day, and Therron told the queen all that Acelyne had shared. Through the hallways of her palace, Eirlys questioned him, testing his recounting of the events. At the door to her room, she hesitated.

"I will write down all you've said, and that of what Dorchmeir told us. I'll send Midna a copy when I'm finished. And I suppose you'd like one as well." Eirlys opened her door and Therron touched her sleeve.

"Your Majesty, in there, when I said the name Max, Dorchmeir replied, 'She's not worthy.' Do you know what he meant?"

Eirlys cocked her head toward her rooms and he entered behind the queen. She strode to a table and washed her hands in the porcelain basin. When finished, she dried them on a thick towel.

"Maxine, or Maxx—with a double x—as she liked to be called, is Dorchmeir's mother. She trained with Labhruinn and Hagan. They were thick as thieves. No offense."

"None taken."

"I used to call Labhruinn and Maxx the Gruesome Twosome. Those women would get up to all sorts of trouble. They usually dragged Hagan into the mix. Brilliant, the three of them. After their training at the Academy, Labhruinn chose to stay here, to be in my personal guard while Hagan and Maxx became intelligence officers." Eirlys called for a servant to bring them tea and sandwiches.

Therron's stomach growled and he put a hand over his gut.

Eirlys eyed him with suspicion. "Aren't they feeding you at Midna's place? For shame." She leaned close and he tensed.

"Your Majesty, I don't wish a repeat of your behavior the last time I was in these rooms. It was an awkward situation I hope to never repeat."

Eirlys waved her hand, as if he were being idiotic. "Oh, posh. I had to try bedding you, didn't I? I mean, before you and Rori consummated your love and you were lost to me forever." She winked at him and grinned. "Don't try to lie—I can see by the tension in your jaw, and the way you look like you'd murder anyone who spoke ill of Rori that you've bedded my spy. I won't stop you, if that's what you're worried about." Eirlys sighed dramatically, even putting a hand to her forehead. "Rori could have been one of my greatest spies ever to grace this kingdom, but her destiny is now tied to yours."

The queen curled her legs around her in the great sofa and looked like a fragile child. For a moment, Therron's heart seized with a need to protect the queen. Despite her being a fierce warrior herself, he saw the fragility in her, much the same as he saw in Midna. Yet both women strove to hide their vulnerability as though it were a flaw meant to be covered with a pretense of indifference. The startling realization that it was the same he was doing to Rori pained him. They did what they must to protect those they loved.

Therron sat opposite the queen and took the teacup offered him by the servant. "You were telling me about Maxx."

"Yes, where was I? Oh, I recall. Time went on. Labhruinn and Hagan got married and had children. Maxx married and had Dorchmeir. His father was killed when he was no more than two and Dorchmeir's nan raised him since Maxx's duties often took her away from home. When Hagan died fifteen years ago, Maxx took it hard. They were never lovers, at least, I don't believe so. Just good friends, and fierce competitors. It was that spirit of rivalry that made them both excellent assassins."

"Where is Maxx now?"

"Dead, for all I know. She disappeared about five years ago. On a mission in the human realm. One day she was alive; the next," Eirlys snapped her fingers, "gone. I sent operatives to find her, but they came home empty-handed. It happens, not often, but enough that I've learned not to mourn when one of my favorites go missing or die."

Therron rubbed his chin and mulled over what Eirlys had told him. "Acelyne said Maxx was the courier. Either there's another Maxx we don't know about, or she's alive and well."

He recalled Acelyne's apparent wanderings from one village to another and the pubs she'd stopped in along the way. His mind was fitting the pieces together, but something was missing. Why would Maxx leave her child? Surely no mother could abandon their flesh and blood without cause? Except, she already had in a way, when she left Dorchmeir's care to his nan. Still, to desert family and friends without a word would take a callous heart.

"It's not much, but I might have a clue how to find this mysterious courier. We need to sort out how they're getting to and from the human realm without notice. Is there a list of all the doorways from Faerie to, well, anywhere?" Therron's mind raced with improbable ideas and impossible solutions. He loved a good challenge.

"Midna and I know of them all."

Therron leaned forward and met her gaze. "Can you risk the lives of your subjects, and your daughter, on that belief?" He knew she couldn't, but had to know if Eirlys would be completely honest with him.

Eirlys held the teacup to her lips, not drinking. Her eyes narrowed to dangerous slits. The queen didn't like being challenged, but Therron didn't care.

"No," she finally admitted.

"Teach me how to use your doorways to go anywhere I please. Midna gave me the words to get here. Now I need you to give me access to them all." Her finger tapped anxiously against the rim of her teacup and Therron added, "I'll find their point of entry. I'll find this missing Maxx for you."

He knew how to control every single doorway not only in Elvenwood, but Faerie's portals, too. If Eirlys learned he had that knowledge, it wouldn't serve his purposes. The less the fae meddled with elves, the better. He needed Eirlys to believe having access to fae doorways would give him the means to track Maxx or even Acelyne's past movements. Everyone who used a doorway left a scent, an invisible signature that could be traced. Fortunately for him, very few elves, let alone any fae, knew how to follow the trail.

If he couldn't be with Rori, the least he could do was help with her mission. He swore to himself he wasn't abandoning Rori to her fate with Midna. He vowed he wasn't running away.

Then why did it feel like he was?

❧ 16 ❧

Nikala eased open the door of Cian's building and turned right, in the opposite direction of his flat. The entry doors were at the corner, thankfully, giving her the option of not having to use the sidewalk where he might see her. The urge to glance up, to see if he stood on his balcony, wrapped in a towel and still wet from his shower, was powerful. She turned up the collar of her coat and hurried up the street, away from the Thames.

What kind of woman did he think she was? First, he took liberties with mending her wound, then he fucked her silly, then he offered to shower with her and later make dinner. *As if.* She didn't need food.

The loud grumble of her empty stomach proved her lie. Of the other claims, she ignored her part in them.

"Fine, I'm hungry. I'll get something on the way to the office." She spoke to herself, shaking her head at the irrationality of her behavior. What had gotten into her? She was supposed to question him, then make him disappear. Her pace quickened and she unwrapped the bandage he'd put on her cut. The wound was almost entirely healed. She shoved the used wrappings in her pocket and ducked her head against the wind.

A large garage door swung open to reveal an underground parking area and she slowed. A figure stepped out of the shadows, into her path.

"Pardon me." She moved to walk past him, but he grabbed her by the collar and shoved her against an internal wall. Shards of old concrete and uneven bricks cut against her coat. "Let go of me, asshole."

If he thought he'd found a quick rape for the night, he was sorely mistaken.

He sniffed the air, like a hound on the scent of a fox, and glared at her. "Where is it?"

Nikala didn't have time for this. She was hangry and exhausted and smelled like—

"Where's what?" She kneed him in the groin, enjoying the flash of anger across his face.

"It's gone. But…" He dipped his head and inhaled from her chest to her lips. Then he made a dreamy sort of sound, as if someone showed him the most decadent chocolate cake and told him he could eat all of it by himself. Calorie- and guilt-free.

Great. Now she wanted a chocolate cake. Her stomach gave a vicious jag and she took a calming breath to center herself.

"I've had a long day, asshole. You don't want to mess with me."

He wasn't listening. His eyes had gone glassy and the whites showed where his irises should've been. An odd tickling started at her scalp and moved downward, over her forehead. The man's mouth opened and a wispy kind of mist floated inside.

"What the actual fuck?" Nikala pressed her arms up through his and pushed outward, breaking his hold on her coat.

His shout was silenced by a punch to his jaw, followed by several more to his temple. He withdrew a knife and she blocked his clumsy attack by grabbing his wrist. In a swift movement, she twisted his hand and used the knife to stab him in the throat. His eyes widened with surprise and a choked gasp came from his lips.

She shoved the blade farther against the bones of his neck. He slumped to the ground, gurgling and flailing his limbs. With practiced efficiency, she dragged him deeper into the garage doorway where he wouldn't be found until, she hoped, much later. After a brief check to make sure he hadn't grabbed any of her hair and that none of her fingerprints could be found on the weapon, she hurried out of the entryway and down a side street to the Tube station.

What the hell had that been? Cian's kiss in the subway and the man in Edinburgh came to mind. A scyver. She hadn't believed him. Still didn't believe him. But that man had done something to her. She put a hand to her forehead where her scalp still tingled. The underside of her wrist shimmered with an iridescence she'd never seen—at least not on herself. It reminded her of the pearly glisten on Cian's forehead when he fucked her. Like glitter beneath their skin.

Nikala shoved her hands into her pockets and sped up. She rushed past the Tube and walked the distance to Malcolm's office. The crisp air helped clear her mind. Dinner was all but forgotten. Too many random events had happened in too small a time. She needed to make notes, to connect the dots, to find a pattern to the randomness. If there was one.

At the entrance to the great glass building, she paused. If she used her keycard, he'd know she'd been there. Her stomach churned despite its emptiness. She didn't want to see him right now, not after what had happened with Yash and Jude. She wasn't ready to confront him about sending a team to trail her, and/or take her out. And for sure she didn't want to tell him she hadn't killed Cian, but murdered some psychopath in an alley.

Shit.

Fuck.

An office worker exited the building and Nikala smiled gratefully while he held the door for her. She recognized him from previous visits, and thankfully he let her through without making small talk. With a quick thanks, she shuffled to the lift reserved for restaurant guests and pressed the button. The front desk where visitors signed in sat empty. The security guard who worked the night shift must be doing his rounds, or whatever it was they did during the long hours when everyone was elsewhere. It was after seven and most of the employees of whatever businesses occupied the ridiculous building would be home with their families, or at the pub for a pint. She didn't care where they were, just that they didn't get in her way.

A bank of lifts faced her, but she ignored those that would take her to offices on other floors. The lift she required pinged and Nikala held her breath. The doors opened to emptiness. She stepped in and pressed the only button available—for the restaurant two floors above Malcolm's office. Another two floors beneath Malcolm's was Hunter's lab. The restaurant dominated the top floor, with breathtaking views of the city, but Nikala wasn't in the mood for it tonight. She'd collect her bags and book a hotel nearby, then grab a kabab or something quick.

The lift doors opened to a lobby with a friendly hostess waiting to help Nikala, but she veered left toward the toilets and stairs. She skipped down two flights of stairs to Malcolm's floor and paused at the door. No sounds came to her from the other side and she carefully worked her lock pick in the tumbler until the door clicked open. She dared not use her keycard as it would record her entry time and when she left. The less Malcolm knew of her movements, the better.

She peered in, relieved to see Malcolm's reception area was dark. It was a rare night Malcolm let his staff go home before nine. He was either expecting her, or had an appointment elsewhere. She hoped for the latter. Nikala closed the exit door behind her and crept to the open area, avoiding Malcolm's security cameras.

A sense of unease rippled through her veins, but she shoved it aside. It might be a coincidence that the receptionist—Nikala didn't even know the poor lass's name—and the security staff downstairs weren't around. She hated coincidences. Hairs rose on her arms and neck as Nikala hurried to her office and unlocked the door without a sound. No sense giving Malcolm warning she'd returned. If he was in his office, which she hoped he wasn't. She opened her laptop and entered her password. As she waited for the ruddy thing, she nibbled on a fingernail, tearing it with her teeth. The screen came to life and she scanned the images from the cameras she'd placed in his office. Malcolm wasn't there.

She let out a long breath and sank into her chair, running her fingers through her hair, loosening the ponytail she wore. Her arms splayed behind her, stretching the muscles across her chest. Several rust specks dotted her coat and she flicked at them. Probably the psychopath's blood. It wouldn't do to be running around with his DNA on her. She'd have to find a hotel with laundry facilities.

After another stretch and crack of her neck, she typed in a hotel search and waited. Her stomach roared, reminding her of its empty state, and her bladder protested its fullness. She closed the laptop and returned her desk chair to where it had been when she entered. Less OCD than it was covering her tracks, Nikala turned off the lights of her office and checked that she'd locked the door before she went to the toilet.

She left the bathroom door open while she relieved herself, listening hard for any sound coming from Malcolm's rooms next to hers. This high up, not even traffic disturbed her. As she washed her hands, she noticed a few spots of blood on her neck. They came away with a quick splash of water, but the dark circles under her eyes would take more effort. Gods, but she was tired. Not just from the day, but everything. Being Malcolm's pet was almost as tedious as being Hunter's prisoner.

Not for the first time, she wondered what her life would be like if she could escape them both.

Also, not for the first time, she shoved that daydream to the bowels of her mind. That was the path of crazy making and death. She'd never be free from Hunter or Malcolm. At least, not while either lived.

Muffled voices in the lobby startled her and she stilled, her heart slowing with each syllable the men spoke.

Malcolm. Shit.

The voices came closer and she flicked off the light, then closed the door of the bathroom. A key scratched in the office door's lock, followed by a squeak as the doorknob turned.

Malcolm clucked his tongue. "Her bags are still here, but she hasn't returned."

"We have business to finish." Hunter's gravelly, slightly slurred words hit Nikala in the abdomen.

Hunter Pearson. Damn. What was he doing here?

The door clicked shut and Nikala let out a long, slow breath. Her head pounded and chest tightened. Her first instinct was to grab her bags and leave the moment they entered Malcolm's office, but she hesitated.

Instead, she relocked her office door even though it was useless if Malcolm had his own key, and sat in her chair, tapping her fingers on the closed laptop. A moment later, she opened it and plugged in her headphones. Voices drowned out the sound of blood rushing through her ears.

On the screen, Hunter helped himself to a glass of vodka without offering anything to Malcolm.

"Viggo McCabe, you said?" Hunter shook his head and swirled ice in his tumbler. "Doesn't ring a bell. But then, I meet so many people, it's hard to keep names and faces straight. Did he mention me at all?"

"Just Acelyne."

"And you told him nothing?"

Malcolm's eyes narrowed to dangerous slits. "How long have we known each other? I'm not stupid, Pearson." He chugged the liquid in his glass and poured more. "Yasheda and Jude lost her. I don't recall giving the order for them to follow Nikala."

Hunter ignored Malcolm's pointed stare and shrugged. "We're at a crucial stage of our testing. We can't afford to lose Nikala's allegiance now."

"You make it sound like a bloody fraternity. Nikala's loyalty has never been in question. You, my friend, are another story." Malcolm pointed his glass at Hunter. "What happened to Maxx? Nikala said she never showed. Then this Viggo character just happens to make an appearance two days later?" He downed the liquor and slammed the glass on the cabinet.

Hunter paced to the window and back to the comfortable chairs set around a coffee table as if it were a bloody lounge in someone's home. He sat down, then rose and paced to the window again. He stood there several moments, his fingers working through his thick beard. He had been handsome once, but she'd erased those memories. He looked as she chose to remember him, with jet-black hair, clear, ocean-blue eyes, and a sloping, pockmarked face he tried to cover with a thick beard.

She'd given him the deformity. At fifteen—after her attempt at seduction was rebuffed—she'd rebelled against him and his endless testing, endless lectures, endless imprisonment. He'd demanded she make coffee for him, such a simple thing, and she'd snapped. Nikala shuddered at the memory of that morning when she'd thrown a vial of blue liquid at him. The chemical inside burned through his skin to the bone, leaving his jaw permanently damaged. It had taken several surgeries to repair his internal and external injuries and even longer for Nikala to forgive herself.

"I haven't spoken to Maxx in weeks. As far as I knew, everything was set. I'll go to Edinburgh tomorrow and find out what's happened." A tremor sounded in Hunter's voice. "With this

McCabe fellow asking about Acelyne, it must mean something's happened on the other side."

Nikala sat up straighter and checked to make sure the memory card was still in her laptop, recording. Satisfied, she held her earbuds in place and listened harder to Hunter and Malcolm's speech patterns. She'd sort out what "other side" meant later. For now, she focused on their body language and words.

"You don't think they know about us, do you?" Malcolm's hands shook as he put ice cubes into his tumbler.

"We have to assume they don't, but take nothing for granted." Hunter turned to face Malcolm, his deformity reddening with his intensity. "Send Nikala away. I don't want her involved in this."

Malcolm scoffed and lifted his lips in a sneer. "Don't play the compassionate father figure now, old friend. We both know the hell you put her through."

"With your blessing."

Nikala's hands shook at the simple admission. She'd always known, but to hear Hunter say it stung. Tears threatened and she fought through her hurt to where she'd been trained not to feel. To act dispassionately and get the job done. That was her purpose. Her reason for living. She was a weapon, not a woman. The words looped through her mind and her hands continued to shake.

"Yes," Malcolm said into his glass, "with my blessing. For this." He waved around the office. "I built an empire so you could play God." His sigh carried through Nikala's headphones.

What the devil were they up to? More than ever, she needed to know what Acelyne was.

"Just…send her away. She's been through enough."

Did Hunter actually have remorse in his tone? Nikala shook her head and stifled a laugh. The day he felt an ounce of sorrow for what he did to her, she'd know it was the end of times.

"Give me the shipment." Hunter tilted his chin toward the safe.

Malcolm fumbled with the keypad twice before getting it right. Hunter watched over his shoulder, clearly able to see the code Malcolm punched in. The door swung open and revealed two shelves: one with Malcolm's laptop, the other empty save for some papers.

"Where are they?"

Malcolm's eyes widened and he searched beneath both shelves. "I don't know. They were here, locked up." A slight tremble to his words made Nikala hunch over the screen. Malcolm had never trembled a moment in her life. He was a damn good actor, though. She almost believed he was frightened.

She watched Hunter's movements, noting the stiffening of his jaw. Something wasn't right. She knew the shipment had been there. Before she left for Edinburgh, she'd personally checked to verify all the amulets, less the one she stole, were in the safe.

Hunter dragged a hand through his hair and swore to the ceiling. "We don't have time for games. Where. Are. The. Boxes?" Each word came out a punch, but Malcolm didn't flinch, didn't waver.

"You tell me. How do I know you didn't take them, then come in here acting innocent? It benefits you far more than me to have them." Malcolm leaned across the desk until he was inches from Hunter's face. "Greed doesn't look good on you, old man. I've supplied you with ten times the specimens needed to be successful, yet you always demand more. Maybe you stole them because you know your project's a failure and you needed someone else to blame."

Through the cameras, Nikala saw the two men face off: Hunter taller, Malcolm with more bulk. The air vibrated—actually shifted—and she stifled a gasp. How the hell could she see air? But it swirled with the slightest green hue.

They stayed locked in a stalemate while the seconds ticked away. Neither man flinched or moved or so much as blinked.

What the actual fuck was going on? Why were the amulets important? She'd thought they were daft trinkets filled with drugs or diamonds perhaps, that Malcolm had taken a fancy to, but now she realized they were far more valuable. Her hand grazed her hip, but where the amulet should've been hidden in a pocket, she felt only fabric and skin. Irrational fear zigged down her throat, choking her. After his impromptu search of her blouse this afternoon, she had no doubt he knew she'd taken one. And now she'd lost it. Malcolm would kill her.

Finally, Hunter blew out a breath and pounded the desk. "Find them." Hunter's voice became low, feral. Nikala dragged her attention away from the missing amulet to the conversation. "The project is close to realization. We need more, Malcolm. At least two hundred. And they must be stronger. The last batch didn't survive the first test."

Survive? Nikala breathed deep and blinked to focus. Hunger and exhaustion were making her hear things. Hunter couldn't have said "survive." Her mind raced to the experiments he'd performed on her and she shuddered. How often had he said he was surprised she had survived? Then he'd pet her hair and call her his beautiful lily, strong and enduring.

In a flash, she was back in his manor house outside Aberdeen —alone, in pain, and in need of companionship. His visits were brief those first few years and she'd begun to long for them in the way one welcomes blissful oblivion from heroin. He became her drug.

"If you're unhappy with the quality, I suggest you and Maxx sort it out." Malcolm shut the safe and leaned against the desk on his fingertips. It wasn't a usual tic of his and she paid closer attention to the way his thumb and forefinger curled in toward his palm. That left three fingers supporting his weight. Three. What did three mean?

"I don't have time. Thanks to your ineptitude, I'll have to scrape together what I can from my research. Send your dogs to find Maxx and make certain she understands there can't be any more mistakes. No lost amulets, nothing broken." Hunter leaned across the desk, mimicking Malcolm's action of a few minutes earlier. "You're getting sloppy, old man. Don't make yourself redundant."

"How dare you." Spittle formed at the corners of Malcolm's mouth. "Without me, none of this is possible."

A sneer twisted Hunter's deformed lips. "Send Nikala away. Suggest a holiday, send her to Venice to check on supplies there. I don't care. Just make her leave for a while."

Malcolm had never been stupid and Nikala saw the mechanics of his brain working in the way his eyes lit and his jaw shunted from side to side. "You send two of my best people after her, and now you want her gone. Why, Hunter? What have you done?"

"Yasheda and Jude were a test. I needed to know how she'd respond to people she was comfortable with. She let them live tonight, but I've no doubt she'd eliminate them if there was a next time. And yes, I like to keep tabs on my experiments, but it wasn't personal. This is. I'm not ready yet to include her in our end game. Until such a time, I don't need her asking questions."

Did Malcolm know Yash and Jude had been enhanced? He had to know. Nikala squirmed in her seat. Maybe the contents of the amulets were what gave them their strength. She put a hand to her chest. Her strength increased with adrenaline, did it work the same with them?

Malcolm's laugh burst through her headphones. "You are a contradiction! Have you forgotten who trained her to ask questions? It's as much a part of her as breathing." At Hunter's glare, Malcolm grinned and waved a hand. "Yes, yes, I'll send her away. Somewhere tropical so she can work on her tan and maybe learn to relax. She's far too high-strung. Or maybe Ireland, where she can drink all the Guinness she pleases."

Nikala should've been annoyed that they spoke about her in unabashed terms, but she was proud of the woman they described. A flush of warmth spread over her cheeks and she giggled to herself. She was the monster they'd created. It served them right that she was too good at being herself.

Hunter strode to the door with Malcolm watching his every move. There was an unspoken—if not respect, then certainly a reluctant alliance—between these two, one that needed further examination. Until this moment, she'd accepted that they were business partners and friends, but what wasn't being said intrigued her as much as what was spoken.

Neither said goodbye and when the door closed behind Hunter, Malcolm sank into his leather chair.

Hunter strode past the office where Nikala quietly tracked his movements. His head swiveled in her direction and for a moment, she felt as exposed and vulnerable as she had every time he'd inspected her after one of his experiments. She knew he couldn't see her, and yet, she felt his probing stare as if he were in the room with her. Felt the immediate need to submit to him no matter how much it hurt.

❧ 17 ☙

Cian walked past the security guards without a glance from either man. The tiny amount of magic he used to blur his movements would also prevent the cameras from capturing his image. At the special lift Nikala had used earlier, he paused. She'd placed her hand on the screen for recognition, but now that he stood before the innocent piece of technology, his senses went on alert.

Undetectable by humans, the scanner had magic imbued in it. Cian glanced at the bank of other lifts. None of them had a scanner, only the one for Malcolm's floor. He ignored the special lift for the restaurant and pressed a button for the closest one, entering quickly when the doors opened. The ping caught the attention of the guards, but neither moved from where they chatted at the front desk. Small mercies.

This particular lift went as high as the floor below Malcolm's then stopped. Cian exited, scanning the area as he did. No one greeted him, nor did he see any employees in the many offices that lined a long hall. He sped down the tiled corridor, his shoes making soft echoes against the walls. At the far end, he found the stairwell and gently pushed on the handle. The stairs were blessedly empty and he made quick work of the steps to the next floor.

There, he was met with a locked door to Malcolm's offices. Cian was fairly certain locking doors to the stairwell was against fire codes, but he wasn't about to bring that to Malcolm's attention. Not at the moment, at least. For now, he used a thread of his magic to unlock the door and ease it open without a sound.

He stepped into the corridor just as a door shut and slipped back into the stairwell before a dark-haired man strode to the lift. He mashed his thumb against the button, clearly agitated. Cian held the door slightly ajar, but couldn't get a good look at the stranger. A moment later, the lift's doors opened and he stepped in without looking back.

Cian slid from the stairwell to the edge of the receptionist area, staying in shadow. He crept to Nikala's closed office door and pressed his ear to the wood. The sound of her retching drifted to his sensitive ears. An overwhelming need to comfort her hit him in the gut. He staggered from the force of it and glared at the closed door. Why would she be ill? And why did he feel the urge to take care of her? It was ridiculous, yes, but crushing in its insistence.

He shook his head to clear that blasphemous thought and made his way silently to Malcolm's office door. No sounds came from within. Cian turned the knob with care, easing the door open a fraction until he could see Malcolm's desk chair was empty. Coughing came from the other side of the office, followed by mumbling. He snuck into the room and closed the door behind him before darting to a closet. Empty hangers hung on rods and shelves waiting for shoes sat unused. The closet could've been a metaphor for his own life. Except, he didn't need anything to make him feel useful. He was a spy. His profession made him invaluable to many.

A nagging at the back of his mind, like a gnat too close to an ear, elevated his irritation level. It was that damned Nikala's fault.

When he'd called out to her from the shower and she hadn't answered, he found his flat empty. He hadn't been surprised, just disappointed. For a full minute, he dripped water on the floorboards, debating his options. Ultimately, he chose to follow her. Not to confront Nikala about her disappearance, but to see what had caused her to rush out. The sex, fast and dirty, had been at her prompting. Yes, Cian wanted it, but there'd been desperation in her movements. It was that vulnerability he needed to explore. If it could help with his mission, he'd not hesitate a moment to exploit her weakness.

Now, as he hid in Malcolm's closet and heard Nikala washing up after being sick, he reminded himself she was not to be trusted. Until he knew what Malcolm was up to, he would use her any way he could. And if that meant fast sex, so be it. He'd never been one to shirk his duties.

Silence descended on the space. Cian counted five breaths. The sound of Malcolm urinating to his left was countered by a muffled noise to his right. Cian pressed his ear against the wall of the empty closet. Quiet sobbing followed by the sound of water rushing from a tap came through the plaster. He listened for any movement from Malcolm. When there was none, he surmised the man hadn't heard Nikala. Not hard to do since the closet where Cian hid was between the two. He returned his ear to the wall.

First, she was sick, then crying. What the hell was going on with her? An image of the scyver in the garage entryway came to mind. He'd arrived in time to see her thrust the knife into the man's throat, then wipe down the blade on his sleeve. He'd hidden behind a pillar as she dragged the man behind trash bins. When she'd hurried away, Cian had followed, stopping first to make sure the scyver was dead, and then to take his wallet and keys.

Perhaps Nikala wasn't accustomed to killing? That would explain the vomiting, but the efficiency with which she'd ended the man's life wasn't beginner's luck. That kind of control came with practice. And execution. Who the hell *was* Nikala St. James?

Cian returned to the closet door to see Malcolm sink into his chair, his face in his hands. A fresh tumbler of clear liquid sat on the desk. He leaned his head back and mumbled to the ceiling. Cian listened harder, distracted now by the sound of Nikala leaving her office and closing the door with a soft click. A moment later, he heard the stairwell door open and close.

Malcolm sipped the drink, his incoherent ramblings white noise to the rest of the office. Minutes ticked by, then the lift pinged and the sound of dress shoes on tile echoed through the lobby area. Cian's heart beat with each step she took. He knew that gait, had studied it on their way to Malcolm's office not more than a few hours past.

Without knocking, Nikala entered, her face flush as if she'd been outside in the cold.

"I thought I might find you here."

"Nikki. Come here, my sweet." Malcolm held out his arms and Nikala went to him. She placed a kiss on his forehead and wrapped her arms around his shoulders as he rested his head at her abdomen.

"Naughty, you." Nikala pulled back to indicate the ajar safe. "You've forgotten to properly shut your safe." She held Malcolm's face in her hands and looked at him with a strange mixture of concern and fury. "Was anyone here when you opened it?"

Malcolm's head swiveled to the safe and he frowned. "Hunter came for the shipment. I thought I closed the damned thing."

"It must've caught on something. Let's change the entry code, shall we? Can't have anyone breaking in again."

Malcolm's glare should've knocked Nikala sideways, but she stood firm. Cian admired the way she stood up to the man.

"I covered for you." Malcolm staggered to the safe and slammed it shut. He punched in a number twice, then a new number three times. Cian memorized each code.

"Did you? About what?" Nikala handed Malcolm his tumbler and helped him to a chair ten feet from where Cian hid.

He closed the door until only a slight crack remained.

"I told him the amulets were stolen. All the amulets," Malcolm slurred. "He was none too happy."

"I told you, I didn't take anything from you. Perhaps you left your safe open another time, I don't know." Nikala sounded sincere in her protestations, but Cian knew it was a lie. "Search me if you don't believe me." She held out her arms, taunting Malcolm to find the amulet.

Except, he wouldn't find anything. Cian wasn't sure whether Nikala was aware he had one of the "stolen" amulets hidden in his flat. He'd found it where her clothes had been tossed, peeking from beneath a rug. It must've dropped during their frantic disrobing, and Cian hid it where he hoped Nikala would never think to look—in a full box of sugary cereal tucked in the middle of his pantry.

Malcolm grabbed Nikala's arm and jerked hard. "Don't fuck with him, Nikki. Not now. Not over this. He'll kill us both."

Nikala sat down beside Malcolm and removed her arm from his grip. "He won't kill us. He needs us."

But Malcolm shook his head. "He won't for long. Not when the Dawn Project is complete."

Nikala stiffened and Cian opened the door a fraction wider.

"What's this mysterious Dawn Project you keep muttering about? Why's it so important?"

"It's nothing. Forget you ever heard of it."

"Let me call for your car and you can tell me all about the project on the way." She pulled her phone from a pocket and dialed. A moment later, she asked that Mr. Dagniss's car be brought around. "Let's get you to your hotel."

"Not hotel, home."

"You bought a bloody house? For Christ's sake, Malcolm, you were only here a week!"

"Not mine." Malcolm grinned at Nikala like a drunken fool. "Hunter's. He's got a place in Chelsea. You have a room, too."

Nikala burst from the sofa and ran her hands through her hair, snagging on the ponytail. She ripped the elastic out and smoothed her hairs back into place before reapplying the band.

"No. I won't go there. I can't see him, not yet."

"That's all in the past, Nikki. He promised me. No more tests. No more lab for you." Malcolm tried to pat her hand, but she pulled it free.

A moment later, she relented and tugged him up from the couch. Her arms went around Malcolm in a hug. Cian saw the tears in Nikala's eyes as she clutched the older man.

Nikala pulled away and smiled at Malcolm. "Let's get you to Hunter's. Don't tell him I stopped by tonight. I need more time. Okay?"

Malcolm nodded and mumbled, "I'm so sorry, Nikki."

"I am too, but what's done is done. Come on, your car's waiting." The tenderness in Nikala's voice stirred something in Cian's heart.

Whatever the relationship between the pair, he needed to find out. And who the hell was Hunter?

Nikala and Malcolm left the office and Cian waited two minutes before he let his Glamour glow just enough to confuse the cameras and eased out of the closet. He darted for the safe and hurriedly entered the codes he saw Malcolm punch in. On the second try, the safe popped open. He drew a breath to calm his nerves and scanned the empty bottom shelf, sensing fae magic. Fury, sorrow, and indignation tightened his chest. He'd been this close to the kidnapped fae, but was useless to retrieve them. At least now he knew who had them. Yet he was no closer to understanding why they'd been taken.

Cian placed his hand on the empty shelf and released a strand of his magic. The energy from Acelyne's magic and that of the kidnapped faeries flowed over and into his skin. He absorbed it with a heavy sigh. In that brief contact, he sensed their doom. Rori would've been one of them if she hadn't broken out of the amulet.

Wave upon wave of rage rippled over his body, chasing his thoughts, disordering his control. Cian struggled to regain equilibrium. No good would come of him racing off without information. He had to know who Hunter was, and where he'd taken the fae.

His thoughts wandered to Nikala, but she was too good at evading his questions. She'd said she wouldn't go with Malcolm to Hunter's, and her hands had been empty when she'd pretended she was returning to Malcolm's office. Which meant her bags were still here and most likely, she would return to gather them. He checked his phone and calculated he had three minutes until she returned.

With relative calm restored, and his focus regained, he searched the upper shelf of the safe, finding several papers and a laptop. All of them he removed and placed on the huge desk, avoiding the empty tumbler.

The laptop wasn't password protected, which made Cian shake his head. It was a boon for him, but Malcolm should know better. His gaze went to the crystal decanters on the sideboard and then to the glass Malcolm had refreshed several times. Perhaps his drinking was making his memory slip. It would be easy enough to exploit the next time they met. Cian filed that tidbit away and opened several folders on Malcolm's computer.

All of SIRE's business dealings were there—legal and not entirely above-board transactions were listed in spreadsheets and graphs that made little sense to Cian. He'd need more than a few minutes with the documents to unravel what Malcolm's company was up to. He searched the drawers of Malcolm's desk and found a memory stick to copy the files to. A quick check of the time gave him less than a minute. Not enough to fully copy the documents, but time enough to get them started.

While the download started, he snapped pictures of the other papers he'd found in the safe. All the while, he listened for the lift's ding to alert him to Nikala's return. As he finished taking the last picture, he heard the sound and rushed to replace the papers. Then he shut the cabinet carefully and tucked the laptop under his arm as he dashed to a room on the opposite side of the office.

Nikala entered just as he slipped into the dark space. He set the laptop on a conference table and returned to the door to see Nikala pick up the two tumblers, a dark scowl on her face. She set the glasses near the decanters and leaned against the sideboard, her head dipped, arms spread wide.

The way her body sagged, and the utter defeat in her sigh, suggested she was in an impossible situation, but what it was, Cian couldn't guess. Seeing her vulnerable again roused the protectiveness that was, until then, reserved for Rori and his mum. His mouth went dry and sweat trickled down his back. The urge to go to her, to take her in his arms and tell her he'd eliminate those who caused her distress, overrode all his senses.

Cian was about to yank open the door when he pulled himself in check.

He didn't know this woman. Despite their mad fuck an hour earlier, he didn't know whether her mood was sorrow or anger or despair. Couldn't afford to get caught up in her business when his wasn't resolved. At least, that's the story he told himself.

Cool reserve washed over him and he inhaled a long breath, centering himself.

Better. Much better.

He checked the download and peered out of the slice of emptiness between the door and jamb. Nikala stretched her toned body and cracked her neck several times before leaving Malcolm's office. Cian quietly slipped from the conference room and strode to the closet he'd hid in earlier. He heard Nikala rummaging around in her office, then she returned to Malcolm's.

She dragged a bag behind her, the same one she'd had on the

train that morning. Dear gods, had it only been twelve hours since they'd met? It felt as though he'd been following her for at least a month. He was shattered and needed sleep, but not until he knew where to find the man with the amulets.

The sound of rushing water came through the wall and Cian crept from his hiding place to the only other door on this side of the office. Nikala had left it open and he peered in. The room was enormous, with a basin and a shower large enough to fit four comfortably, which made Nikala look tiny in the glass box. On his right, a door led to the toilet, and at the far end was a wooden door, leading to a steam room, if he were to guess. Swanky place. SIRE must be doing well to afford such luxury. He'd bet a day's wages there was a bed somewhere in the vast office, too.

Why would she stay here and not go to her own flat, or a hotel if she didn't have a place? Cian shuffled to conceal himself better. She'd only stay here if she felt safe. Which meant she felt safer here than at Hunter's place. Again, a surge of protectiveness asserted itself. Hunter became enemy number one where Nikala was concerned. An image of the dark-haired man leaving as he arrived at Malcolm's office swept past his thoughts. Possibly Hunter. He hoped the downloaded information could shine a light on who the mystery man was.

Nikala stood with her head tilted upward, letting the water flow over her skin. Her blonde hair hung down her back nearly to her buttocks. Cian studied her like a master his sculpture. Physically, she was perfect: muscular without being bulky, gorgeous, pert breasts, and an ass that his hands twitched to grab hold of once more.

She swept her hair aside and his appreciation of her body turned to horror. Icy chills pierced his heart as a slow burn infused his veins. Across her back, pinkish scars marred the delicate creaminess of her skin. She turned and he saw more scars on her abdomen. Two more dotted her left bicep. That pair, and another two near her collarbone, were roundish, like bullet wounds, but the others—Cian breathed in and out, his nostrils flaring. The others were precise, as if she'd been cut with a scalpel. He counted twenty-three in all.

The protectiveness turned to violent rage at whoever had done this to her and he twisted himself to lean against the outer wall of the bathroom where she couldn't see him. His heart tripped in its beating and a muffled roar drowned out all sound. When she'd left her shirt on at his flat, he hadn't thought anything of it. He'd been too focused on her face and lips, believing erroneously there would be time later to explore her body.

Now he understood why she'd left his flat in such a hurry. His heart ached for her, for whatever torture she'd had to endure to receive such scars.

"No more tests. No more lab for you," Malcolm had said to Nikala. Is this what he meant? No more brutality that ended with mutilating her body?

The need to punch something, to hurt someone, to utterly destroy, pulsed through Cian. He breathed in deep and out again, but it didn't help. To hell with not knowing Nikala well enough —he couldn't allow anyone to be subjected to what she'd been through.

A sharp intake of air ripped down his throat.

The faeries. A wild possibility was forming in Cian's mind. He didn't like where it was going, nor did he like what he saw in the shower fifteen feet from where he stood.

He jogged back to the conference room to check on the download. It had one minute remaining. He kept watch on the bathroom, thankful that Nikala was taking her time. When it finished, he ejected the memory stick and secured it in his pocket. He waited for Nikala to emerge from the shower and return to her office, wrapped in a towel, dragging her bag. Her wet hair dripped a path on the carpet, but she didn't notice and, from the grim determination on her face, didn't care.

The moment the office door clicked shut, Cian dashed to the safe and returned the laptop to where it was when he found it. Then he left Malcolm's office. On his way to the stairs, he paused. His mind screamed at him to leave, to let Nikala work out whatever issues she had with Malcolm on her own, but his heart stayed his legs.

He pressed his ear against the door and listened as she moved around the office, humming a song he didn't recognize. The sound of a hairdryer drowned out everything else and Cian placed his palm upon the wood. He sent his magic through the door to her. Why? He wasn't sure. But he needed that connection. Needed to know she'd be safe. His magic wouldn't protect her from the horrors of her past, but it would prevent any harm coming to her this night. It was all he could do.

Then he turned away from her to the stairs with a promise to himself that he'd forget what he saw tonight and remember she was the enemy.

❦ 18 ❦

Rori stretched on the huge bed, delighting in the feel of soft cotton on her naked skin. She grinned and reached out for Therron, but the other side of the bed was empty. She propped herself on an elbow and squinted against the bright sunlight that streamed into the room. No noise came from the vast suite. She scanned the area, noting the dwindling fire and empty chairs.

"Therron?"

No answer came.

She flopped onto her back and stared at the canopy above her bed. It was well past morning. Therron probably was up and doing whatever it was elves did during the day. She had no idea, but would remedy that today. She'd also remedy her empty stomach. With another full body stretch, she slid from the huge mattress to the floor and shuffled to the bathroom.

After fiddling with the tub faucets for the perfect water temperature, she emptied her bladder and pondered why her body was sluggish this morning. In fact, she'd been physically off since being captured in Acelyne's amulet. Perhaps not all of the drug had worn off and if so, what kind of potion could knock someone out and make them sleep for weeks at a time? Maybe Meg would know. She'd send a message to the witch after breakfast.

While the tub filled, she called for a servant and rummaged through the silky, frilly, floaty gowns in the wardrobe. Midna had to be freaking kidding. Nothing in there was decent, or practical, or even remotely Rori's style. Apparently, one of Midna's conditions for Rori staying at the Unseelie palace was that she had to dress appropriately. Appropriate for Midna, but not Rori.

She cobbled together a temporary covering using two dressing gowns and a robe. The three layers provided enough coverage she didn't feel exposed.

Despite her desire to train at Midna's, she wasn't quite ready to jump in—not feet first as the saying goes—but naked body first. In fact, with each layer, she questioned her enthusiasm. It had been an excellent idea yesterday, but now? Not so much. She knew why, but didn't want to admit the reason. As she finished tying the robe, a knock sounded at her door. Rori's heart beat faster, but when she opened the door, it wasn't Therron in the hallway.

A handsome servant with copper hair and patrician features bowed his head. "Miss rang?"

"I'd like some breakfast, please. Or lunch. I'm not quite sure what time it is."

"Just before midday, miss."

Rori nodded and mentally did the math for how many hours she'd slept. Remembering herself, and the servant waiting for a reply, she blushed. "Whatever they have in the kitchens is fine. And tea, please."

He bowed again and sauntered down the carpeted hallway. She studied his gait, the haughty way his shoulders swayed, and the elongated stride of his legs. The cream-colored satin court trousers he wore and matching vest set off the russet tones of his skin. If she wasn't mistaken, he was from the southern lands of Faerie, and definitely not a servant.

She set her musings aside and checked on her bath. Several jars of sweet-smelling crystals sat on a shelf and she tossed a handful from one into the water. Bubbles and foam covered the surface and she stripped off her garments, leaving them in a heap on the floor.

The sting of hot water bit at her ankles, then calves as she lowered into the tub. The stitches on her thigh protested against the heat. Meg would probably tell her a bath wasn't good for her wound, but Meg wasn't there and Rori craved the calm a nice bath would provide.

She shut off the water with her toes and lay her head against the cool porcelain. In a matter of moments, she was drifting in a dreamy state of contentment. Her mind rewound to Therron waking her from a nightmare—she shut out the replay of that horrific scene—and focused on what came after, when Therron made love to her.

Her hands snaked to where he'd touched her and a low thrill warmed her from the inside out. Tingles crept across her skin at the memory of his kisses. She slipped a hand between her legs and thumbed herself, her other hand massaging her breast. Little gasps rent the quiet air as she replayed every touch, every moan. Flutters of something dangerous tickled her heart, but she ignored those and concentrated on the physical sensations lower. She panted and rubbed harder, fighting her emotions. It wouldn't do to get caught up in her feelings for Therron. Hell, she didn't even understand them. They were tangled and complicated and ooooooooh, gods, so, so good.

A knock at the door halted her cresting orgasm and she cursed at whoever had interrupted a perfectly lovely moment.

"Go away!" she yelled from the bathroom, her anger fueled with frustration. Her head throbbed and body clenched with a need to release.

"I have your breakfast, miss."

The sharksniffing servant. She thought he'd take longer. Efficient asshole.

"Leave it on a table, please."

The door opened and she heard him setting the dishes on one of the tables in her room. Instead of leaving, he stood in the doorway to the bathroom and asked, "Is there anything else I can assist you with?"

An embarrassed flush covered her neck and cheeks. The nerve of the man! She slid her hands to her sides. Despite the bubbles hiding her solitary activity, a slice of guilt cut into her heart. She hadn't cheated on anyone, so why did she feel as if she had?

He remained where he stood and a shocking realization spiraled in cool waves from her hair to her toes.

"You're not just a servant, are you?" Rori adjusted the bubbles, making sure they covered her nakedness.

"I'm not sure what you mean?" The non-servant cocked his head, his eyes roving the tub.

The angle of his posture, and haughty sneer he couldn't quite hide, gave away the game.

"What's your name?" Rori's eyes narrowed, and her lips pursed.

"Lor—" He caught himself in time, then said with a bow, "Justin, miss."

"Mmm-hmmm. Tell me, Justin, if I were to order you to pleasure me, would you?"

"Without hesitation, miss."

"And what else do you do for your queen?" She knew the answer before he even spoke.

"Anything she demands. It's an honor to serve her." He stood to his full height and flexed his shoulders back.

"What do you get out of serving her?" Rori was genuinely curious now.

"Pleasure. Humility. Control of my emotions. I've learned a

great deal from the queen. How to serve, among those lessons." Not an ounce of humor shone from his eyes. He spoke with quiet sincerity.

"So that one day you will be a better master of your domain?" Rori asked and delighted when his lips pinched. She'd guessed correctly. "Does Midna make all of her guests act as servants? Or did you choose this?"

"I misbehaved." He hung his head for effect. "This is my penance."

Laughter burst from her and his glare brought about another ripple.

"What would someone have to do in *this* palace to be punished?" Giggles punctuated her words.

An imperious veneer covered his features. "Does miss require anything from me?"

The bulge in his pants was evidence he wouldn't mind a tumble in her bed, even if she had embarrassed him.

"Thank you, but not at this time."

With another bow he left, but not before giving her a look of resignation or regret, she wasn't sure which. She lay her head against the porcelain and tried to recover her thoughts of Therron, but they were gone. That stupid Justin had chased her lovely memories away.

She rose and dripped across the tiled floor to where the towels were kept. Rori made quick work of drying and dressing—in the filmy gowns, tripled up for coverage—then she settled in for her meal. Twice while she was eating, her mind wandered to Therron and his prolonged absence. She didn't expect him to stay with her while she slept, but a part of her wished he would have. That he hadn't checked on her yet left her disappointed. A feeling she wasn't accustomed to having, nor did she particularly enjoy.

Stomach full, she decided sitting in her room all day moping wasn't going to happen. She traipsed down the long halls of Midna's palace, keeping her eyes forward, but noting all the couples or small groups along the way. No one acted inappropriate, nor were there any hints of distress from the people she passed. It was, as she'd noticed on her first visit, remarkably unremarkable.

Snippets of conversation drifted to her. Gossip, mostly about who the queen would choose as her partners for the evening's entertainments, and some about Rori. She listened to both without appearing to do so, although the urge to yell, "I can hear you!" was strong.

The MacNairs were not unknown to the Unseelie Court, and by the whispered conversations she overheard, a bit of a mystery. Cian, it seemed, by refusing to sleep with the queen, caused quite a stir. Now the courtiers placed wagers on whether Rori would follow his lead.

A servant scuttled past, averting his eyes, and Rori turned to follow in the hopes he might point her in the direction of Midna's rooms. She couldn't be expected to simply wander all day, could she? There were lessons to be learned, an education to be gleaned.

Just as she opened her mouth to speak, a hand clamped over her lips and she was jerked backward into an alcove. An arm reached around her middle, immobilizing her movements. Rori's muffled curses went unheard as a female hissed near her ear, "Aurora MacNair, your life is in danger. You cannot stay at this palace."

Rori reached for daggers that weren't there—stupid asinine dresses—and struggled against the hold her assailant had on her. The grip was like steel. Rather than fight, she relaxed. As she'd hoped, the woman loosened the grip on her mouth, but not her waist.

"Who are you?" Rori mumbled beneath the hand.

"Continue the work your brother started. Faerie cannot afford another traitor. Time is short. Do not linger here lest you be caught in Midna's web."

"Midna wishes me harm?" Rori's mind spun with everything that had happened in the past week. All the words said, unsaid, and simple expressions she'd not noticed.

A soft chuckle tickled her neck. "Midna would have you as her trophy. When Cian denied her, she took it badly. If she could snare you, that would be a boon for her status. But she does not wish you injured or dead."

The last was said without emotion.

"Why are you telling me this?" For all Rori knew, the assailant was a jealous courtier who wanted Midna all to themselves.

"Follow the enchantress. Do not, under any circumstances, go to the human realm."

"The enchantress is dead," Rori argued, but the hand around her waist was gone, as was the woman.

She spun around, but a blank wall met her searching gaze. The faint scent of ylang-ylang and citrus hovered in the air. Rori knew the smell, but couldn't place it. She pressed her fingertips to the wall and it inched inward. More pressure revealed a hidden doorway within the alcove. Clever. Of course Midna's palace would be riddled with secret passageways.

Rori glanced around at the near-empty hallway and slipped into the darkness. She made a ball of drossfire and plunged ahead. The secret passageways were a rat warren of turns and dead ends. Rori chased the mysterious woman down one cramped space and through another, hoping all the while she'd catch up to her and failing. After several minutes, Rori admitted defeat. She bent at the waist, hands on knees. Breathing wasn't exactly difficult in the musty passage, just uncomfortable. The wound on her thigh throbbed and she took a moment to calm her tumbling heartbeat.

A bump on the wall to her right drew her attention and Rori pressed her ear against the cold stone. Muffled voices came from the other side and Rori cursed the stupid woman who'd led her into this place. What good were secret passageways if you didn't know where the doorways were?

Rori straightened and directed her drossfire to one side, then the next. She decided to forge ahead, taking a slim passage to her right. Muffled sounds continued the farther she went, and she took that as a good sign.

As she walked, with her fingertips floating across the stones, she parsed the woman's warnings. Don't sleep with Midna. The woman could be a past lover and jealous of Midna having a new favorite. But then, why would she warn Rori from going to the human realm? If she were truly a jealous lover, she'd want Rori as far from the Unseelie Court as possible; the human realm didn't get much farther. And why tell Rori to follow the enchantress when Acelyne was dead?

Unless she meant follow Acelyne's past behavior to discover how she was able to kidnap so many fae. Rori's hands fisted and she scraped her knuckles on the rough stone. If she could kill the witch a second time, she'd gladly do it.

Where were the missing faeries?

And why had Acelyne told Rori *she* knew how to free them?

Questions and more questions swirled in her mind. With each new query, Rori became increasingly certain she couldn't stay in the palace. The fae needed her and she was honor bound to help them first. And she couldn't do that lounging around with álainn obedience.

Strangely enough, she didn't mind postponing—or even cancelling—her education with Midna. What she'd been searching for might still be with the álainn obedience, but her heart told another story. Leaving the Unseelie Court meant leaving Therron. She could ask him to come with her, but this wasn't his fight. Hadn't he said as much? He didn't get involved with fae politics. Besides, he hadn't bothered staying with her all night; why would she think he'd want anything to do with her now? She told herself it was a hookup, nothing more. Her breath caught in her throat as the thought of him filled her senses.

A niggling at the back of her mind reminded her she'd never actually had a hookup, and if she had, she didn't think they were like last night. Therron had made proper love to her and she'd responded in the most delightful way. Weren't hookups all grunts and grinding? A flush crept up her neck and she was grateful for the dim light and solitude. If anyone caught her blushing over an elf, she'd be mortified. There was plenty of grunts last night and she certainly had been grinding. But it wasn't quick and dirty. Hell no.

Warmth spread from her cheeks to her toes and she forced thoughts of Therron from her mind. She had work to do and couldn't afford to be distracted. She'd find him once she spoke to the queen, then she'd say a quick farewell and be on her way to retrace Acelyne's steps.

A lightness in her chest sparked hope and she bounced on the balls of her feet. Therron had said he'd been following Acelyne—he could help in her mission. She'd ask politely, of course, and he could always deny her, but the least she could do was give him an option.

It wouldn't do to simply leave without saying goodbye.

❦ 19 ❦

Prickles of apprehension covered Nikala's skin and she turned off the blow-dryer to listen. The faint sound of footsteps across tile rose the hairs on her neck. She set the dryer down and picked up the gun she'd taken from Malcolm and set on the coffee table. He didn't share her revulsion of the things and with the amount of alcohol he'd consumed, she hadn't trusted him with the weapon. Without making a sound, she crept to the door and listened. A click to her left was followed by silence. Whoever it was, they were gone. She hoped.

Ignoring the thump-bump of her heart, she opened her office door with a jerk. The lobby sat stark and empty. For a wild moment, she thought maybe Hunter had returned.

She held the gun low, with both hands, and checked that the door to the stairwell was locked, then moved into Malcolm's office. Nothing was out of place, but an unease settled in the pit of her stomach. A slight shift, perhaps. As if a spirit had drifted through, disturbing the air, but nothing else.

"Get a grip, St. James." Nikala tucked the pistol into the waistband of her jeans and breathed out. Ghosts and phantom footsteps. She was losing it.

Before she conjured more imaginary boogiemen, she grabbed her leather jacket and phone. Food and sleep. That's what she needed. In a matter of seconds, she had her boots zipped and was heading out of her office. She'd grab something quick, then come back to grab her bags. With Malcolm shipped off to Hunter's, her stuff would be fine for the half an hour it would take to eat, then she'd get a hotel and sleep for a year.

The shower had been to help clear her mind, help her think about what Malcolm had said. He'd hidden the pendants somewhere, she was sure of it. Otherwise, why say he'd covered for her? Clearly he knew she stole one amulet, but why hide all of them from Hunter? And if he confessed to covering for her, why not just tell her where they were? Her gaze took in all the luxe fabrics and furniture of the reception area. It was another test. This time from Malcolm. She was sick of tests. Yes, she stole one damned pendant. That didn't mean he needed to keep testing her loyalty. It was bloody asinine. Yet, that little voice chided from the back of her mind, it was her own damn fault.

She'd find his hiding place and return the amulet. Maybe then he'd trust her again. She smoothed her hair off her face and breathed deep. Where would Malcolm hide them?

A floral scent wafted to her from the lift when the doors opened and she inhaled with a smile. Hadn't Malcolm told Hunter he'd send her somewhere tropical? Maybe she should go on holiday. Disappear for a few weeks or months. Lay low until this business with Hunter was completed. Malcolm was ridiculous for believing Hunter would get rid of them. If anything, Hunter needed Malcolm very much alive. It was Malcolm's money that kept Hunter's lab operating. Yet the way Malcolm shuddered when he'd spoken set an alarm in Nikala's mind.

Whatever the Dawn Project was, she had to find out. That meant sneaking into Hunter's lab. Drips of apprehension clung to the thought. The last time she'd seen Hunter was in that lab. Far more sophisticated than what he'd built in Aberdeen, the London laboratory was Hunter's dream and Nikala's nightmare.

Her hand went to the two scars on her left bicep—the ones Hunter had given her when he'd shot her at point-blank range. Then she traced her fingertips to the scars on her collarbone, where her quick movement made his bullet miss her heart by mere inches.

A test, he'd said. A test to see how quickly she healed, but also if a bullet could kill her.

Nikala's fingers shook as she stroked the place where her loyalty to Hunter had finally snapped. Tonight he'd said Yasheda and Jude were a test—for her. But what if he was testing them as well?

The lift doors opened and Nikala walked in a fog through the lobby. One of the night watchmen said something and she mumbled a reply.

"The last batch didn't survive the first test," Hunter had said to Malcolm. Nikala's mind whirled with details and snippets of overheard conversations.

Malcolm had always supported Hunter's experiments. At one time or another, they both had told Nikala that what Hunter was doing was to benefit all mankind. She'd convinced herself they were making cures for diseases. And why not? She'd never been sick a day in her life. Certainly the tests they performed on her worked—she was proof of that.

Why didn't the last batch survive? And what constituted a batch?

And what did Cian MacNair have to do with all of this?

She braced against the chilly air and strode across the broad walkway toward the pub, her thoughts churning as quickly as her empty stomach. An idea was forming that she didn't like—the amulets were filled with pathogens that Hunter tested on unsuspecting patients. Acelyne might be the one providing the test subjects. But why? Nikala shook her fists at her side. Something was eluding her. Something simple and it pissed her off to not grasp it.

The sound of a motorbike revving broke her reverie and she glanced up in time to see two black-clad riders heading straight for her. Time slowed to microseconds and she took in tiny details. The first rider's eyes were hidden behind a windscreen, but the second rider's eyes were dark and mean. *Yasheda.* Hunter must've sent them to test her again. Or this time it was Malcolm who gave the order. Either way, they were nearing, and she had to make a decision.

A woman crossing the narrow alley opposite Nikala didn't seem to hear or see the bikers and, at the rate she was walking, would collide with them.

Nikala lunged toward the lady, knocking her backward as the motorbikes sped past. A stinging burn sliced across her lower back and she turned in time to see a flash from Yasheda's blade. The bitch cut her. Nikala cursed under her breath and swore that by the end of the night, neither Yash nor Jude would see the light of day.

The woman floundered beneath Nikala's grip, then found her footing and swung her head from Nikala to the retreating motorbikes with a look of surprised fury crossing her features.

"Are you all right?" Nikala scanned the woman's features and aside from an ashen face, she looked unhurt.

"Thank you," she stammered. Her gaze settled on Nikala and the rage turned to something softer, like regret, or ruefulness. "I thought I was looking at a ghost." The last was mumbled with a slow shake of her head.

"Bloody kids and their bikes. They should get a warning for dangerous driving." Nikala straightened her leather jacket, wincing as it swished over the wound Yash inflicted.

"Too right. Well, thank you again." The woman dipped her

head and scrambled off in the direction she'd been walking, taking her past the entrance to Malcolm's building. She pulled the collar of her saffron-colored coat up, leaving only a tuft of her auburn hair visible.

"You're welcome," Nikala mumbled. But she wasn't angry with the woman. Why should she be? The poor thing was in the wrong place at the wrong time.

For a long minute, she listened for the motorbikes, but heard only London traffic. If it was her, she'd return to finish the job. Maybe it was their plan to make sneak attacks all night to keep her unbalanced and paranoid. Good plan, but it wouldn't work. She felt for the dagger up her sleeve and grinned. If they wanted to play games, she was ready.

She hesitated where to go—she was hungry and needed food, but she had bandages in her bags upstairs in her office and the cut on her back felt sticky. Beneath everything, one question played on constant loop—where would Malcolm hide the amulets? Her stomach grumbled and she decided Donyatella could patch her up, at least until she returned to the safety of her office. She shuffled down the cobblestoned alley toward the pub. With each uneven step, her shirt rubbed against her skin and with each prick of pain, she imagined how she'd repay Jude and Yasheda. If Hunter wanted to test her, she'd show him where her loyalties really lay—with herself.

On the sidewalk outside the pub, she paused to glance up at the empty flat on the top right of the building. In all the times she'd frequented the place, she'd never seen anyone there. No lights flickering on or off, nor did the curtains ever move, but always, she felt a presence coming from the flat. Nothing hostile or worrisome, just—there.

Donyatella wasn't at her usual spot by the door, so Nikala eased to the back table where she always sat. It gave her a view of the room and both entrances. Within moments, the hostess appeared and handed her a menu.

"Where's Dony?" Nikala asked the girl as she settled onto the leather seat, doing her best not to rub her back against the booth.

The girl, who couldn't have been more than eighteen, rolled her eyes and shrugged. "Dunno. In the kitchens, maybe. Want me to find her?"

"If you could. And I'll have a Guinness, please, plus a steak pie."

A snap of bubblegum served as the girl's reply. She snatched the menu off the table and skulked away.

Hadn't Malcolm said Ireland? A cool shiver snaked down her spine. Because Nikala loved Guinness. She took in her surroundings, taking note of everywhere a bag could be stashed. Would Malcolm be so bold as to hide the shipment here, in a public place? Nikala's breath caught and her nostrils flared. Yes, the madman would be that bold. And that rash.

Donyatella emerged from the kitchen with a huge grin on her ancient face.

"Nikala, it's good to see you again." The woman kissed Nikala on each cheek, then pulled back to study her eyes. "You are in pain, no?"

"Just a scratch. Can you take a look?" Nikala leaned forward to let Dony see the wound.

"It's no too bad. You come with me, yes?"

Nikala obediently followed the woman to a small room off the bar that Dony called her office. It looked more like a charity shop with bits and bobs on every surface.

"Stand here, and I'll get you sorted." The aged woman grabbed a tin box from a shelf and rummaged through it while Nikala leaned forward across a desk scattered with bills and receipts.

The cooling sting of surgical spirits swiped from left to right, then a moment later, again, from right to left. Dony sucked at her teeth while she worked, making little harrumphs and tsks. Nikala distracted herself by reading the notices on the board in front of her. Shift changes, notes about delivery dates, street works schedules—all the mundane necessities of running a pub. Tucked behind one of the pinned pages, Nikala saw the corner of a childlike drawing. She balanced on one hand and nudged the top page over until she saw the complete image. Two stick figures held hands with a rainbow behind them.

"A gift from an admirer?" Nikala teased.

"A young girl who used to live above the pub. She once called me Nona Dony."

Something in Dony's tone unsettled Nikala. "Used to? Did something happen to her?"

Donyatella smoothed a plaster over Nikala's skin and pulled her shirt carefully over her jeans. "She moved on, as everyone must." A wistfulness filled the emptiness of her words. "Be more careful in the future, yes?" Dony clapped her hands and opened the door for Nikala to exit.

She cast a last glance at the picture. Scribbled beneath the stick figures the artist had written, "Nona Dony," and another name, but it had been erased. Nikala could make out a y, but not much else. Her gaze drifted lower and there, tucked between two boxes, she saw a leather strap she recognized from Malcolm's safe. Her mind buzzed and throat went dry.

"Did Malcolm leave anything for me?"

Dony's stony stare unnerved her. The way the woman's lips pressed into a line made her wrinkles appear like veins in marble.

"You ask the wrong question. Perhaps you need food first." Dony prodded her out of the office and closed the door behind them.

Nikala glanced over her shoulder to the small room. As long as the bag was safe in Dony's office, she could take a few minutes to eat.

At her table, the much-needed Guinness waited for her and Nikala sat with a satisfied sigh. The wound stung, but not nearly as much as it had a few minutes earlier. Whatever Dony put on it was working. She could practically feel her skin knitting back together.

After a quiet, but mentally distracted meal, Nikala paid her bill. Donyatella had disappeared from her seat and Nikala wavered whether she should take the bag from Dony's office without asking. Deciding that was rude, she hovered near the kitchen, hoping the woman would show.

Curiosity burned in Nikala's gut. When certain no one looked, she darted into the kitchen, where she knew back stairs led to the flats. A few workers frowned at her being in their space, but she ignored them. Three steps in, she turned to the stairs and left them behind.

Sounds of cooking and conversations from the pub drifted through the walls, but no one halted her progression to the third floor. With each boot placed on the old wooden planks, her heart raced a second faster. By the time she reached the top floor, a sheen of sweat covered her forehead and her lungs swelled beneath her ribs. Every nerve ending was lit like a Christmas tree, ready to pop from too much voltage.

No sound came from the flats she passed. At the end of the hall, she paused in front of the door. If she did this, she'd be betraying Donyatella and whoever lived here. For some reason, the latter bothered her more than upsetting her longtime friend.

Nikala reached for the door handle and before she made contact with it, the door swung open with a soft groan. Her head swiveled from side to side, but the hallway was empty.

"Hello?" she whispered into the room. Silence answered.

She pushed the door farther open and stepped a boot inside. When nothing happened, she took another step, and another. Rivulets of sweat ran down her back, over the plasters Dony applied, and pooled in the divots above her ass.

The flat was comfortable and homey, yet sparse. No pictures

lined the walls; no personal items were left lying around. It was a serviceable flat, and yet Nikala felt at once loved and protected as she stood in the middle of the lounge. A fireplace—long gone cold—dominated one wall and a comfortable rocker nestled in front of it. She sat in the chair and smelled cigar smoke and cologne. The kind older gentlemen wore.

She closed her eyes and heard someone, a female, whisper, "It is time."

Nikala sat up, eyes wide, pulse racing like a Formula One car. The empty room sat motionless and, oddly enough, lonely.

"They are archaeologists. At least, that is what they wish the world to believe," Donyatella said from the doorway. "They travel often and use this flat as their base when they are in London." Wistfulness lingered in her words.

"I'm sorry. I know I'm trespassing, but I couldn't stay away, not any longer." Nikala stood, guilt sliding over her like a scratchy sweater.

"It wasn't time for you to know about them, but now maybe it is." Donyatella entered the room and ran her fingertips across the overflowing bookshelf. "I do not know when they will return, but I keep their home ready, just in case."

"I don't understand." Pounding began in her head and the Guinness she drank sloshed in her belly.

Donyatella studied Nikala for a moment, her lips pursed, eyes narrowed. "He's kept you in the dark for so long, I don't know what trouble the light will cause."

"Who? Malcolm?" Nikala's head spun and bile splashed against the roof of her mouth. She braced herself against the chair.

"When the time comes, on whose side will you fight?" Donyatella stroked a glass lily figurine and for one mad moment, Nikala thought she saw it glimmer and flutter as if it were alive.

"Fight? For what? What are you talking about?" Nikala

stared, transfixed, at the glass lily. "You're not making any sense, Dony."

"War is coming." Her voice lowered. "It can't be avoided. Isn't that right, child of Faerie?"

Nikala scrunched her face in confusion. "Faerie?"

"Not if I can help it." Cian's body filled the doorframe and Donyatella hissed beneath her breath. Cian extended his empty hands. "You have nothing to fear from me, Guardian."

Nikala looked from Cian to Dony and back. "What am I missing?" The landlady's naturally gruff exterior melted away to reveal her fear. "Dony, what does he mean?"

Cian stepped into the room and inhaled deeply. "Tell me, who lived here?"

Donyatella shuffled from foot to foot, eyes downcast. "Please, don't make me. I am sworn to their protection and cannot break my vow."

"Someone tell me what the bloody hell is going on." An implied threat hung on Nikala's words. It had been a long day and she was done playing games.

When Donyatella remained silent, Cian's jaw tightened and his lips pursed. "She needs to know. Just as I need to know who lived here and what they have to do with Faerie."

Again, that Faerie. They said it as if it were a place, not a thing. Nikala fisted her hands to keep from yanking on her hair. With each passing second, she sensed both of her companions were inching closer to losing their shit.

"I made a vow," Dony repeated. "I cannot break it, no matter how much I want to help. We are neutral in these affairs."

What affairs? Nikala wanted to scream at them to make sense. Instead, she jammed a thumb between her teeth and gnawed on an invisible hangnail. Something was happening here and she was caught up in it. The more she listened, the more she'd learn, and hopefully, the better chance she had to stay alive.

Cian took Donyatella's hands in his and the landlady stiffened. "The honor of Stone Guardians is legendary. I've seen first-hand what happens to gargoyles when they break an oath. Forgive me."

Nikala's attention snapped to Cian. Gargoyles? Faerie? What the hell parallel dimension did she fall into? And how the fuck could she get out?

❧ 20 ❧

Cian had no intention of breaking the guardian's vow, but he had to know who had lived there. It drove his every need, his utmost desire. He released Donyatella's cold grip and strode to the fireplace. The ashes were long since burned, but he hoped to find something to help him identify the tenants. A presence in the flat—calm, serene—drove his curiosity. He knelt and swiped two fingers over the ashes. For a long minute, he knelt in silence, rubbing his fingers together, then finally tasted the ash.

What the soot told him was far more than he'd hoped to discover, and also set his heart beating at triple speed.

"Her protector was called Brandt, and she went by Taryn." A hollowness rang with each syllable, as if he were speaking in a trance. Cian blinked and swiveled his head to Donyatella. "I know this name, Taryn. She came to my sister in a vision."

"Aurora MacNair is known to us," the guardian said. "But I do not have providence over her protection."

Fury flashed through his veins. "Why is she known to you? What does she have to do with what is happening?"

The guardian swayed and gripped the bookcase to steady

herself. Nikala went to her side and helped her to sit in the chair. Once settled, Nikala knelt in front of the woman.

"I don't understand any of this. What's going on, Dony? We're old friends. Please."

Tears filled the old woman's eyes and she shook her head. "Don't ask this of me. I can't."

"Nikala," Cian put a hand on her shoulder, "we should go."

Scraping came from the roof and Nikala looked first to him, then to the guardian. The others were vexed with them for upsetting Donyatella.

"I'll answer any questions you have. But we have to go. Now." Cian placed his other hand on Donyatella and knelt so she could see his face. "Is my sister in danger?"

The guardian shook her head. "Not yet. Go now. They're here."

Scraping sounds came from the windows and Cian grabbed Nikala by the hand. He tugged her up as he bolted for the door. They stumbled down the hallway to the back stairs and raced down, down, down until they reached the kitchen. Not much unnerved Cian MacNair, but hostile gargoyles were definitely on the list.

By the time they skidded to a stop, breathless and flushed, the scritching had stopped. He stood still a moment and listened, noting the soft shuffling of Donyatella as she made her way down the hallway to the front stairs. She muttered to the others as she moved along, thanking them for their assistance, and reassuring them Cian and Nikala meant no harm.

"Have you ever heard this name, Taryn?" Cian asked Nikala and she jumped at the sound of his voice.

"No, never. Who is she?"

"I'm not sure." Instead of exiting through the kitchen, Cian led Nikala to the cellar where he'd found the doorway earlier that day.

Sounds rumbled above them as they descended into the

near darkness, but down here was empty of people. He covered the five feet of space between the stairs and doorway in two steps, then rested his hands on his hips as he studied the oak planks.

"It's a door." Nikala managed to sound bored and mocking at the same time.

"Not just any door." Cian spun around and grabbed her by the collar of her leather jacket. The scent of hibiscus wafted to his nose and he fought the urge to kiss her. Why did this woman have to be such a pain in his ass? One second, he was ready to throttle her; the next, he wanted to bed her.

"I suggest you unhand me, unless you fancy a knife in your throat." Her steady gaze showed no fear, just chilling calculation.

"I saw your handiwork earlier. You're good with a blade. What else should I know about you?"

A grin lifted her lips and laughter entered her eyes. "I could ask the same of you. What's Faerie? Why did you call Dony a Stone Guardian? And why are you obsessed with Malcolm?"

The feel of cold steel against his throat had the reverse effect he suspected Nikala was going for—instead of instilling angst, it made his heart lurch and cock pulsate. Damn her for being irresistible.

His lips covered hers, hungry for more of her sweetness. She'd left him wanting when she disappeared from his flat. That want surged into his kiss as he ground his hips against hers and thrust his tongue into the warmth of her mouth.

Nikala's gasp turned to a moan. Her tongue greeted his like a welcoming lover. His grip lessened on her jacket and his hands tangled in her hair, luxuriating in the silkiness. The knife disappeared from his throat and she pressed her body against his. The distinct shape of a gun pushed against his abdomen.

Blood pumped through his brain, killing all rational thought. Her hands wandered beneath his jacket and across his chest, feeling their way to his pants. A few inches more and she'd feel more than his aching cock. She'd find the memory stick he'd stolen from Malcolm's office.

Cian released his grip with a groan and stepped back, breaking physical contact with her. The emptiness that engulfed him was suffocating.

"Not here. Not like this." Cian raked a hand through his hair and looked at the ground, then the door, and finally to Nikala. "I want you, but proper. Not hard and fast in some dingy cellar."

"So, you're a gentleman now," Nikala teased. She tossed her hair and he was mesmerized by the golden glints that sparked in the light.

He hovered over her, protective, consuming. Her scent intoxicated him. Cian traced his fingertips across her forehead and down her temple, over her cheekbones to her jaw. His thumb scraped along her lips and a low growl came from deep in his throat.

She worried her bottom lip with her teeth and he moved his fingers lower to skim her neck and collarbones. A flicker of apprehension crossed her eyes as he slipped his fingers beneath the fabric of her T-shirt. The pads of his fingers lingered on a scar, memorizing the feel of twisted skin.

"What you do to me should be illegal." His eyes bore into hers and for a moment he was lost in the sea of lust he saw reflected back to him. "I have no doubt you would kill me if necessary, but what terrifies me more is I'm afraid you'll break my heart."

Regret, raw and intense, flashed over her features. "I'm incapable of loving, Cian. If that's the sort of relationship you're looking for, I suggest you wander elsewhere." Her eyes narrowed and a cheeky grin lifted her lips. "Although, something tells me you aren't all you've made me believe you are. There's a darkness in you that I quite like, but I, too, feel you'd kill me in an instant if it came to that."

Cian lowered his lips to brush against hers. She sighed into the kiss and he lingered there, barely touching, but connected.

Blood rushed against his hearing, drowning out the sounds above them until he was certain she could hear each rapid beat of his heart. This wasn't part of the assignment. He was breaking his own vow by remaining here, but he didn't care. No one had ever made him feel like this and he feared once their kiss ended, he'd never reclaim the joy of this moment.

"You're not making this easy, you know." Nikala eased him away from her with a sad smile. "Mad shags are my thing. Love 'em and leave 'em, as you know." The joking of her tone didn't reach her eyes. They remained clouded with remorse.

"Put your hand on that door." Cian cocked his head to indicate the door behind him. It was a hunch he had to see through.

"What?"

"Just humor me, please."

Nikala studied the door, then shrugged and stepped forward to press her palm against the wood.

Runes glowed orange around the doorframe and Cian memorized their order and structure.

"Satisfied?" She tapped her fingertips on the oak. "It's a cellar door." Again, she shrugged.

"You see nothing?"

"Nope. And please, don't tell me you see something because after the day I've had, I might be tempted to believe whatever ridiculous story you make up." She removed her hand from the door and wiped it on her blue jeans.

Only beings with magic could use the doorways. If she couldn't see the runes, it meant either he was wrong about her, or that she was heavily warded. Cian wavered between the two options. Rarely was he wrong about someone, but it was possible she didn't have magical abilities herself. Which could mean she was a scyver and very good at deceiving him because a scyver would've seen the magic runes. He seriously doubted she was a scyver or had deceived him. Which meant, most likely she was warded. But by whom and why?

He took her hand in his and placed it against the wood. His hand covered hers and the glow returned, brighter. More runes appeared; several he recognized as symbols for Faerie. Most, he didn't know. "Do you see anything now?"

Nikala's eyes were huge disks of midnight in her pale face. "How'd you do that?"

Her phone rang and she gave him an apologetic look before tugging it from a pocket.

"Yes?" she said by way of answering.

"Where are you? Not at the office, I hope. Something's happened."

Cian clearly heard the male voice on the other end, and the rise of panic in his words.

"No, I'm not there. What's going on?" Nikala lowered her voice and turned her back to Cian, but in the small space it did no good.

"Get here right away. I'll send you the address. There's no time for a car to retrieve you. Grab a cab." The man on the other end took a deep breath and sighed. "I'd thought—never mind what I thought. Just get here soon."

"What happened?" Impatience rang in her words, but also a note of concern.

"There's been an incident at SIRE. Someone destroyed the lab."

"You're kidding?"

Cian saw the shake of Nikala's shoulders, the tremor that ran down her body. She ducked her head and held the phone against her ear at the same time she leaned against the wall. He resisted the urge to wrap her in his arms. Instead, he placed a steadying hand on her shoulder and gave a small squeeze. The muscles beneath his touch were wound tight, ready to spring with the slightest provocation.

"I wish I was. Years of work, gone." Silence stretched across the line. Then, "You didn't do it, did you?"

"Seriously? You think I'd do that? I'm not an idiot. Besides, I was at the pub with Dony. You can ask her." The tremors beneath his hand turned to full-on spasms and Cian stepped closer until his body curved against hers. She relaxed into him. "I can't believe someone did that. Why?"

"Get here as soon as you can. We'll discuss this further then." Nikala was about to reply when the voice asked, "Are you alone?"

"I'm still at the pub. Why?"

"Speak to no one. Do you hear me? Not even Donyatella."

"You don't have to be so dramatic. I get it. Silence and sealed lips." Nikala took a deep breath. "Where's Malcolm?"

"We'll discuss him when you get here."

Nikala held the phone in front of her and said, "Well, goodbye to you, too." She turned and looked up at Cian with something close to terror in her eyes. "I suppose you heard that?"

"It was hard not to. I'm sorry."

She pushed a hand through her hair and rolled her bottom lip between her teeth. A blip sounded from her phone and she glanced at the text message. "I can't go there. I don't know what's going on, but I can't go there. Not tonight."

Cian didn't reply. Her musings were more for herself than him.

"Can I stay with you?" When she glanced at him, it was with fear and something else. Not remorse or lust or longing, but hope. The word sanctuary came to mind.

"I thought you'd never ask." Then he did enfold her in his arms and held her tightly against him. "I won't let anything hurt you."

Her laughter bubbled from within his hug.

"I'm not a princess. I can take care of myself."

Cian rested his chin on her head and inhaled her scent. "I

know plenty of kickass princesses. They're not all damsels waiting to be rescued."

She pulled away and grimaced. "I don't even know if you're joking right now and that's disturbing." She headed for the stairs and beckoned he follow. "I need to get something from Dony first." A shadow crossed her features.

They found the gargoyle at her usual seat by the front door. Nikala leaned in and whispered, "I need what Malcolm left here for me."

Donyatella didn't move for a moment, then she reluctantly rose and hitched her head toward the office. Cian studied the pair, noting the slight flaring of Nikala's nostrils and the tightness of Dony's jaw. After a brief hesitation, he followed the women.

He felt Nikala's fury before he heard her angry words. "Where is it?"

"It was here, where you last saw it. I swear to you, I have not moved it." Donyatella's granite eyes flicked from shelf to shelf and razed the floor. "Guardians are neutral in these affairs, but if asked, we will provide assistance. Malcolm asked me to keep the bag until someone came to us and retrieved it. He did not specify you, but I assumed."

Nikala blew out a breath and spun away from the office, her face red, eyes narrowed. "Fuck."

Dony called over a waiter and asked if anyone had been in the office. His gaze slid to Nikala and his face blanched. "You said if anyone came here asking for the bag, to fetch you, but you weren't around. I gave it to them. I hope you don't mind."

"Don't mind? I could bloody kill you." Nikala advanced on the boy and Cian stepped to keep her from seeing through her threat.

"Perhaps a calmer head should prevail." Cian stared down Nikala until she backed off. To the waiter, he said, "Can you describe them?"

His flustered words came out halted, but he said enough that

Cian recognized the pair as the same thugs who had followed him from Malcolm's building.

Sirens sounded in the distance. "We should go."

Nikala fumed and pounded a fist against her palm. "They stole it while we were upstairs. Now Hunter has the shipment." She turned in a semi-circle then back to Cian. "We can catch them. Let's go."

They left through a side door and headed east on Lower Thames Street. Sirens and flashing police lights came from one hundred meters up the alley, where SIRE's offices were located.

Their hurried steps were drowned out by the chorus of onlookers who'd gathered to see what the excitement was all about. Cian listened for any clue as to what had happened, but all he could make out was fire and explosion. A few whispers mentioned terrorists and a wave of anxiety rippled through the crowd.

Nikala searched the street, her flushed face unreadable. "They're gone. Bollocks." She touched a hand to her back and winced.

Cian turned them away from the activity, toward Tower Hill and the Underground. Half a block from the Tube entrance, Nikala's pace slowed and she darted inside a doorway. He scanned the area as he joined her, noting the two black-clad bikers. They circled the street, then revved their engines and rode off, away from where they hid.

"Asshole sent the B-team." She shook her head, a scowl cutting across her features.

"Nikala, if you're in some kind of danger, I can help."

She looked up at him with a wry smile. "It's not your problem to fix, but thanks."

A group of tourists ambled along the sidewalk, lugging their bags to the subway. Cian and Nikala skirted them and jogged to the brightly lit entry. She whipped out her card and he waved his hand over the reader, using a spark of magic to confuse the machine and allow him access. She glared at him with a sardonic grin, which made his belly pinch in the most delightful way.

Two figures rose from their lazy, reclining positions against a wall and his senses went on full alert. What were two scyvers doing together? As far as he knew, they didn't travel in packs, yet here they were, eyeing him and Nikala like lions sizing up a gazelle.

As Rori would say, futnuckers and cocklespaz. The Tube was the fastest route to his flat. It wasn't coincidence they were here, waiting.

$\maltese$ 2 1 $\maltese$

Cian grabbed Nikala's elbow and spun them toward the exit. She started to protest, but saw the grim determination in his scowl. They hopped through the turnstiles and she turned in time to see a spark of silver flow from his fingertips to the machines. If she'd blinked, she would've missed it.

Two men moved quickly through the crowded station and she hurried out of the building. Angry shouts came from behind them.

"Who were those men? I don't recognize them." Nikala glanced over her shoulder and kept walking.

"Scyvers."

"Do they normally run in pairs?" She easily kept pace with his long strides.

"This way."

They turned toward the Tower and embankment. At this time of night, there would be plenty of people to hide them.

"Not that I've ever seen. And they don't usually stake out a place. They were waiting for us, or someone else, I'm sure of it." Cian kept hold of her elbow as they jogged across the street.

A slow tremor worked its way through her veins. Hunter had sent not only the B-team, but backups of his backups. He had the amulets and Malcolm. All he needed now was her. She had to get away from the men following them and clear her mind. At the moment, Cian was her best bet for survival.

The smell of roasted nuts came from a street vendor and Cian stopped to buy a cup. He paid the man and resumed his hastened pace.

"Eat some." He handed the cup to her after taking a large handful for himself. "Almonds confuse scyvers."

"Really?" She shoved a bunch of the warm mess into her mouth. It was delicious, but she didn't linger on the taste. "Although," she said between chews, "you could tell me witches and vampires are real and I would probably believe you."

The grin Cian gave her made her knees go weak and stomach roil. Nikala made a mental note never to ask if vampires were real. The day had already proved anything was possible.

They wove in and out of crowds, with Cian directing her to rub along as many people as she could without being obvious. Something about transferring magic and keeping the scyvers off their trail. Every so often she'd chance a glance behind them and see a head bob above the others, searching. She didn't get a good enough look at the men to know if these were the same ones from the station, and she didn't really care. They were being followed and in her experience, she could either keep running, or stay and fight.

"We can't keep up this pace all the way to your flat." She held onto Cian's sleeve, slowing him down. "You and I can easily handle them."

"Murder isn't always the answer, Nikala."

"And running is?"

Cian ran a hand through his hair, and swore under his breath. "Once we're at my place, we'll be safe. I'd rather they not follow us the entire way."

"Then what do you suggest?" She fanned her jacket, allowing cool air to run beneath the leather. The gun melded against her side, pinching her skin. After a moment's hesitation, she took it out and handed it to Cian. "Something tells me you'd be better with this than me."

He took it with a low chuckle. "You never cease to surprise me." He tucked the gun into an inner pocket of his coat. "Let's keep moving."

They strode past a restaurant to a small grassy area dotted with trees. The budding leaves gave slim cover. In the distance, a pair of golden eyes surrounded by dark fur emerged from beneath a shrub and Nikala took a step backward. "Please tell me that's not a wolf. Why is there a wolf in London?"

Cian followed her outstretched hand and squinted into the darkness.

"Not a wolf—a lycan." He took several steps toward the huge beast and knelt, his hand outstretched.

"What the fuck is a lycan? Do you really think that's a good idea? It looks hungry." Nikala stayed firmly behind him, ready to bolt in the opposite direction if the creature so much as snarled.

"Not hungry, injured. See how it's limping?"

Nikala only saw the shimmering black fur and glowing golden eyes. Well, and the huge paws. And yes, one was bent at an odd angle, making the thing stagger a little. A crack in her heart opened toward the beast.

"I won't hurt you," Cian cooed to the lycan. "Who did this to you?"

The lycan limped forward with a whimper. Its head came to the same height as her waist, and it probably weighed a stone more than her. About a foot from Cian's outstretched hand, it stopped and glared up at Nikala.

"She's a friend. She means you no harm." To Nikala, Cian said, "Kneel down beside me and put out your hand."

Nikala glanced behind her to where the scyvers were

certainly catching up to them. Should she risk getting mauled by a wolf, or murdered by psychos? What was wrong with her life that those were her only choices? She seriously needed a holiday. Somewhere tropical, like Malcolm had suggested, without crazy men or magic hunters or whatever the hell a lycan was.

She knelt beside Cian and held out a shaking hand. The lycan crept forward and sniffed her fingers. The beast's fangs dripped slobber on her and she held her breath, hoping the thing didn't see her as a tasty snack. A cold nose sniffed her fingertips while golden eyes held her stare.

"That's it, boy, come here." Cian stroked a hand over the lycan's fur and down his left leg to his paw.

The beast snarled and Nikala swallowed a whimper. She rather liked her fingers where they were—attached to her hand. One wrong move and the beast could end her life before she drew her blade.

"We don't have time for this," Nikala whispered, fully aware the lycan could hear the blood rushing through her veins.

"No, but should I ever need the kindness of strangers, I would hope they don't pass me by."

Properly chastised, Nikala flexed her fingers to stroke the beast's muzzle. "What happened to him?"

"Hard to say." A faint glow emanated from Cian's palm and covered the lycan's paw. He whined and tugged to get away, but Cian kept a firm grip on his leg. "Easy now. That's it. You've got a nasty cut that needs time to heal." He sucked in a breath and shook his head. "How'd you get here?"

The lycan looked over his shoulder toward the river.

"Do you have somewhere safe to stay tonight? I can't take you with me, but I'll come back to check on you tomorrow." Cian released the beast's paw and patted him on the shoulder.

To Nikala's astonishment, the lycan dropped his head and nudged Cian's hand so that he could pet the beast's ruff. If she didn't know any better, she would've thought it was a domesticated dog looking for a tummy rub.

"Off you go now." Cian rose and Nikala followed. The lycan shuffled to the shrubs and disappeared with a swish of his tail. "It pains me to leave him, but as you said, we can't spare the time."

As they hurried past the bushes, Nikala felt the glowing eyes following her and shuddered. She raised a hand in farewell, hoping the thing survived the night.

They kept close to the wall as they sprinted toward Temple Church and Cian's flat. Without warning, he turned right and she skidded to adjust the trajectory of her run. As she did, she glanced toward where they'd come and saw two figures bobbing through the shadows a short distance away.

"They're close." She caught up to Cian and heard a slight wheeze in his breath. He couldn't keep this pace up the entire way to his flat. "What's your plan?"

He tilted his chin toward the busy street in front of them where several cabs waited at a taxi rank. They ran full out to the first one and jumped into the backseat, startling the driver. Cian gave the address, with instructions to drive across the river and back on another bridge a mile away. Within moments, they were speeding away.

Nikala checked behind them, but didn't see the scyvers. She settled into her seat, too amped to relax.

The day's events played on a loop through her mind as the cab wove in and out of traffic, turning where Cian directed, and backtracking across several streets. By the time they reached Cian's flat, Nikala was dizzy from all the twists and turns they'd made.

She checked the street as she waited for Cian to pay. Nothing out of the ordinary caught her attention. No scyvers waited in doorways, no wolves huddled in bushes. The street was quiet, but not too quiet.

Cian strode past her without a word and waved his hand over

the entry door's lock. It clicked open and she followed him inside. They jogged up the stairs to the long hallway leading to his flat. Cian paused to listen before striding across the thick carpet to his door. Once again he waved his hand over the lock and it opened.

"That's a pretty neat trick. Does it work on every lock?"

"Most." Cian grinned. "Some are harder than others."

The look he gave went straight to the apex of her legs. A little thrill curled itself around her heart. She'd forgotten her warning of that morning—*this man was Dangerous.*

Once he'd locked the door behind them and drew all the curtains, he cracked his neck and flexed his hands. Nikala stood in the middle of the lounge, unsure what to do. It hadn't been that long ago that she'd been in this very room, against that very wall, with Cian. At the time, she thought she'd never see him again and was fine with that, but now everything had changed. She couldn't just bang him for information and kill him. He'd helped her—she owed him at least a little debt of gratitude.

Plus, the way he'd cared for the lycan, despite being pursued, pinched her in places she never thought to feel again.

She shifted from foot to foot and jammed her thumb between her teeth to gnaw on a nonexistent cuticle. When they'd been running from the scyvers, it seemed only natural they'd seek refuge in Cian's apartment—she didn't have a place to go, after all. But now that she was there, that plan seemed a bit short-sighted. What if they found them? Cian said they'd be safe, but could she fully trust him? He had a lot of secrets and that made her nervous.

And there was Hunter's call she'd have to deal with sooner or later. When she didn't show up at his place, he'd send people searching for her. It was doubtful they'd track her to Cian's, but after her day and night, she believed anything was possible.

Cian blew out a breath and leaned against the table, his arms wide, head dipped low. "I need to do something, and please don't ask me to explain it because I can't." His hazel eyes met hers and in them she saw a silent plea.

"Is it dangerous?" Of all the hundreds of questions swirling in her mind, that was the one that popped out. She shook her head at the naivete of her question. What about their night *hadn't* been dangerous?

"Only to those who wish us harm." Cian removed his coat and lay it over the back of a chair.

Next, he stretched his arms wide and wiggled his fingertips. Nikala suppressed a giggle at the image of a magician about to perform a trick. She half expected to see a bunny appear in his hand. Instead of a bunny, sparks lit from his fingertips to form a blaze a foot high. Blue-black flames licked up his arms toward his serene face.

She stared in horror as the flames danced closer. A moment later, they spread outward, toward her.

"Stay calm. Don't move." Cian's voice came from within the inferno.

Nikala remained where she stood, her heart spinning as wildly as the fast-moving flames. If she couldn't trust Cian, now was the time she'd fine out for sure. A voice whispered in the back of her mind that yes, she could trust him. With her life. With her heart. With everything. She told the voice to shut up, but not with much urgency.

Cian clapped his hands and the fire became a solid wall of bluish light that covered the entire flat, from floor to ceiling, and everywhere in between.

When the light touched her, she flinched, but there was no burning sensation or warmth or anything. Just a soft probing that settled into her skin and moved on. A sharp crackle came from Cian's coat and something the size of her pinky fingernail fell to the table. The chip she'd stuck to his collar that morning. Another crack came from inside her jacket and she peered into the inner pocket to see a tiny disc smoking in the corner.

She picked it out of the fabric and held it aloft. "Where did you come from?" It wasn't one of hers. Most likely, it was one of Malcolm's inventions. "You sneaky little bugger."

The bluish light continued its trek through the flat and Nikala's attention was drawn to a cupboard to the right of the kitchen. A strong pull, one she knew well, came from somewhere inside. Her gaze shifted to Cian, who was watching her with bemused interest.

"We're safe now. Whoever was tracking us won't get any further information." He picked up the chip on the table and inspected it. With two steps, he closed the gap between them and took the disc from her fingertips. "Two separate trackers."

Nikala bit her lower lip and shrugged. "I might've put that one on your coat this morning. But this disc, I'm pretty sure is Malcolm's. Which surprises me, but shouldn't."

Cian tossed them into the fireplace. "I was curious how you found me this afternoon."

The lack of emotion in his voice unsettled her as much as the indifference his body language showed. Was he brooding, or just accepting? Either way, it unsettled her to see him so calm about the trackers. She was livid she hadn't thought to check her cloth-ing. But then, had there been time?

"Sometimes it's hard to know who to trust." At the moment, she wasn't sure anyone was trustworthy, not even herself. Hadn't Malcolm ordered her to take out Cian a few hours earlier? And here she was, back in his flat, admitting she was following him.

"It's late. We're both exhausted." Cian turned toward the bedroom and paused a moment to run a fingertip along her jaw. "In the morning, we can talk."

That tiny connection of touch sent rivulets of desire through her ribs and down her spine. The man knew his way around seduction, she'd give him that.

"You take the bed. I'll sleep on the couch."

She blinked in surprise. "Are you sure?"

She'd been preparing herself mentally for sleeping with him and now to have the choice taken away made her long for it even more.

"I'm not sure of anything at the moment." A wistful grin lifted his lips and a tiny dimple formed in his right cheek. A day's worth of stubble covered his chin and she nearly reached up to rub her hand along its roughness. To stroke that small scar hidden beneath the hair.

He left her standing there and went to the bedroom. She watched him leave, studied the way his shoulders hunched and the slowed pace of his steps. He was right—they were both exhausted. When he returned a moment later with his arms full of linens, a sense of guilt washed over her.

"It's your flat. I'll take the couch." She reached for the bundle, but he shook her off.

"There are towels in the shower if you need them. I laid out a T-shirt if you'd like something clean to sleep in."

Nikala mumbled a thanks and shuffled to the bedroom. This wasn't at all how she'd expected the night to go. Then again, nothing about today had been as planned.

After she slipped out of her clothing and into the T-shirt he'd left for her, she climbed onto his comfortable mattress and slid between the cool sheets. All around her, a pale-blue twinkling shimmered along the walls, ceiling, and floors. Cian would have her believe it was magic. She reached toward the ceiling and stifled a gasp at the shimmering beneath her skin. It was getting worse.

When she'd killed the scyver, only a small patch had shown on her forearm, but now her entire arm from bicep to wrist sparkled. She could shrug it off as aftereffects from Hunter's tests, but she knew that was a lie. From deep inside, the truth emerged like a lava flow, covering her thoughts and emotions with a searing realization.

Her eyes widened as she took in the tiny flickers around her.

It *was* magic. Faerie was a place and a people. Lycans roamed London. Scyvers hunted magic and were very real. As she lay gazing at the wonder surrounding her, her mind and heart shifted. Something had happened to her and nothing would ever be the same.

❧ 2 2 ❧

Snickertits. Rori had gotten herself lost, *again.* She scrunched her nose and peered in the direction from where she'd just come and then down the hall in the opposite direction. There were only the two options. Yet somehow, she'd managed to end up in the exact same spot where she'd been five minutes before.

Someone had to be messing with her. Someone or something was leading her here, but why? And who? Acelyne came to mind, but the enchantress was dead and Rori doubted she could make illusions now that she was dust. Still, why direct her to this spot?

She glanced at the furnishings and wall hangings. They were finer than elsewhere in the palace. Perhaps this wing was reserved for important guests, or—Rori's heart beat in her throat and her adrenaline surged—a princess. Perhaps even the sister of the queen. She drew in a long breath—this was Mairead's floor.

As Rori turned toward the closed doors behind her, she heard a soft click come from her right. She crept toward the sound, keeping aware of her surroundings and any sudden movements.

Why lead Rori to her chambers? A door opened on its own and Rori peeked inside. A sitting room, in pinks and greens, two colors Rori would never put together, sat empty. Despite the wild color scheme, the room was attractive in its welcoming arrangement of chairs and sofas.

"Hello?" Rori called into the room, unsurprised when no one answered.

She eased farther into the apartments, checking first the drawing room, then the study before the intimate areas of the dressing room, bath, and bedroom. A floral, powdery scent followed Rori's movements. She touched a dressing gown's sleeve and an image of raven hair came to her, followed by searing pain. She snatched her fingers away and wiped them on the flimsy fabric of her gowns.

The image had a masculine quality to it, but these rooms were clearly meant for a woman. Rori skipped past the hanging dressing gown to a vanity covered with ornate bottles, hairbrushes, and other womanly accoutrements. Most of the things Rori had little time or patience for.

She touched the bristles of the nearest brush, letting the silky strands of strawberry-blonde curls twist around her fingers. Another image—this time of a young woman smiling gaily and dancing beneath the stars—came to her.

Mairead.

Midna's missing sister.

Rori gathered several of the curls and wrapped them in a piece of cloth she found in a drawer of the vanity. The ridiculous gowns Midna had provided her didn't have pockets, nor did they have anywhere she could conveniently carry the tiny parcel. With a snarl for her hostess's lack of propriety, Rori tucked the cloth between her breasts.

She returned to the gown in the dressing room and stood before it for several seconds before reaching out. Being prepared for the image and sensation of pain didn't lessen the impact of sensing Mairead's emotions in the garment. They ripped through Rori as if they were her own.

For a long minute, she breathed in and out, letting the feelings settle. Heat infused her as if she stood before a fire, warmth cocooning her from within as well as without. When the discordant buzzing in her ears became a gentle hum, she opened herself to what the dressing gown could tell her.

A man, with raven hair and dark eyes, young, happy, yet tormented, had worn the gown on many occasions. Rori focused on his eyes. They were deep brown, with flecks of gold in them. He was fae. From the Unseelie Court, but not nobility.

Anguish tore through Rori's psyche and she released her hold of the fabric. Tears blurred her vision and she said to the unsettled air, "Please forgive me. I didn't know."

Who or what she was apologizing to, and for what, she had no clue, but the words slipped past her lips before she could stop them.

She stumbled backward, against a bookcase, and brushed her fingers along the spine of a leather-bound novel. She stood, stuck—unable to move, unable to blink.

Rivulets of ice started at her crown and ran down her face to her torso, down her spine to the tops of her buttocks. A chill entered her marrow where only moments earlier she'd been basking in heat. The shift in temperature came not from her surroundings, but from a memory that bullied its way to the forefront of her mind.

Acelyne spoke true—Rori knew where to find the dark spells to free the trapped fae.

The day her father went missing, Rori had been practicing warping and weaving spells, but then her words twisted into dark magic and she'd chanted an incantation she scarcely remembered.

Sweat dotted her brow and her mouth went dry. That spell wasn't the only one she knew.

Rori pressed her fists against her forehead and squeezed her eyes shut to block out the dark words surrounding her thoughts. Someone had taught her dozens of forbidden spells when she was too young to comprehend their meaning. As Rori stood in the empty space, shivering with the memory, she fought to remember who. Nothing came to mind. No face, no voice, no touch— nothing. It was as if she'd learned by osmosis, but that wasn't possible. Or was it? She didn't know anymore.

She shook out her fists and breathed in the musty air, taking it deep into her lungs. That was long ago. Whatever she'd learned as a child, she wouldn't let it harm anyone now. If she had knowledge to release the fae, she'd use it, but not until she was certain she had the right words.

If she got them wrong, Rori would be little more than a murderer.

She bent to inspect the book and those sitting in perfect order on the shelf. It wasn't a spell book, nor did it dredge anymore memories. Yet something about it caused a trigger. Books. Not these books. Where? She slammed her fist on the wood and swore at the ceiling.

More confused than ever, and distraught over what she'd encountered in Mairead's rooms, Rori hastened out of the chambers and sped down the hallway. She made a left, then a right, and jogged up a flight of stairs before stopping, out of breath and unable to outpace the demons that followed her. Images of the handsome young man and Mairead dancing beneath the moon. They'd been in love, the pair. Happy. What had driven them apart? For as long as Rori could remember, Mairead hadn't had a lover, or at least not one spoken about at the Seelie Court. In the robe, she'd sensed unfathomable sadness. Whatever had happened to their love, it had been enough to drive a sane person to madness.

A bitter aftertaste coated her tongue and she swallowed to rid herself of the sensations lingering like a gentleman's aftershave in a lift. Cloying enough to make her gag.

Two guards stood at attention outside an enormous, gilded

door and Rori shook her head. Of course she'd find Midna's rooms now, after the ordeal she suffered.

"Is the queen in?" Rori stood and huffed a deep breath. "I need to see her."

Both guards scrutinized her, from the disheveled hair falling over her shoulders to the velvet court slippers that didn't quite fit her feet. They were the only shoes in her wardrobe besides a pair of bath slippers that she didn't think would be acceptable for walking through a palace. Even though they were, in truth, more comfortable.

She shifted her gown that had slipped off one shoulder and surreptitiously checked to make sure the cloth was between her breasts. Faerie needed to rethink some of their "nothing modern" rules. Like bras. She could really use a bra right now—a good, supportive garment that she could hide shit in—but all Faerie had was a camisole-like blouse that wasn't even close to what she needed.

"Guys, come on. The sooner you let me in, the sooner I can leave the Unseelie Court, and we all know you'd prefer not to have a MacNair in residence, right?"

One of the guards disappeared into Midna's rooms and she was left waiting with a surly-looking chap. A few minutes later, the guard returned and held the door open for her. She floated into Midna's domain with a sassy thanks to the men. Neither replied nor even glanced at her as she passed.

The Unseelie queen beckoned Rori join her in the lavish sitting area. The gorgeous fae who Rori always saw by Midna's side hovered in the background, his presence neither a comfort nor a distraction.

"Why have you interrupted my morning? I've not yet break-fasted and yet here you are, demanding an audience." Midna's nasally whine was unlike the queen and Rori took care not to offend her more than she already had. Which meant she bit back her reply that she hadn't demanded anything, just simply asked to see the queen.

"I'm sorry to disturb you, Your Majesty." Rori's quick curtsey was met with a nod and indication to sit. She did as told, then said in measured beats, "I'm grateful you allowed me to stay with you, but in light of recent events, I feel my services are needed elsewhere."

She kept her verbiage vague on purpose in case anyone was eavesdropping.

Midna weighed Rori's words, her nails scraping along a pleat of pale-green gossamer.

"What events?" The queen's head cocked to the side and a forest-colored tendril curled around her neck.

Rori scrunched her nose. She wasn't sure what to make of the revelation she'd had in Mairead's room, and she couldn't tell Midna she'd changed her mind about becoming an álainn obedience after just one night with Therron. But that was the truth. Would the queen laugh at her? Kick her out of her palace? Did it matter?

She dragged in a long breath. "I thought this was where I needed to be—and maybe it still is; maybe I do need to learn to control my emotions—but there are faeries in danger and I can't relax knowing there is something I can do to help. Even if I stayed, I wouldn't be fully committed and for that, I'm sorry. I didn't mean to waste your generosity."

Midna's smile warmed Rori from the middle outward to the tips of her toes.

"I was wondering if you'd have a change of heart." Midna beckoned Rori forward and she knelt before the queen. "Darling, this palace was never the place for you. Your emotions serve you well. Don't let Cian or anyone else tell you otherwise. You needed to discover this on your own, however." A flicker of regret crossed Midna's features. "I'll admit, I will grieve the lack of knowing you carnally."

An indelicate snort came from deep in Rori's throat. Embarrassed, she covered it with a quick cough. "I, erm, thank you?" What was the proper response to a statement like that?

A soft giggle, sort of like the sound of unicorn hiccups, eased the awkwardness. Midna stroked Rori's cheek. "Where will you go?"

"I was hoping you'd allow me to search Cian's rooms here, in case he left any notes or letters that might help me continue the work he was doing." It was a deflection from her actual mission. Midna might not approve of her chasing after a dead enchantress and send her somewhere else. The queen didn't seem bothered about ordering Eirlys's agents to do her bidding. Besides, although she sincerely doubted Cian would leave anything, and if he had, he would've told her, he might've forgotten something seemingly insignificant. Or possibly, he left a clue just for her.

"You may search them, but I assure you, there is nothing to be found." The grimace Midna wore told Rori she'd already had the rooms searched, several times, probably. From her tone, Rori guessed the queen hadn't found anything.

"Then, if your, erm…" Rori glanced at the handsome fae reclining several feet away and pretending he wasn't paying attention to their conversation. "If someone could direct me to Therron's rooms, I'd like to see if he wants to join me."

Midna's perfect brows dipped and her lips flatlined. "Therron's gone."

"What do you mean, gone? Where?" A scorching chasm opened in her heart, threatening to swallow her whole and burn her to a crisp.

"He left quite early this morning for the Seelie Court." A flicker of something mean lit from deep in her eyes. "Didn't he say farewell?"

Rori bit down her disappointment and secured a look of passive indifference to her face. "He probably didn't want to disturb me. I'll catch up to him soon, I'm sure." She could scarcely breathe for the pounding of her heart and ringing in her ears. Therron had left her.

Softness replaced the meanness Rori saw, and Midna's body sunk into the sofa. "Darling, you couldn't have expected him to stay here while you were busy with your *education*, now could you?"

Guilt slid through her mortification. She had hoped he'd be the one doing the educating, but that wouldn't happen now—or ever. Their night together *had* been a hookup. She just hadn't realized it. Even now, she was loath to accept the fact. Her gaze went to the faerie, who regarded her with a look of profound sadness drooping his features. She felt a kinship to him in that brief moment. They loved someone who couldn't or wouldn't return that love.

Her body vibrated with the realization. She loved Therron. When had that happened? Her emotions flicked through their time together, settling on the kiss he'd given her at her cottage. Surprised by the depth of anguish his absence brought, she fought hard to push her feelings into a dark corner where she could forget they existed.

"I don't see how it would make any difference," Rori said at last. "I mean, it's not like he loves me and being subjected to seeing me with dozens of men wouldn't be terrible for him, right?"

The fae blinked and looked down, his face turned away.

Midna's gasp stung Rori's heart.

"Of course it would torment him. If you think that elf doesn't love you, you're not nearly as smart as you'd have us all believe."

Rori stopped her protest before it reached her lips. Therron had left her for the Seelie Court—for Eirlys. If he loved her, he wouldn't have done that. Even so, outlandish fluttering tickled her belly and Rori struggled to keep a firm grasp on her indifferent features. It wouldn't do to let Midna know how much her words had thrilled—and confused—Rori. Maybe Midna was right—she wasn't smart about the mysteries of the heart. Maybe Therron left *because* he loved her.

With renewed purpose and a stupid grin on her face, she gripped Midna's fingertips in her own and kissed them before rising. "Thank you for everything. A final request?" Midna looked at her with a bemused smile. "May I use your Room of Mirrors?"

"Of course, darling." Midna waved her off. Her hand covered her lips and her eyes clouded as if she saw something Rori and the other fae couldn't see.

At the doorway, Rori turned back to the queen. "By the way, it wasn't just Therron I was talking about."

The Unseelie queen stared at her with tears shimmering in her eyes. Whatever the history between her and the gorgeous fae, they were fools not to see how much they loved each other. The nagging question of why Midna wouldn't commit to one faerie dragged at Rori's thoughts as she left the queen's chambers and hustled to her own rooms. There was a reason, but not a clear one that she could imagine.

She changed into her own clothes, being careful as she slid her jeans over the stitches in her thigh. The wound was healing, but not quick enough for her. Meg had said nothing strenuous for a few weeks and Rori had every intention of heeding the healer's advice. The last thing she needed was to visit Meg with a busted-open cut. She shivered at the thought of Meg's shrieks if she turned up wounded so soon after her fight with Acelyne.

Daggers firmly secured to her person, she shrugged into her leather jacket and made her way to Cian's room. He had plenty of opportunities to take her aside and give her information, but with spies lurking around every corner, she knew her brother well enough to know he wouldn't say anything aloud that was of vital importance. He'd hide a clue or papers where only she would find them. At the door to Cian's room, Rori paused. If she were Cian — She stopped that line of thinking and changed it to herself. If *she* had important information she wanted only Cian to find, where would she hide them?

The answer came to her like a brilliant light popping in her mind.

Sneaky bastard.

He'd already told her where to look—at their mum's.

Out of due diligence, she searched his rooms thoroughly. Two tiny scraps of paper were all she found, and she couldn't be certain they were from Cian or leftover from previous occupants. All the same, she tucked them into the pocket that now held the parcel with Mairead's curls.

On her way to the Room of Mirrors, she scanned the hallway for the mysterious woman, but saw only courtiers going about their day. She tugged open the door and entered the mirrored room with a plan. She'd hop from doorway to doorway, and another, inching closer to her mum's without making a direct route to where she was going. If anyone wished to follow her, she wouldn't make it easy on them.

And, a voice whispered in the back of her mind, perhaps she might run into a certain thief along her journey. At the first mirror, she paused. Before she could change her mind, she spoke the incantation that would take her to the Shoogly Dragon.

23

His magic protected them from anything entering the flat, but as Cian lay on the couch staring at the unmoving ceiling, he worried about what they'd encounter outside. The lycan he'd healed near the Thames was far from home and should never have been in the heart of the city. Yet something had drawn it out. The poor creature was too long removed from his humanoid form to make much sense.

All he'd been able to gather from him was that he'd been lured to the embankment and attacked. Physically as well as magically. Someone had knocked the creature unconscious with a bottle and stolen his magic. Barbarous. Cian had never heard of such a thing. If he was in Faerie, he'd have gone to Eirlys and demanded something be done.

But he was in the human world, where lycans were myths and feared.

He placed a hand over his face to stop from seeing the pleading in the lycan's glowing golden eyes. The image remained rooted at the forefront of his memory. He'd all but begged Cian to end his life. A sworn assassin, unable to kill a defenseless dog.

"Hey." The sound of Nikala's voice startled him and he sat

upright, eyes wide, alert to danger. "I'm sorry, I didn't mean to alarm you." Her warm hand covered his. For a split second, he thought he saw Glamour shimmering beneath her skin.

"What's happened?" Cian stood to his full height and scanned the flat.

"Nothing. I, erm…" She ran a hand through her hair, clearly agitated. "I shouldn't have bothered you. Go back to sleep."

As if he could. She turned to leave and Cian put a hand on her shoulder. "I'm here, Nikala. Talk to me."

"I don't want to talk."

His breathing hitched as she slid a hand down his arm and slipped it into his hand. He followed her to the bedroom, where she turned to face him.

"Proper, like you said."

The words pooled in his heart, turning it molten. Slowly, he lowered his head to hers and brushed his lips across her forehead, then down her nose, to her waiting mouth. A small gasp came from her and he felt the trembling of her legs as he pressed his body against her.

One hand cradled her head and the other wrapped around her waist to keep her as close to him as possible. Her heat seared his senses, but he didn't care. Proper. That's what he told her, and that's what she wanted.

Giving himself to her, now, with his magic cocooning the room and his every nerve alight, was dangerous. He'd already let her see more of him than anyone ever had. He'd made himself vulnerable.

Her hands snaked up his chest to his jaw, where she rubbed her palms along the scruff of stubble. Her eyes stayed locked on his. They shone with an inner light that went straight to his core.

She wasn't human.

She was fae.

Did she know? He doubted it. He'd been right in the pub's cellar to guess she was warded. His magic cut through some of the barriers placed on her—but not all of them. A nagging pulled his thoughts from her, from her sweet face and those lips. If she was fae, who were her parents? Did they leave Faerie to have her? Or was she born there and moved to the human realm? Was she one of the kidnapped fae who somehow managed to escape? With a growl, he shuttled the bothersome questions aside and returned to the here and now. Answers would come later.

A soft shimmer glowed beneath her skin and he wondered whether she could see it, or if that was blocked from her as well. There was no telling the amount of magic she possessed, not with the wards on her, but he guessed it was substantial. Whoever had hid her magic didn't want her or anyone else to know she was fae, of that he was certain.

His lips traveled to her eyelids, where he kissed each one, then grazed over her cheek to nuzzle behind her ear. She whimpered and squirmed, pushing her pelvis into him, but he couldn't be tempted to rush this. Proper was what he'd promised.

But damn, it was hard.

His hands and lips traveled the length of her, skimming over the T-shirt she wore to her bare legs. Cian knelt in front of her, like a devotee worshiping his goddess. The tremble in her legs was slight, but noticeable. She was scared. Frankly, so was he.

His hands caressed her legs from her ankle to her hips, all the while her fingertips raked across his scalp. The soothing sensation of her touch lulled him into a state of bliss and he kissed her thigh, nudging her shirt up as he went.

As he rose, he continued lifting the fabric. Her shaking quickened to near spasms, but he wouldn't stop. When he brought the shirt up to her face, there was a silent plea in her eyes that nearly broke his heart.

He knew her scars, understood her pain. Like her, he'd been injured, but he'd never had to endure the kind of abuse she must've suffered to receive so many disfigurements. With a flourish, the shirt cleared her head and fell to the floor. She stood before him wearing only her panties. Tears shone in her gorgeous blue orbs and he wiped them away with a thumb.

"Don't hide. Not from me." His hands smoothed the hairs from her face and stroked down to her neck. His lips followed until he reached the first scars above her left clavicle. There, he paused to place several featherlight kisses on the mangled skin.

Her sharp intake of breath and stiffened body troubled him, but he continued. She would be loved tonight. Proper. Scars and all.

"You're beautiful, Nikala."

Her hands were on his shoulders, pushing slightly as if she wanted him away from her, but also not to stop. This was no longer about his needs, but hers. He was driven to show her she had nothing to hide, nothing to be ashamed of.

"Who did this to you?"

She shook her head, and the pressure on his shoulders increased. "It doesn't matter. He's in my past."

Cian pressed his lips to hers. "I won't hurt you, Nikala."

His caresses and kisses continued across her body until each of her blemishes were soothed, every inch of her body memorized. Only then did he lift her from where she stood and place her on the bed, where she gazed at him with a look of awe and terror. Whatever hell she'd been through, she'd survived and for that, she had his deepest respect. The scars she bore were a mixture of fighting and intentional cuts. A few were from burns, not cigarette, but some kind of liquid that spread like a rash. The geography of her disfigurements was like that of a lab experiment gone bad.

And she'd lived through whatever had done this to her.

He stripped off his shirt and boxers, kicking them to the floor before returning to the gorgeous woman lying on his bed, waiting. He snaked his hands up her shins to her thighs and hooked his fingers into the cotton panties she wore. Her hips lifted and he tugged them off without any sort of pretense of patience. The need to fill her, to meld his body to hers and give his strength, his healing, his love to her overwhelmed him to the point where nothing else mattered. No lycans, no fae, not even the threat of scyvers could distract his focus.

Nikala was all he saw. All he felt.

He leaned forward and kissed her softly, delighting in the murmurs and moans that tickled his lips. Her legs wrapped around his as her mouth opened. He entered her far slower than he'd like, almost losing control at the warmth that embraced his cock. This was nothing like earlier, when it had been too fast, too hard to notice subtleties and shifts of movement. A tweak to her hips there, a lift of his bum here, made their connection deeper, richer.

They moved as one in a steady rhythm. The shimmer beneath her skin brightened the closer she came to orgasm. He glanced at his arm and saw his Glamour. Muted, but there. A sense of wonder covered him that this woman should bring out the one thing he swore no one would ever see unless he allowed it.

Perhaps he was allowing it and didn't realize.

Nikala traced a finger over his chest and arched until her neck stretched tantalizingly beneath his mouth. He sucked on the soft skin, earning a sultry moan from her, and a spasm went straight to his cock. Another minute and he'd be undone.

Her thrusts quickened, and her legs tightened around his back. That was all he needed.

They panted and cried out as they came together, a mass of writhing and sweat and Glamour mixing with his protective magic.

The air shifted and thickened with their orgasms. As if some unseen force added to his protective barrier. Almost imperceptible, but Cian noticed and by the wide-eyed stare Nikala gave him, she noticed it as well. A wildness entered her eyes, followed by a cheeky grin.

She gripped his face between her hands and brought his lips to hers. The warmth of her kiss burned through his limbs.

They lay together, fingers trailing across skin, occasionally brushing lips, but not speaking. Cian's thoughts spun with shoulds and woulds and couldn'ts. His queen would tell him to interrogate Nikala, then dispose of her if necessary. But his heart was a traitor.

He fell asleep with absolute clarity he'd defy everyone for this woman. They were connected by a tether he'd never known existed—not just from their lovemaking and shared experiences, but by something deeper he couldn't yet articulate. What he knew, though, was that he would die protecting that bond.

He woke the next morning to an empty bed. His breath stilled with the horrible thought that she'd left him again. He envisioned her on the streets, being hunted by scyvers, and his heart beat hard against his chest. Then he heard a noise come from the lounge and relaxed, but not enough to quiet his spinning thoughts.

A ray of light shone through his drapes as he grabbed a fresh pair of boxers from his drawer and dragged on a clean T-shirt. The floor was empty of Nikala's clothing, which was a shame. He'd quite like to see her naked in his kitchen.

He'd like even more to hear what she'd call him if he told her as much.

She sat at the table he'd never used for meals with a bowl in front of her, a cup of tea to her right. Beside the tea was something that made his blood chill.

The box of sugary cereal he'd hidden in his pantry.

And there, to the left of her bowl, was the amulet. Next to it was the memory stick he'd stolen from Malcolm's office.

"Good morning," she said with a cheery smile. "Breakfast?" She indicated the cereal and he blanched.

"Do I have any coffee?" He shuffled to the kitchen, his mind scrambling to sort out how to get the amulet and memory stick from her.

"In the fridge. You're low on milk, though."

This alternate reality he woke up to was messing with him. Since when did he start putting coffee in the fridge? It hadn't been that long since he'd been in London—a few months, maybe? His thoughts were muddied, as if his brain trekked through sludge.

"What's happening here?" He took a pod from the refrigerator door and placed it in the coffeemaker.

Nikala rose and completed the process of making coffee for him. "You tell me." She cocked her head and planted a fist on her hip. "Why was my pendant in your cereal?"

"Where did you get the pendant in the first place?"

Her stance shifted. Still defiant, her eyes softened. "That doesn't matter. Why were you hiding it?"

Cian grabbed a bowl and poured himself cereal. He dragged his hands over his face and glanced at the clock. Nine fifteen. He'd slept less than seven hours in the past two days.

"What do you know about that pendant?" He indicated the amulet without making a move to touch it.

Nikala sat opposite and held the pretty glass ornament. "Nothing. It's pretty. I liked it, so I picked it up."

"Where did you get it?"

"I can't tell you."

Cian sniffed the milk before pouring some into his bowl. It was still fresh. "Well, when you decide to be honest with me, then I'll tell you why it was hidden."

They ate in silence, each eyeing the other like fighters at a prize match waiting for the starting bell. A few minutes later, Cian rose and poured himself a cup of coffee. He held the pot out to her, but she shook her head.

Once the bitter liquid touched his tongue, his thoughts

started to clear. Relief washed over him like a cool blanket. At least she hadn't poisoned him. He hoped.

The second hand of the clock ticked as they toyed with their spoons, their cups, their hesitation. Finally, Nikala took a deep breath and stretched her arms wide. The amulet's chain dangled from her fingertips.

"I stole it from Malcolm." The words came out in a rush, barely audible.

"Where did he get it?"

"I don't know." She glared at him. "I swear."

"Do you have any idea what's inside of it?" Cian watched her features as she shook her head slowly.

"I really don't. At first I just thought they were trinkets, but after Malcolm freaked that one was missing, I figured maybe some kind of biochemical weapon, or poison. With him, it could be anything."

He noted her use of the plural. She knew where all the amulets were, not just the one. A flutter of lightheadedness gave him hope. "I need to get them and return them to where they belong. You said Hunter had the shipment, do you know where he'd keep them?"

Nikala inspected the glass and traced a fingertip over the metalwork that looked like tiny branches. Whoever made the amulets was a talented craftsman. Cian doubted it was Acelyne, which meant someone else in Faerie was involved. The list of those to track down kept growing. Which meant he had to get word to Rori. She could find the bastards in Faerie while he stayed in London. He ran a hand through his hair, knowing the reason he put off leaving the human realm sat across the table from him. And he didn't mean the amulet.

Finally, Nikala slowly shook her head. "If I had to guess, I'd say at Hunter's place. He won't forgive me for this." Nikala hesitated, then continued, "Someone destroyed his lab last night."

Cian processed her words, the way she looked down when

she spoke. A subtle submissiveness entered her actions. "Was this the man who called when we were at the pub?" Cian's mind was working like gears in a clock, setting plans in motion, making alternate plans if the first fell through.

Her nod was more of a full body rocking. "He told me to meet him at his place, but I came here with you instead." The warble in her voice sent fury racing through Cian's veins.

The man had ordered her to his house and she'd denied him. The change in her tone indicated she feared the man. He'd be dealt with in time. Cian needed more answers from Nikala first.

"The amulets come from somewhere, Nikala. I need to know where."

She took a sip of her tea and sighed. "Someone in Edinburgh brings them. From where, I have no clue. I was supposed to meet her when you arrived."

"Her?" Cian sat up straighter. "Was it Acelyne?"

Nikala shook her head, letting her blonde waves cover her face. "I don't know. All I was given was a description. Red hair, shorter than me, trim build." Her eyes widened and she swore under her breath.

"What is it?" Cian prodded when she didn't elaborate.

"Red hair." She toyed with the pendant, slipping it between her fingers like a magician with his cards. "The woman from last night." Nikala snapped her attention to Cian. "There was a woman near SIRE's building last night. Saffron coat, auburn hair. She seemed startled to see me. I'm not saying she's the woman, but it was definitely strange."

"Acelyne had blonde hair, golden like yours. As tall as you, perhaps an inch taller. The woman you were to meet must've been her courier."

Nikala bit her lower lip and rolled it between her teeth. "I overheard Malcolm talking about someone named Max."

Cian felt sucker-punched. The air swooshed from his lungs and he choked on the coffee in his mouth. It couldn't be. Not the same Maxx who was his mum's best mate. Not the Maxx he knew to be one of Faerie's greatest spies. According to his queen, Maxx died five years ago on a mission in the human realm. He sifted through memories and data. Had she died or gone missing?

Slick tendrils of dread latched onto his spine.

He'd been there last night when Nikala had risked her own life to save the woman from getting hit by the bikers. By their body language, he hadn't thought they knew each other, but upon reflection, the woman in the mustard coat *had* looked at Nikala strangely—as if she recognized her and was afraid.

The dread slipped into his throat, constricting his breath.

He'd not seen Maxx in years, seven or eight at least, and she'd had dark-brown hair, if he recalled correctly. It wouldn't be hard for her to change her appearance, but why would she be hiding from Faerie? And if she was the courier, why was she selling kidnapped fae to Malcolm?

"What's going on, Cian?" Nikala reached across the table to take his hand. "I think it's time we both told the truth."

As much as the idea terrified him, and as much as it went against everything he believed, she was right. Last night he spoke the truth with his body; now he'd speak the truth with his words. He could only hope she wouldn't betray him.

❧ 24 ❧

At a quarter to one, Nikala left Cian's flat with the promise she'd see him soon. The quiet, fog- drenched streets matched her mood. He'd told her many things over the last few hours. Things she never thought could be possible, but for every argument she'd had, he could point to an event that proved his story. In the end, she'd had to accept that what he'd told her was not only conceivable, but highly feasible.

Beyond the reality of this world, was another. Faerie, he'd called it. And not just that one, but many other worlds that existed in tandem to Earth. Some were parallel timelines, like Faerie, and others were in the future or past.

The tea she'd drunk and cereal she'd eaten had long since turned to an agonizing mush in her gut. She'd listened to Cian as he told his wild stories of assassins and queens, of elven thieves, and sweet-natured giants. The world he created sounded too fantastical to be true, yet something nagged at the back of her mind every time he said Faerie.

The most astonishing admission he made was telling her he wasn't human. He was fae, he'd said with a straight face and not an ounce of mischief. A faerie. Even when she'd asked about his wings, he didn't smile or chortle or say he was joking.

"They're here," he'd told her, "beneath my skin. When I need them, they'll be revealed, but not until then. Only if you're royalty can you always display your wings." Then his face became somber and his voice lowered. "When a fae is close to death, their wings will curl around them in a protective embrace, like a cocoon."

She'd held the amulet the entire time he spoke. Not once did he try to take it from her, although she saw the desire in his eyes. It was when he'd told her each amulet contained at least one kidnapped faerie that she'd thought he'd really lost his mind.

One question she hadn't asked—and he hadn't mentioned— was the glistening of her own skin. She told herself it was from Hunter's tests, but a seed of doubt or hope or despair had been planted in her psyche.

When she said she needed time to process what he told her, he didn't argue for her to stay. Instead, he stood quietly and kissed her on the lips before helping her into her leather jacket. Then he stooped to pick up the memory disk she'd found in his trouser pockets and handed it to her.

"Whatever Malcolm's up to, it's on here." He'd pressed his warm lips against her forehead and inhaled, as if marking her scent. "I've told you everything I can. Now it's up to you to find your own truth."

Something in the way he said the words, with a wistfulness she'd not expected, set her nerves jangling. As if he knew something about her he didn't reveal. Or something about Malcolm. But there was an unspoken fear lodged in his goodbye.

She bounded down the steps to the Blackfriars Underground station and swiped her card for entry. A shadow in her peripheral eased from the wall and followed. It could've been one of the scyvers from last night, or another of Malcolm's henchmen. She didn't care. If they came too close, she'd take care they couldn't follow her ever again.

They kept their distance, whoever it was. On the platform, she checked her phone, surreptitiously trying to peek beneath the hoodie. Their face was too covered to know if it was anyone she recognized. Last night she didn't get a good look at the scyvers, but she sensed it wasn't one of them. Nor was it Jude or Yash. From the height, it could be the mysterious Maxx. She looked closer, but could only make out a pale chin. Not enough to assume anything.

Nikala boarded the train that pulled up with a whoosh of hot air and settled into a corner where she could see most of the passengers. The door between carriages to her right had its window lowered, and loud screeching assaulted her ears as the train pulled out of the station. The hooded figure stood facing her, about thirty feet away. As long as they kept their distance, she'd keep hers.

Sweat dripped down her back to the wound Donyatella had dressed the previous night. Cian had spent several excruciating minutes examining her body—every scar, each mole, even that damned cut Yash had given her. She'd stood still during his probing, but every instinct had wanted her to grab her clothes and run as far and as fast as she could, putting as much distance and space between her and Cian as was humanly possible.

But with each caress, every kiss, she'd melted a little more. By the time he'd lain her on his bed, she didn't fear the disfigurements as much as she feared his unabashed delight in her body. The way he'd looked at her, as if she were whole and beautiful, was harrowing. How could a man not be disgusted by the marks on her flesh? Cian hadn't flinched when he saw them. He hadn't shuddered and looked away. He'd loved her.

Tears pricked her eyes and she crammed her fingernails into the soft spot of her palms to keep from crying. This would not do. Crying was for simpletons, not for her.

She'd do well to forget all about Cian MacNair and his sweet kisses and gentle touch. He was a distraction she didn't need in her mountingly convoluted life. A distraction she welcomed, nonetheless.

The train pulled into her station and the hooded figure exited before Nikala. Perhaps she was getting too paranoid. Maybe they weren't following her after all.

She made her way through the throng of people to the street where the sounds of city traffic chimed like welcome bells in her mind. The quiet of Cian's street had been unnatural. She remembered the blue haze he'd made appear in his flat and wondered whether that somehow had flowed out onto the street.

Magic, he'd called it. Said every being in Faerie had some kind of magic in their blood. Then he'd explained how different races could do different things with their magic. Fae were excellent at illusion, deception, healing, and nurturing. Trolls worked their magic through nature, and elves—hell, she forgot what elves were good at. It had all blended together at that point. Magic was something she thought of as parlor tricks or Vegas shows. Not something people had or did.

She inspected her hands and farther up her wrist to her forearm. The slight luster was gone. Cian had shown her his Glamour and said it was helpful in confusing cameras and other things in the human realm.

"You were in Malcolm's office last night when I was there, weren't you?" she'd asked him.

"I was." He'd answered without elaborating.

She'd known someone was there, but had worried it was Hunter. It hadn't crossed her mind that the intruder might be Cian. He was good, she gave him that much.

At SIRE's building, she paused. The police cars were gone and from where she stood, it didn't look as though anything was out of the ordinary. Yet Hunter had said someone destroyed the lab.

Her stomach coiled in on itself. Shit. Hunter had told her to go to his place last night and she ignored him. He was going to be pissed. She rubbed her hands together and crossed them over her chest. When wasn't he upset with her over one thing or another?

Another sliver of their conversation slipped into her mind. He hadn't answered her when she asked about Malcolm. Nikala gazed up at the glass building. No way would Malcolm destroy Hunter's lab. Not after investing a billion pounds in the stupid thing. Top-notch technology, Malcolm had beamed when he showed her the plans. The latest in medical equipment so Hunter could continue his work.

She shivered and forced the thought out of her mind. His work was that of a mad scientist and should be shut down, not rewarded. Her right hand slipped beneath her jacket and she rubbed the two bullet wounds Hunter had given her. Whoever had destroyed the lab did the world a favor. If only she could bring herself to kill the man. It wasn't Malcolm that kept her from going through with it. Nikala shook with the realization that every time she thought of killing Hunter, another, fiercer need to protect him overrode her thoughts. She couldn't control it or get rid of it, but it was visceral and all-consuming.

As if someone had fucked with her brain.

Shit. She had to find Malcolm.

A movement across the street caught her attention and she turned in time to see the hooded figure duck into a recessed doorway. With another glance toward the office building, she turned and jogged across the street. The figure darted from their hiding place and ran down an alley, with Nikala close behind.

The alley twisted to the right and she swung wide in case the runner thought to attack from the inside. They did. A gloved fist came from the corner of a brick building, missing Nikala's temple by an inch. She heard the rush of air as the fist clipped her ear.

She dodged another punch and kicked hard into the assailant's midsection.

They *oofed* as they were thrown backward, into the wall. A crack sounded when their head hit stone, but Nikala didn't let up. She kicked and jabbed, ducking to avoid punches, and side-stepping kicks as much as she could. The hooded figure—adept at martial arts and seeming to know Nikala's moves before she made them—didn't give her any advantage.

Nor did the limited space allow for improvisation, yet she found ways to reach her assailant's soft middle again and again. Her elbow connected with a cheekbone and the figure's head snapped to the left. The hood slipped and Nikala caught sight of auburn hair pulled into a tight ponytail.

"Maxx?" The name was forced between breathless gasps.

The woman backed away, hazel eyes huge in her tanned face. "You know who I am?"

Confused, Nikala shook her head. "Not really. I heard your name and put the pieces together. I was supposed to meet you in Edinburgh, but you never showed."

"Because Acelyne never arrived. I've been hiding from Malcolm ever since." Maxx straightened her jacket and replaced the hood over her head.

Nikala leaned against the wall to catch her breath. With only a few hours' sleep, tea, and sugary cereal to keep her fueled, she was lagging in energy.

"Why hide? Why attack me?" Everything Cian had told her about Maxx slipped between her thoughts. This woman was a skilled assassin. If she wanted Nikala dead, she'd be dead.

"I'm trying to warn you."

"You could've just said something."

"I had to know if you could be trusted." Maxx snorted. "Or at the very least, if you'd listen. We aren't really the trusting sorts, are we?" They shared a grin, then Maxx said, "That blade last night could've been meant for me, but you risked your life to save a stranger. You earned more than my respect."

She did a funny thing then. She placed the tip of her thumb against her lips, then to her forehead. If Nikala was supposed to understand the meaning, she didn't.

"Malcolm's not right." Maxx leaned in close. "I believe he has the madness."

"Madness? What, like Alzheimer's?"

"Similar, but different for our kind." Maxx looked from one end of the alley to the other. "You're not safe here. None of us are."

"Why? What's going to happen?" Maxx was right; they weren't the trusting kind and nothing she said could be taken for truth. She was the reason Hunter now had all the amulets. Nikala crossed her arms over her chest and lifted her chin. "Why should I believe you when all this time you've been selling those—" She couldn't bring herself to say faeries, wasn't willing to believe it was true. Not yet. "You've been helping Malcolm."

Maxx glanced down at her hands. "I want my freedom, nothing more. I didn't want to help him. I was forced to." She tugged the hood over her head until it masked her face and turned away from Nikala. "If you're smart, you'll get away from him, right now."

Maxx pivoted and ran full out down the alley. Nikala let her go with a frustrated growl. She had too many unanswered questions and too little patience. She strode back toward SIRE's offices, where she hoped there would be answers. Her knuckles were bruised where she'd hit Maxx, and her ribs ached where she'd been kicked. Maxx wanted her freedom? Did that mean it was Malcolm who had forced her to help? Or Hunter? And why?

A chilling prickle tracked over her skin. Or was there a third player on the board? One Nikala didn't know, but perhaps Cian did?

Police tape covered one of the lifts and she glanced at the ceiling. If the firefighters were able to contain the fire to the one floor, that meant her laptop and everything were still safe in her office. She jammed her hand on the reader to their private lift and waited while it blipped and hummed. A moment later, the doors opened and she stepped inside. Whatever Malcolm was up to, she was going to find out. She fumbled in her pocket for the memory stick Cian had stolen from Malcolm's office. All of SIRE's business dealings were on there, according to Cian. But Nikala wanted to hear the truth from Malcolm before she looked at what was on the stick.

She ignored the receptionist and went straight to Malcolm's offices, but they were empty. The poor dear raced after her, mumbling apologies, and asking questions. Mr. Dagniss hadn't shown up for work today and wasn't taking her calls; did Nikala know what she should say to those who he had appointments with?

"Fuck if I care," Nikala groused and stormed into her office.

Her heart seized at the sight of her broken laptop. At least she knew Cian hadn't been the one to vandalize her property. Yasheda and Jude came immediately to mind. Those assholes. She scanned the rest of the room, noting the state of her luggage and mess of belongings tossed willy-nilly behind her desk.

She put a hand to her chest where the amulet rested in her cleavage. If they'd come for it, she had Cian to thank for them not finding the pendant. Her gaze went to her laptop and the empty slot where the memory card had been when she left the night before. Great. Now Malcolm would know she'd been spying on him.

Well, that was kind of what he paid her for. Not spying on *him*, exactly, but spying on others. It was poetic justice of a sort. Except, she didn't think he'd see it that way. She locked the office and turned to the receptionist, who stood beside her huge desk, wringing her hands.

"Don't let anyone in there. No one. Do you understand?"

Not that she thought the clueless lass could stop anyone, but what the hell, she might as well try.

The receptionist nodded and glanced furtively around the lobby. "Will Mr. Dagniss be in today?"

"I'm not sure, but I'll find out." Nikala calmed her voice and said, "Cancel his appointments, just in case."

The girl nodded again and scampered to her chair. Nikala strode into Malcolm's office and opened the cupboard where he kept his safe. An error code displayed on the readout, meaning someone had tried to open it and failed after three attempts. She punched in the code and breathed a sigh of relief when the door sprang open. Malcolm's laptop and important papers were still there.

Nikala chewed on a cuticle while she debated what to do with the laptop. Ultimately, keeping it in the safe would be best. She re-entered the code, then changed it, using a six-digit numerical and alphabetical sequence she doubted Malcolm would ever guess. Until she knew who had broken into the offices last night, she trusted no one.

She stared out the window and rifled through everything she'd learned in the past two days. Had his three fingers on the desk been a clue? Her gaze went to the safe. Did he mean three amulets were missing? What was going on with him? She arched her back and stared at the ceiling. Why would Malcolm hide the pendants from Hunter? If he'd had a change of heart and no longer wished to help with Hunter's experiments, that might explain his actions, but Hunter would never allow Malcolm to walk away. Where the fuck was he? Malcolm rarely missed work and even rarer did he get to the office past nine.

Anxiety pooled in her gut, churning her tea to a sour mess. Hunter. He had both Malcolm and the amulets. She had to get to them before Hunter did something crazy. There was only one thing to do—confront him.

Out on the street, she flagged a cab and gave him Hunter's

address. They drove to a nice neighborhood in Chelsea where all the homes were white and sparkling. Her senses went on overdrive as they approached a lovely detached five-story with a tidy front garden and inviting green door. The Victorian glass overhang above the door balanced the property nicely. This was outrageous, even for Malcolm, but Hunter? Totally not in character. When had he bought the place?

"Drop me off up a little. I want to surprise them." The cab parked alongside the curb a half block away and she paid cash for the fare. As he pulled away, she scanned the neighboring houses. All of them were understated elegance worthy of a prince or high-powered CEO. Prices in this area were in the millions of pounds. They must've bought it as an investment. Had to be. No other explanation made sense as to why he'd buy a home on a quaint, upper-class English street.

She strolled along the sidewalk as if she belonged there. A white workman's lorry sat in the small drive, hiding a side gate that led to the back garden. Nikala glanced inside the lorry as she passed, noting the toolbox, heavy blankets, and rope. To an unsuspecting passerby, they looked like basic equipment for a painter, perhaps, or a joiner. Nikala saw them for what they could be—items necessary for kidnapping and possibly torture. She quickened her pace and quietly unlatched the gate. The street was silent as she crept across rough slate pavers. Despite the chilly air, perspiration covered the back of her neck and forehead.

Voices drifted to her from somewhere in the house and she crouched beneath a windowsill. She continued on to the garden, where green cast-iron furniture sat pleasantly beneath a closed umbrella. It all looked too conventional. Too normal.

A glass door with the blinds drawn were to her right, and steps leading to a small balcony were in front of her. She skirted the patio doors and took the steps one at a time, easing her boot down on each stair. Two doors off the balcony stood ajar, giving her access to a dining room on one side, a drawing room on the other. She slipped into the drawing room and plastered herself against the wall.

The voices carried up the stairs to reach where she crept along the wall, doing her best to stay hidden. A mansion like this would certainly have security cameras, but why make herself known when she could be stealthy? The challenge made it more exciting. Weaving between the many chairs and sofas hampered her quest, but eventually she broke through the scads of floral fabrics and furnishings.

She reached the landing and looked down to a well-appointed foyer with tile and parquet flooring. This was a far cry from Hunter's manor in Aberdeenshire. There, wood paneling covered all the walls, with thick rugs thrown over ancient stones. The décor was decidedly masculine and definitely unkempt. Here, everything shouted old money and wealth, but with under-stated opulence.

As Nikala stood at the balcony looking down on a crystal chandelier and thousands of pounds' worth of indulgence, she was jealous. A place like this would've been a more acceptable place to raise a child. On a proper street where she could've made friends. Far more suitable than the wild Highland estate where Hunter had abandoned her more often than not. Except, she knew why Hunter had kept her in the Highlands—to isolate her from the world. As much as she might wish she'd grown up on a nice street like this one, that would've been counter to everything Hunter meant to accomplish.

Cian's raised voice came from her left and she froze. *What the bloody hell was he doing there?* She hurried down the carpeted staircase to the ground floor. Malcolm's shout reached her as she slid behind a pillar.

Shit. When Cian had said he needed to confront Malcolm about the amulets, she didn't think he meant right away. Cheeky bastard. That's why he was so keen to let her leave his flat. He was planning to sneak over to Hunter's before she got there. A dash of rage twisted with sorrow pierced her heart. If he'd trusted her, he would've asked her to come along. Or, her mind offered hopefully, he cared about her and wanted to protect her from unforeseen danger. Of the two options, she preferred the latter, but had to accept it might be the former. Both made her suppress a snort. If only he knew how much she loathed Hunter and would've gladly helped. That was on her. They'd spent too much time discussing fairy tales; she hadn't had a chance to tell him of her past.

The men's voices dropped and she strained to hear what they said.

"Deny it if you want, but I know you're behind the rise in scyver activity. Whatever you're planning, Dagniss, we'll uncover it and you'll account for your treachery." The threat in Cian's voice slid over her.

Who was the "we" in his statement? Those in Faerie? Or were others coming?

"You're becoming tedious, McCabe. I don't know anything about scyvers, or lycans, or these amulets you keep blathering on about."

"They don't belong to you, Dagniss. Whatever you're doing with them is wrong. Those are innocent lives you're taking. At least Acelyne can't supply you anymore and whoever was her courier, we'll find them as well. You're not as shielded as you believe."

Nikala imagined Cian leaning over Malcolm's desk, glaring at the man.

"I've told you, I don't know Acelyne, and I have no idea what you're talking about with these amulets. Now, please leave my home or I'll call the police."

"I'm not leaving without those amulets."

Malcolm gave a dramatic sigh. "Yash, Jude, please see this man to the door."

Nikala's heart seized. Of course Yasheda and Jude were there.

That would explain the white lorry. Something was going on here, and the fact that Malcolm kept it from her burned. She'd lost his trust. She'd known better than to push him and he finally had had enough. It was her own damn fault. Or, that same stupid hopeful voice whispered, he was trying to protect her.

Men and their ridiculous code of honor. How bloody chivalric.

From inside the other room, she heard Yash and Jude struggle with Cian. They'd be coming through the door soon and find her.

She darted up the stairs two at a time and pinned herself against the far wall of the landing. Her heart tripled its beating and her mind swam with her next steps.

Sounds of fighting drifted through the door below her. She wavered a moment with indecision. Help Cian, or find the amulets? She had no doubt Cian could fend for himself, but a need—foreign in its intensity—tugged her toward the room downstairs. To see him again, to let him know she wasn't the enemy, to protect him. Yet he'd made it clear the amulets were more important. If she retrieved the amulets for Cian, she'd be betraying Malcolm. Cian or Malcolm: where did her loyalty lie?

A movement on the floor above gave her a moment's warning before Hunter emerged from a room, dressed in a black turtleneck and blue jeans. She slipped into the drawing room before he saw her, but not before she noted the scars on his chin glowed red and his dark eyes were like granite. He strode past the open drawing room door without stopping and bounded down the stairs toward where Cian was.

Nikala counted to ten before she rushed up the stairs and closed the door behind her. She'd let the men fight it out while she searched for the amulets. It's what Cian would want. She hoped.

The room she found herself in was vast, a master suite with attached bath. Fucking hell, it could fit an entire village. She scanned the room with a quick glance. Her gaze settled and a slow burn moved up her sternum. The final betrayal in a lifetime of deception.

The leather bag with all the wooden boxes inside sat on a chair beside an unmade bed. Hunter's suitcase was next to it.

Her heart rammed in her throat and blood rushed through her ears, pulsing against her skull. He was leaving. Hunter was leaving again. How many times had she seen that stupid suitcase and worried whether she'd ever see him again?

How many times did she fear his return?

Nikala grabbed the messenger bag and slung it over her shoulder. She clambered out a window and shimmied down a drainpipe to the ground. She darted across the patio to the little side yard and bolted to the lorry. With no time to think, or make a plan, she stashed the bag behind the passenger's seat beneath a blanket. She was just closing the car door when she heard the gunshot.

Her world spiraled in a tempest of faces and words and images. *Cian. No, please not Cian.* Shouts came from inside the mansion and she raced to the front steps. Nikala paused and remembered her training. Calm washed over her.

This was no time to panic. She should run, she knew. Grab the amulets and get as far from the house as possible before the authorities arrived, but she had to know. Had to know Cian wasn't dead.

With a steady hand, she turned the huge knob and entered the house proper. Silence descended through the rooms. Only the *tick, tick, tick* of a clock broke the quiet.

At the door to her right, where the men had argued, she heard shuffling. Nikala yanked open the door and saw Malcolm splayed on the floor, a dark-red stain spreading across his chest. No. Nooooooo. She shuttled her emotions to the dark place where they couldn't hurt her. To the place of detached indifference she'd mastered in Hunter's lab. If she allowed herself to process what she saw on the floor, she might lose control for good. Her hands fisted and she pressed her nails into her palms, embracing the soft sting of skin tearing.

Her gaze slid to the left, where Cian swayed. Bloodied and bruised, his jaw hitched at an odd angle. His right hand hung limp at his side. In his left hand was a revolver.

❧ 25 ❧

The ringing in his ears blurred all other sound in the house. His lip bled where Jude had punched him, and he was certain his right wrist was broken. They'd worked him over good. He should've been stronger than both of them, but their speed and might was equal to his. It wasn't possible. Humans were slower and weaker than the fae.

Cian shook his head and a spittle of blood dropped to the floor. *Blood.* Not dust or glitter, but blood the color of crimson. He hadn't been in the human realm long enough to bleed. This didn't make sense. He wiped his lips with his mangled right hand and held up the gun in his left. Where had the gun come from?

"How could you?" Nikala's voice came from far away. A snarl of words edged with betrayal. "Why? Why kill him?"

Kill him? Cian looked at the gun, then to where Malcolm's body sprawled across the carpet. His lifeless eyes stared at Cian with bitter judgment.

"I didn't." Cian started to protest, but the pain in his jaw prevented him from saying more.

Nikala knelt over the dead man, her face a mixture of remorse and fury. The pair who had beaten him lingered in the shadows, their faces masks of indifference. Their inaction confused him. Why didn't they kill him? His gaze slid to the door to where the man had lurched into the room and shot Malcolm. He was nowhere to be seen.

The other man. Something about him tugged on Cian's memory. Of a time or place out of time and place.

He tapped his temple with the barrel of the gun. Shit. He'd have to get rid of it or the police might think he'd actually killed Malcolm.

Did he kill him? Or was it the other man? Pain disoriented his memories. He fought through the confusion, laying out his actions since entering the house. He'd come for the amulets. Even now, he sensed their presence, but he hadn't gotten far in his search. Malcolm Dagniss had interrupted him, here, in this room.

They'd been arguing, Cian and Dagniss. Cian's vision wavered and he swayed where he stood. Nikala eyed him suspiciously, then he saw a spark of something—acknowledgment, perhaps; an understanding that he hadn't killed Dagniss, he hoped—dawn in her eyes.

When had she arrived? He'd hoped she would go to the office and not come here. He needed her to stay away while he confronted Dagniss. It had been important that she stay away. *Why?*

Nikala bent over the dead man, trying in vain to revive him. Two fingers pressed against his neck and Cian watched helplessly as she performed CPR. It would do no good. The bullet had hit true, straight through Malcolm's heart.

"Yash, Jude, help me. Get some towels, anything to stop the bleeding." Nikala gave the order, but they remained impassive. She stared at the pair, unblinking.

Cian watched the three of them, his head swerving from the left to the right. Finally, the flunkies exited through a door to his left. When his gaze returned to her, Nikala was watching him.

There was meaning in her look, but his brain wasn't functioning at full capacity. Whatever she meant to convey, it was lost to him.

He staggered backward and sat on an uncomfortable chair. The gun slid from his grip and he reached to retrieve it. The movement shoved bile up the back of his throat and he sputtered a blood-bile cough on the rug.

"You're hurt," Nikala whispered.

When had she moved beside him?

"I've been worse." He did his best to smile, but his jaw refused.

"Who shot Malcolm?" She tucked the gun in the back of her jeans and held his face in her cold hands, her eyes searching, always searching.

Would she ever find what she needed to be at peace?

Cian shook his head. "I didn't see him." He reached up to stroke her cheek. "So beautiful."

For half a heartbeat, she smiled and tilted her face into his touch. "Why did you come here alone? I could've helped."

He saw the despair in her eyes, the wariness and need for an answer. "I didn't want you involved. Didn't want you to be hurt ever again." The amount of effort it took to speak those few words was astonishing.

Tears shimmered in her eyes. "I could've protected you." Her sad little smile softened the hard angles she usually wore. Without another word, she returned to her place at Malcolm's side and leaned over the body.

"I'm so sorry I failed you," she whispered in the dead man's ear. She spoke low, but Cian heard every word. "I had one job and failed. Can you ever forgive me?" A lone tear dripped on the dead man's cheek. Nikala swiped her eyes against her sleeve and cleared her throat.

The sentiment and tenderness in her tone tore at Cian's equilibrium. Dagniss was the enemy. He didn't deserve Nikala's compassion. Fury bit at the broken ends of his nerves and he ground out a curse through his broken jaw. Nikala glared at him, and in that look he saw anguish and torment that he understood far too well. It was how he'd felt the day his dad was murdered. He looked from Nikala back to Dagniss, a dawning realization taking hold. His body softened and his rage simmered.

The next thing Cian knew, Nikala screamed obscenities at him and accused him of murdering Dagniss.

The shouting hurt his ears. His head cocked and he withdrew from the moment, a trick he'd learned long ago. It was to help visualize the scenario without passion. The way she ranted, more to herself than at him, gave the impression she wanted someone else to believe her rage. Or was that just wishful thinking? She cast a finger in his direction and called him a murderer.

Before the gunshot, Cian had been arguing with Dagniss about the amulets. Then Malcolm had his goons beat the crap out of Cian. But why had the other man shot Malcolm? What had Dagniss said just before the gun went off?

Cian sucked in a breath and tasted his own blood. Malcolm had hovered close to him and whispered in his ear, "You'll never see those fae again and everything you hold dear in Faerie will be destroyed."

Cian had lunged at the man just as the shot rang out.

"It was meant for me," Cian forced out between his broken jaw.

"What?" Nikala stopped her tirade and stared at Cian.

"He meant to shoot me, but Dagniss got in the way."

A veil of dispassion covered Nikala's features and she stood. Blood covered her hands and stained her jeans. "I'll kill the motherfucker."

"Tsk, tsk, tsk. What have I told you about cursing?"

A voice came from Cian's right and he swiveled his head to see who had spoken. The man kept his face turned away from Cian, his body at an angle. Nikala he saw clearly.

Behind him, the two thugs stood with their hands clasped in

front of their bodies. Nikala took in the man and his henchmen with a nod.

"You told me a lot of things I'd hoped to forget." A gleam of rebellion lit her eyes.

The man moved into the room, keeping his body at the odd angle to Cian. When he reached Nikala, a hand snaked up to stroke her hair and Cian saw the faintest of flinches from her.

"You always were a challenge, my lily." The gravelly voice rasped, as if his face were misshapen, and Cian struggled to see past the short tufts of raven hair that hid his features.

"Why, Hunter?" Nikala's eyes brimmed with tears.

"He'd outgrown his purpose." The cold, detached words chilled Cian. The man, Hunter, cradled Nikala's cheek in his palm and Cian sat upright, ready to spring from his seat. "Stay where you are, fiend." Hunter's free hand whipped toward Cian and a thread of magic pulsed into his chest.

Cian roared with pain. The man's magic tore through his broken body. Molten lava seared his being, wreaking havoc in his mind, engorging his heart until it might burst. Something was off about the magic. It was too focused, too powerful. Too advanced. Cian whimpered through his mangled jaw. The stranger's magic was fae-born and enhanced with technology. How it was possible, he had no idea. The realization stunned him.

Cian struggled against the assault, outwardly writhing in pain and inwardly sucking the man's magic into his pores. Coaxing it through his veins until it mingled with his own magic, infusing his blood with the man's power.

What he did was forbidden—using dark magic to heal himself—but under the circumstances, he hoped his queen would understand.

The man growled and snapped his power with a muttered spell. Cian countered the spell and grabbed Hunter's power. With a grunt, he warped it to his bidding. By the twitch of Hunter's shoulder, he wasn't accustomed to someone knowing dark magic.

Cian suppressed a chuckle as he felt his bones knit together. The man's power was restorative instead of deadly. Never having encountered this before, Cian was dumbfounded how Hunter's magic could heal his many wounds, but he wasn't about to question it. The man believed he was killing Cian and he'd do all he could to perpetuate the lie. With another loud groan, Cian writhed in his seat, selling it for all he could.

"Stop it! What are you doing to him?" Nikala's wail assaulted Cian's fragile hearing.

Hunter's laugh was anything but human. He'd called Cian a fiend, but by the hollowness of his rasping, the title was more suitable to Hunter. He might be fae, or elven, or even a demi-god from another world. Whatever he was, it wasn't human like he wanted everyone to believe.

"What, do you fancy yourself in love with him?" Hunter's magic eased and Cian drew a long, ragged breath. The possessive tone enraged Cian, but not as much as the jealousy that edged Hunter's words. "Did he call you beautiful and promise you an eternity of happiness?"

"Don't be ridiculous." Nikala stared at the man, her lips pinched.

Cian bit against his own feelings of resentfulness toward Hunter's casual dominance of Nikala.

Hunter grabbed a handful of her glorious golden hair and yanked her head backward.

"Unhand her." Cian wheezed. He staggered on his still-strengthening legs.

One of the thugs—Jude, Cian guessed—backhanded him and he wobbled into the chair.

"Pathetic," Hunter spat over his shoulder. He released Nikala's hair and stroked her as if she were a pet. "You've grown soft in my absence, my lily. We'll have to begin our instructions again."

Nikala visibly shuddered and clenched her fists, but she said nothing.

Cian studied the two of them, noting the rippling of muscles beneath Hunter's turtleneck and the flexing of Nikala's fingers. Whatever the relationship between these two, it was well-established and complicated. His heart wobbled at the sudden awareness that this man, this Hunter, was responsible for all of Nikala's scars. He'd tortured her to twist her into a weapon. He kept himself passive, his nostrils flaring with each breath. The veins on his neck corded with his suppressed rage. Hunter had brutally murdered Malcolm. Until he knew the man's potential strength, he'd play along. But if he laid another possessive finger on Nikala, Cian wouldn't be responsible for his actions.

"Take them to the warehouse," Hunter ordered Yasheda and Jude, circling a finger to indicate Cian and Malcolm. "Dispose of them properly. If you fail me this time, I'll no longer have need of your services." He continued to stroke Nikala's hair. Her eyes were bits of blue granite as she stood mute before him.

"What about her?" Yasheda asked, a nervous tic to her voice.

"Make sure she sees everything. I'd hate for her to miss all the fun." Hunter pointed to Cian, still keeping his face hidden. "Prolong his torture. She needs to understand the price of her treason."

"Do you really think watching you maim him will teach me anything I don't already know?" Nikala's chin jutted out and Cian's heart slowed. He feared more for her life than his own.

"Perhaps a reminder is what you need." Hunter's fingers stroked her cheek. Tiny fissure-like scars ran across his skin. "We'll discuss your insubordination when they've finished." His fingertips dug into her face and pain etched across her eyes.

"Let her go. Do what you will with me, but leave her out of this." Cian teetered to a stand and took a step toward Hunter.

A punch caught him in the gut and he doubled over. As much as the man's magic worked to heal his broken body, it wasn't yet complete. The force from the blow undid some of his healing.

Rough hands grabbed him and half-dragged him from the house. They went through the dining room to a back garden, where sun streamed onto flagstones and tidy flowerbeds. Cian squinted against the bright light as the pair rushed along a side yard to a waiting lorry.

The van hadn't been there when he'd come to Malcolm's home. Two things crashed into his mind at once: Malcolm wasn't in charge of operations at SIRE; Hunter was. And, he was going to die.

Not only was he going to die, but Nikala as well.

He needed a plan.

Yasheda and Jude tossed him roughly inside the van and while Yash held him down, Jude bound his ankles and wrists. A gag was shoved into his mouth and tape secured across his lips. With his mouth muted, he had to breathe through his nose. They shut the back doors and went around the front of the lorry to enter the house.

Cian contorted his legs to shorten the length of rope attached from his hands to his feet, but he couldn't reach the knots. He shimmied his arms beneath him and rolled to his side, hoping that angle might prove more useful. A blanket shifted and he spied a leather messenger bag hidden in the shadows. He scooted closer and pulled the blanket away with a thread of magic. There, tumbled on their sides, were several wooden caskets.

The ephemeral magic he sensed from them could only mean one thing—they were the missing amulets. His breath bottled in his chest. He could save himself, Nikala, and the captured fae. Somehow.

Voices came from the back garden and he used a spark of magic to tug the blanket over the bag. The doors opened and a heavy bundle wrapped in a blanket was tossed atop him. He shifted until the clump rolled toward the driver's seat. Malcolm's hair stuck out from one end of the blanket.

The doors slammed shut and Cian was left alone with the

dead man. He lay calm, working through his options. Each one presented a challenge, but ultimately, he'd have to risk using even more magic if he wanted to survive. Hunter had unleashed a stream of magic that, as far as Cian could tell, hadn't attracted any scyvers. Yash and Jude's indifference could mean they were used to being near magic, or it could've been they didn't see the magic and only saw Cian suffering. In any case, he had to assume they understood magic even if they didn't have their own.

Which made his options even more difficult.

He eased a thread of magic to the knots in his bindings and worked to loosen them. Bit by bit, they slackened. Hope, small and unsure, took hold in his heart. If he could get them unfastened by the time they reached the warehouse, he and Nikala might have a chance of survival.

When the doors opened a second time, Nikala was shoved into the back. Her hands were bound same as his, with a strip of tape covering her mouth. A cut on her temple dripped blood onto her cheek and the beginnings of a black eye ringed her right eye.

She sat rigid against the side of the lorry, her eyes staring straight ahead, her knuckles white. Cian stretched his bound leg until it brushed against hers. He needed that physical connection, to let her know he wouldn't abandon her. He'd meant it the previous night when he said he wouldn't hurt her, and now more than ever, he'd make sure no one else did either. The feel of her warmth against him settled in his nerves, calming his frustrations. If they worked together, they'd survive.

The lorry lurched as it began to move. Cian squirmed to his side and looked out the windscreen. His mind froze and bowels turned to water. There, in the top window of the elegant house, stood a man. Raven hair and dark eyes, similar in shade and shape to Cian's, the man wore a beard over his misshapen chin. The man's steely gaze locked to his. He didn't blink as he stared at the figure. Even when the van sped off, he didn't look away. Couldn't look away from his past.

The memory of that day long ago on the battlements of Edinburgh Castle strangled Cian as he was tossed unceremoniously against Malcolm's corpse. His ribs rebelled at hitting the metal and his wrist seared with fresh pain. He struggled to look out the back window, but the man was gone.

As they bumped and jostled over the road, Cian replayed the memory of his father's death again and again. He knew with absolute clarity that the shadow man who had killed his dad was the same man he saw in the window.

26

Nikala breathed out a long, chilling breath.

Don't lose it. Don't lose your shit now, St. James.

Cian looked bad. His right wrist was broken, and possibly his jaw. The way he favored his left leg meant a possible fracture in his tibia. Yasheda and Jude worked him over hard. She shuddered at the memory of their fight the day before, when she'd defeated both of them, but that was one-on-one. If they'd both taken her on, she might've looked like Cian, or worse.

She'd be dead, like Malcolm, a voice in the back of her mind taunted.

She bit her cheek to keep the tears at bay. Who shot him? Hunter hadn't actually admitted to shooting Malcolm. Cian was holding the gun when she'd entered the room, but in his left hand and from what she'd observed over the course of their day together, he was right-handed. Was it Yash or Jude? Or Hunter? He'd said Malcolm had lost his usefulness. What did he mean by that? Or had he meant Cian? How would Cian be useful to Hunter? Had Cian been lying to her this whole time?

He pressed his leg against hers and warmth infused her soul. He'd been gentle the night before, even promising to never hurt her. She blinked to focus. Hunter seemed agitated with Cian's presence. More possessive, even. As if he were jealous of the man. She'd have to consider the possibility that everything Cian had told her was the truth, and he wasn't working with Malcolm or Hunter. For now, he was an ally.

The lorry creaked as they made a sharp turn and she listened to Hunter's thugs with renewed interest. They spoke low, of how they should proceed, who would go first. Their emotionless voices were a shock to Nikala. When had they become these automatons? She'd always given them a grudging respect because they were dutiful employees, but the pair in the front seats were strangers to her.

And when had they begun obeying Hunter over Malcolm?

She was missing something and it irritated her that she didn't know what. She clasped and unclasped her hands. Where Malcolm's dried blood had been, motes of glitter stuck to her skin. She stared at the tiny sparkles.

Her heart stilled and her breathing deepened.

It couldn't be true. She rubbed her fingers, but it wouldn't come off. She looked at Cian, who was lying on his side next to Malcolm, his face a study in concentration. A similar luster covered his jaw where he'd been bleeding only minutes ago.

What was happening?

Tears bit against her closed eyelids, but she refused to let them flow. She wouldn't let Yash or Jude or Cian see her as weak.

I'm so sorry, Malcolm. I know I failed you, but I will avenge your death. It's the least I can do. She stopped short of saying, "Blessed be." Something she'd heard somewhere and it had stuck with her.

The van slowed and she shifted to look out the front windscreen. A wide door opened and Jude eased the van into a dark warehouse. She needed a plan. Yash and Jude weren't expecting her to fight. Or maybe they were. Maybe they hoped she'd fight and they could "accidentally" kill her. They were fools to think she'd sit idly by while they murdered Cian. Maybe that's exactly what she needed to do. Be docile, show that he meant nothing to her. Let them tire themselves out before she acted.

She glanced at Cian, at the grimace of pain he wore, and doubted he had much left in him.

For the first time she could remember, she was afraid. Truly, in her marrow, terrified. This was a stupid plan. It wasn't even a plan—it was a wild escape into madness.

They were going to die. She was a fool. She'd let Malcolm down, and now she'd sent Cian to certain death. She wasn't strong enough to fight Yasheda *and* Jude, not with them being enhanced and her on her own. God knew Cian couldn't help, injured as he was. Well, she told herself as she gazed at the dark space of SIRE's newest warehouse facility, if she was going to die, it might as well be with the man she loved. She just wished she'd had a chance to tell him.

Hunter's taunts had hit close to home, but not for anything Cian might've said to her. It was the undertone of dominance that had cut into her heart. She was used to his being possessive, but this was deeper, darker. Perhaps it was jealousy of Cian, but it felt like something else. As if Hunter were jealous of *her*. What a concept.

Perhaps, her mind coaxed, ever hopeful, he was also a tiny bit afraid of her.

She pulled her legs into a tight fold as Yash and Jude exited the van. Her fingertips could barely reach the rope securing her ankles. She fumbled, trying to grasp it, before she gave up. A warm tingling came over her skin and she looked at Cian. His grin lifted the tape over his mouth and it was like an arrow to her heart.

What a silly old fool she was being. But right then, with Cian encouraging her, she believed she was capable of anything.

The prickles continued and goose bumps rose upon her skin. He was using his magic—the very magic she didn't quite believe existed—to untie her knots. The first one loosened and she was able to kick her feet out of the ropes. The binding on his hands fell away and he scooched close enough to finish untying her wrists.

She glanced out the window at the two figures who were setting up chairs a few feet away. They didn't even look to see what Nikala and Cian were doing. Idiots. Confidence only worked when your plan was foolproof. It was Nikala's experience no plan was ever fully guaranteed. Always have backups of your backups.

Cian's magic and nimble fingers had her knots undone in a matter of moments and she shook out her wrists before removing the tape from her mouth. She spat out the disgusting cloth they'd shoved against her tongue and swiped her sleeve against her lips.

"Don't worry," she whispered close to Cian. "I won't let them hurt you."

He tugged at the tape and removed the gag from his mouth. "Funny, I was about to say the same to you."

She leaned forward and kissed him. "Don't die."

"I'll do my best." He jerked his chin toward the hidden messenger bag. "In case I do, the amulets are under there in a leather satchel."

"I know." She nuzzled his nose with her own. "I put them there."

His smile lit up his entire face. "You devious little beauty."

The sound of footsteps silenced the words on her lips. Cian curled into himself to hide the fact he was no longer bound. Nikala wasn't as stealthy.

When the door opened, she kicked it hard and sent Yasheda sprawling backward. Jude grunted and reached for her jacket, but she was too quick. She grabbed his hand and jerked hard, slamming his head against the frame of the lorry.

Cian sprang from his crouched position toward Yasheda. Nikala kicked Jude in the gut and launched herself out of the van. Cian and Yash were locked in combat to her left. He moved like a man in good form. He favored his right hand a little, but that was all she could see of his injuries. Twenty minutes ago, she'd thought he was a foot from the grave, but now he was somehow—miraculously or magically—restored. Sweet niblets, she was *not* prepared for this. Fairy tales and superheroes, or were they supervillains? She didn't know anymore.

Jude regained his balance and lumbered toward her, a knife in his hand. He swiveled and twirled it, flashing the blade again and again in front of his face.

One of the things Nikala couldn't tolerate was a braggart and show-off.

She crouched and circled him like a tiger its prey. The knife flashed once, twice, at the third rotation, she leapt. With her right hand, she grabbed his wrist and twisted it until the blade cut into his flesh. Jude cried out and she plunged the knife deeper.

Her legs wrapped around his waist and the impact of her weight sent them sprawling backward. Nikala was prepared for the landing. Jude was not.

She rolled off him and hopped up while he remained on the floor, winded. Maybe he wasn't as enhanced as she'd thought. She whipped around to slam the knife into his heart. His hands came up in a half-hearted attempt to strangle her. She broke his left arm at the elbow and grabbed his head with both hands. Giving a vicious jerk, she broke his neck and pushed off him.

Jude's eyes stared up at her, bewildered.

Perhaps he thought she wouldn't kill him. Or perhaps he thought he could best her. Whatever his thoughts were, he was wrong.

She reached inside his jacket to the leather holster he always wore and calmly took the gun. A low groan came from his frothing lips and she tucked the gun into her waistband. He no longer had need of the weapon.

A shriek from the other side of the lorry drew her attention and she jogged around the front of the van to see Yash bent over a table and Cian wielding a surgical blade close to her face. Yash's nails scraped down Cian's face, drawing blood. Not glitter, blood.

Yash twisted and rammed a sharpened pipe into Cian's side. His animal-like cry filled Nikala with dread. She grasped Jude's gun and held it with both hands, aimed at Yash's head. If only Cian would stop struggling for a moment, she could take the shot. As if reading her mind, Cian glanced over to her and nodded.

The gun fired with a deafening bang and Nikala watched in slow motion as the bullet traveled from the muzzle to penetrate Yasheda's temple, messily decorating the table with the contents of her skull. The woman's arms flopped to her side and her body went limp.

Cian staggered backward. The pipe stuck out of his side at an agonizing angle. He reached down as if to pull it free.

"Don't." Nikala ran toward him. "You'll do more damage than good. Let me."

She lay him on the hard concrete and sprinted to the van for one of the blankets. When she returned, Cian's eyes were hazy and his face ashen.

"Oh, come now. You survived their beatings—surely you can overcome a simple little pipe stuck in your guts." Nikala gingerly placed the blanket underneath his right side and sat back on her heels.

"That was a good shot, by the way." Cian wheezed.

"Did I ever tell you how much I hate guns?"

He shook his head. "There's a lot you haven't told me. So much I wanted to discover." His hand reached up to stroke her cheek and she bit her tongue to keep from crying.

"There's still time. Just relax. Don't talk."

Nikala refused to believe this was the end. She grabbed a handful of rags from the table Yash and Jude had set up for their torture station. She scanned the tools for anything that might help. Most of the items were to cause pain and death. Not many of them were for saving a life. Yash wore a jacket that looked much cleaner than the rags and Nikala stripped the woman of the garment.

She returned to Cian's side and gave him a wan smile. "This is beyond my medical skills. If I remove the pipe, you'll bleed to death."

"Fae are excellent healers, Nikala."

"I don't...I can't...I don't know what to do."

"Heal me."

"I can't, Cian. I'm sorry."

His palm cupped her cheek. "Take out the pipe. Do it."

It would kill him if she did. His eyes bore into hers and she took a staggering breath. "This is going to hurt."

She didn't wait for a reply. With both hands, she gripped the pipe and eased it out with a pop. A horrid sucking sound followed and she shoved the jacket into the gap left from the pipe. Cian put his hand over hers and closed his eyes.

Warmth vibrated through her body and thousands of years of history flooded her psyche. All of it familiar, none of it known to her. Tears filled her eyes and through her blurred vision, she saw the shimmer beneath her skin.

Malcolm had left a glittery luster where he'd bled on her.

"What are you doing to me?"

"Breaking wards meant to keep you from your true potential."

A force, insistent and powerful, twisted in her core, spiraling outward. Her hands shook as she pressed the fabric against Cian's wound. A hurricane whirled through her veins, igniting every cell until she was aflame. A cool clamminess covered her brow and her palms were slick. She licked her lips, tasting salt from her own sweat.

"What's happening to me?" Whatever this was, she didn't like it.

"Kiss me." Cian's gorgeous brown/hazel/autumnal eyes bore into hers.

She leaned forward and put her lips to his.

Stars burst behind her closed lids and images played out against a backdrop of fields of wildflowers. People, places, names, buildings, creatures of myth, and there, standing in the center of it all, was a woman with strawberry-blonde hair and Nikala's sky-blue eyes.

In a flash, it was gone. The meadow, the woman, all of it. Gone as if it had never been.

Yet Nikala knew and remembered. Serenity from that knowledge washed over her. She stayed hunched over Cian, their lips connected. Reluctantly, she drew apart. "Was that magic?"

"It *is* magic. Yours and mine combined."

Cian guided and directed her power to the puncture in his side. She removed the jacket and grimaced at the wound. At least the bleeding had stopped. Her feeble, too-new magic wasn't enough to fully heal him, but it might keep him from dying.

"You need a doctor. A proper hospital."

"I need to return to Faerie." Cian struggled to sit and Nikala helped him. "Can you drive that thing?" He pointed to the lorry.

"Of course. Can't you?"

He shook his head. "Never had a need."

"What should we do about them?" Nikala meant Yash and Jude. "And Malcolm. Should he be returned to, erm, where he's from?"

"He's a traitor to Faerie. They'd never allow it."

Again, Cian said "they" as if she knew who he meant.

Cian used a chair to help him stand. He shuffled to where Yasheda's body draped over the table. With a heavy sigh, he placed his hands on her abdomen and mumbled beneath his breath. Yash's body shriveled and turned to dust. The smell of sulphur lingered in the air. Next, Cian shuffled to where she'd left Jude's body. He knelt and repeated his mumbling, his hands on

Jude's head. Like Yash, his corpse curled and shriveled, then became nothing but dust. Not a shimmering radiance like Malcolm's blood, but ordinary ashes.

Nikala wavered at the back of the lorry. Despite everything, Malcolm deserved more than this. But what, exactly, he deserved, she wasn't sure. Cian tugged on the blanket covering Malcolm's body and Nikala helped him drag the corpse out of the lorry to lay beside Jude's ashes.

"Do you mind if I say a few words?" Nikala put a hand on Cian's forearm.

She knelt beside Malcolm and smoothed the blanket. She was grateful she couldn't see his face, but also needed to look on him one last time. To know for certain he was dead, or to mourn, she wasn't sure.

The blanket peeled away to reveal the visage of a man who could've been sleeping. His lashes were soft against the hard lines of his cheekbones. She stroked his forehead and brushed a few hairs into place. Everything she'd ever wanted to say to him left her mind. All the angst, the fury, the bitter resentments were gone. All she was left with was a deep regret.

Regret for all the time they'd squandered. All the memories they never made.

Finally, she said simply, "Be at peace."

Cian knelt beside her and placed his hands on Malcolm's chest. As he mumbled the words and the dead man's body began to shift, Nikala let the tears flow over her cheeks to drip on the concrete floor. In a matter of seconds, it was over. Malcolm could never use her or hurt her again. It was the freedom she wanted, but not the ending she'd imagined.

27

Cian had Nikala stop off at the little park where they'd found the lycan the night before. He limped to the bushes where he'd last seen the beast and knelt low. The sun was setting across the Thames and darkness would soon blanket the city. Another long night alone in a strange place wouldn't be the lycan's fate.

The gaping wound in his side rebelled at every movement he made. Nikala had healed him as much as she could, but her magic was too untested. That his instincts about her had been correct did little to ease his anguish for what she suffered to learn of her fate. The death of Malcolm, his beating—he sensed her conflicting emotions.

She'd need strength and perseverance in the coming days, but mostly she'd need understanding and compassion. In a perfect world, he'd take her to his mum's, where she could grow and explore without restraint or judgment. Without the queen's permission, Nikala's fate in Faerie might be the same as Malcolm's in the human realm. Even though Cian trusted her, she was unknown, a possible traitor or spy, and he doubted very much if the queens of Faerie would welcome her without first interrogating her. He was certain at the very least, Nikala would be accused of being Acelyne's courier.

For now, she was safer in the human realm. The best he could do was ask Donyatella to keep an eye on Nikala until he returned.

A rustling came from deep in the bushes and relief surprised Cian. He'd hoped the lycan was still there, but had feared he wouldn't find him alive.

"What will you do with him?" Nikala knelt beside Cian, her gaze firmly set on the bushes. Her unease around the creature was palpable, but she would grow used to living with strange beings. In time.

"He won't survive long in this world. I'm going to take him somewhere he can thrive and have a semblance of the life he was meant to live." He still couldn't ascertain how someone had stolen the beast's magic so thoroughly he'd become more dog than lycanthrope.

"Will you come back once he's settled and you're healed?"

Cian took her hand in his. "Nothing could stop me. What will you do?"

Nikala glanced toward SIRE's offices, two blocks away. "I have some unfinished work to see to."

She meant Hunter, Cian was certain. The man who killed his father. He touched his wound and flinched. No human doctor could save him. Hell, he wasn't even sure if Meg could, but she was his best hope. Even now, he felt Nikala's magic waning, the wound growing. He couldn't linger long and yet he loathed leaving.

It was an impossible situation. She couldn't go to his world, and he couldn't stay in hers.

"I'd prefer you wait until I return." Cian grinned at the tightening of her jaw. "But I doubt that's likely. Be careful. Please."

"I was about to say the same to you."

Nikala squeezed his hand and rose. The lycan emerged from

the bushes and sniffed the air. His muzzle turned toward Nikala and his mouth opened, his tongue flopped to the side.

"I think he's smiling." Cian stroked the creature's ruff and stood beside Nikala with more effort than he cared to admit. "He senses the change in you."

She held her hands out and turned them from one side to the other. Her Glamour was muted beneath the paleness of her skin.

"About that. I know some crazy stuff happened in the warehouse and at Hunter's, and I'm not sure I fully understand what it all means."

The lycan licked her fingers and nudged her hand to his head. Cian shifted his weight and breathed through a jag of pain.

"You're not human, Nikala. Someone brought you to the human realm. I don't believe you're a changeling. I think both your parents are fae." Cian scratched the beast behind his ears.

Nikala's lips pursed, but she didn't reply. After a long hesitation, she turned to him. "What does that mean for me? For us? Can I still live here?"

Cian caressed her cheek and kissed her softly. "It means you can live wherever you want. Don't overthink it too much. When I return, we'll sort it out together. I'll be gone a few days at the most."

"Then go, so you can return to me sooner."

Their parting kiss was filled with enough emotion to fill a year's worth of days. There was too much to tell her and not enough time. His wish was to take her with him to Faerie, but not until he'd had a chance to speak with the queens. When she returned, it would be without a stigma hanging over her head.

His lips lingered on hers, not wanting to lose the physical connection. Her hands wrapped around his back and he absorbed her strength. It was all that kept him standing. Reluctantly, he withdrew, inhaling her scent, imprinting it and everything about her to his memory. The few days he'd be gone would be an eternity.

They strolled hand-in-hand to the lorry, where she reached behind the passenger's seat for the messenger bag. He slung it over his shoulder and placed a protective hand on the flap. She rolled her bottom lip between her teeth, her eyes narrowed.

"Hunter took the amulet I had, and there were two more missing when Malcolm gave the rest to Hunter. I'll try to get them back."

"Please." Cian put a hand on her shoulder. "Stay away from that man. Or at least wait for my return."

"I'll wait." Nikala patted his hand and walked around to the driver's side. "Be safe on your journey. You know where to find me." She tilted her chin toward the huge glass building that dominated the skyline.

Some of Malcolm's Glamour shone on Nikala's skin. It was another mystery he would have to solve—how Malcolm's blood had remained pure fae despite his long stay in the human realm.

Cian held up a hand in farewell. He knew she would ignore him and seek out Hunter. He could only hope he'd return in time. First, he had to get the lycan to Faerie and himself to Meg. The way his heart was pounding, he wasn't sure he'd make it that far. But then, it might've been beating for reasons other than being half dead. He glanced one last time at Nikala, then at the sky. *Protect her*, he begged the gods. *Please.*

"Come on, mutt." Cian touched the beast's fur and they stumbled across the street toward Donyatella's pub.

The old Stone Guardian was sitting at her table when he approached with the lycan. Her gaze went from Cian to the beast and back.

"I need to use your cellar, if I may." Cian placed two fingers over his heart, a silent signal that he would never betray her secret portal.

"And that? Are you taking it with you?"

"I am."

Donyatella looked past him to the busy street. "Where's Nikala?"

Cian's heart rattled beneath his rib cage and his breath hitched. "She's going to her office. You'll keep watch over her?" It wasn't so much a question as an order, one he wasn't authorized to make, but did anyway.

The snort that came from the woman was comical in its absurdness. "You fae. Think you command the worlds. Of course I'll keep watch over her, as I was instructed long ago, and not by you."

Cian cocked his head. "You knew what she was and didn't tell her. Why? And how could you let her be abused by that monster?"

"The guardians remain neutral."

He clenched his fists and breathed several shallow breaths. "Your neutrality will get her killed."

"We have seen civilizations come and go. It is not for us to choose sides."

Cian sucked in a breath. "That wasn't always the case."

"To our immortal shame. But, who's to say if we were right or wrong," Donyatella replied, eyes downcast. "I'll put someone I trust close to Nikala. She'll be safe until your return. I give you my word."

He knew he shouldn't push his luck, that with one wrong move the gargoyle might refuse his request to use the doorway in the cellar, but he had to know.

"My sister, Rori. You said she's known to the guardians. Can you tell me why?" His life force was ebbing away and time precious, but he had to know.

Donyatella shook her head and took a sip of water from an ornate goblet. "Nikala will know soon enough. War is coming. To this world and Faerie. There's nothing any of us can do to stop it. Tell your queens they best be prepared." She set the goblet down. "I've said too much. Now, go." She waved a wrinkled hand in dismissal.

It wasn't the first time he'd heard the warning about war, but something in the old woman's tone uncovered a dread he'd buried deep in his past.

The lycan limped down the stairs beside Cian and stopped in front of the doorway that would take them to Faerie. As he placed his hand upon the old oak planks, he burned with the knowledge he was letting Nikala down. He'd left her to deal with the aftermath of Malcolm's treachery on her own. How far the betrayal went, Cian could only guess. He pushed his free hand against the wound in his gut. He wouldn't be much good to Nikala dead.

Once in Faerie, he'd track down Rori and together, they would uncover who Nikala's parents were. Then, he'd return to the human realm and help her claim her fae legacy.

28

Rori stood in the center of the Shoogly Dragon, having an out-of-body experience in the darkened pub. She left the present and returned to the night Acelyne had captured her. In her memories, she had been surrounded by friends and a dozen strangers. Her gaze roved from the bar to a corner table where she recalled an attractive man had sat the night Acelyne captured her. Her eyes narrowed and she focused her sight to a pinpoint.

Therron. That bloomin' elf had been there that night. She put a hand to her head. Of course—he said he'd been following Acelyne. She pivoted and went to the bar where her friend Sal had brought her a drink.

The barkeep entered through a side door and jumped when he saw her. "We ain't opened yet."

"Have you seen Sal?"

The barkeep looked toward the street. "Sal's dead. Got himself stuck on the pointy end of someone's blade in the market."

Sal dead. Acelyne dead. Coincidence? She didn't think so. Why had she come back? She should've left the Shoogly Dragon alone and used other doorways to get to her mum's. But the pull had been too great. Not just in the hopes of bumping into Therron, but to get answers about what happened that night.

As she turned, a flash of blonde hair caught her attention and she thought Acelyne had returned. A deep spasm of anxiety rocked her, but when she looked closer, it wasn't the enchantress at all, but a ruggedly handsome elf who stared at her as if he'd seen a nightmare.

"What are you doing here?" His tone didn't convey the same horror of his expression. In fact, it was riddled with relief.

"I, erm, I couldn't stay at Midna's knowing fae were in danger." A half-truth was better than none.

He approached, cautiously, and the sounds of the barkeep yammering at them to come back when the pub was opened dimmed. Rori stayed rooted where she was, not trusting her legs to keep her aloft for all the trembling they were doing. When he was a foot from her, he stopped, his eyes searching.

"Will you return to the Unseelie Court when this is all over?"

What she saw in his eyes tore at her heart. He'd left to give her freedom to explore her needs. They were both fools. Him for not seeing how much she cared for him, and her for believing she needed anyone but him to teach her how to love.

"No, I won't be returning. At least, not as an álainn obedience."

Relief swept over his face and the scar on his cheek reddened.

A piercing scream rent her mind and she doubled over against the pain. Her breaths came in gasps and she saw a vision of Cian, hurt.

"Rori, what is it?" Therron's arm wrapped around her and he dragged her to a booth. "What's happening? Talk to me."

Words wouldn't come. All she could do was stare into the distance where she saw a woman with blonde hair and sea-blue eyes hovering over Cian's body. A moment later, the image popped and her hearing returned. Her breathing slowed. But her heart galloped at an alarming pace.

"Cian's hurt. It's bad, Therron."

"Where is he?"

"The human realm. I don't know. He's with someone, a friend, I hope."

"Can you get to him?" Therron beckoned to the barkeep and asked for a pitcher of water.

"He's coming back to Faerie." Her voice sounded far away, even to her. "He's not alone."

"Which doorway is he coming through?"

"I don't know." She drank straight from the pitcher, not bothering with the glasses the barkeep brought. The cool water slaked her thirst, but did nothing to clear the sludge from her brain. "He'll need a healer." She set the pitcher on the table and wiped her lips with the sleeve of her jacket.

"Is Meg still at Rowan's?"

"We'll find out." Rori was off the bench and heading to the cellar by the time she'd finished her sentence. If Cian was hurt, he'd need fae healers and Meg was the best. With any luck, she'd be at Rowan's and the pair could mend Cian's wound.

At the doorway, she spoke the words that would take them to Rowan's private portal. Therron watched passively and for once, she didn't care whether he saw or heard what she did. Cian's life was in mortal danger and now wasn't the time to play one-upmanship.

They stepped through into the darkness and she clasped Therron's hand in hers. The warmth of his skin helped offset the chill that had settled in her heart. Cian had only been gone two days. What the hell had that fool man gotten involved in?

The void wobbled and Rori pulled her thoughts away from her brother. She fixed Rowan's study in her mind and breathed through her nose. Calm. Serenity. There was no telling what lurked in the shadows of the in-between and she didn't care to find out.

The light of Rowan's study pierced the blackness and she grabbed it with her mind, propelling them faster to their destination.

A startled Rowan glanced up from his desk as they stumbled through the portal. He rose, questions in his aging eyes.

"Is Meg still here?" Rori asked by way of greeting.

"She is, but may I ask what could be so important you abuse my sacred trust and burst into my private chambers?"

Feeling the sting of his recrimination, Rori slowed and drew a long breath. "I'm sorry, Rowan. I know you said to never use your doorway, much less to ever speak of it to anyone, but this is an emergency. Cian's hurt and I fear he won't make it unless you and Meg heal him together."

Therron stepped forward and grasped the old wizard's forearm in his own. "We appreciate your need for discretion and will never speak of this to anyone."

Rowan nodded and mumbled an affirmation. It took another minute to soothe his frazzled nerves, then he led them to Meg's room, where the witch answered before they had a chance to knock. By the harrowed look on her face, Rori guessed she already knew why they were there. She looked past the woman to where medicines and tools were laid out on her bed.

"You were expecting us."

"I was expecting someone, young Rori, but I wasn't sure who." Meg grinned and patted Rori's arm. "To be fair, it's usually you or your brother, so in a way, yes. I was expecting you."

They moved Meg's supplies to a larger room where she and Rowan would be unencumbered in their work. Rori helped to keep her mind off Cian, but his presence battered her mind. She'd never had a connection like this with him, certainly not from Faerie to the human realm. When they were little, she'd always known where he was, but had grown out of the ability with adolescence. She'd missed the sense of having him with her, even in a detached sort of way.

Now that it had returned, and with such insistence, she questioned the timing.

"How will we get him here?" Rori touched the frame of an ornate mirror.

"What, dear?" Meg's hands hovered over her scissors.

"We don't know what doorway he's using, or if he's even coming back to Rowan's."

Therron set a box of wrappings on a desk and stood, his gaze going from Meg to Rowan. Something in the way he held himself put Rori on edge. Would he leave her again? She knew he and Cian weren't friends.

"I hadn't considered this complication." Rowan scratched at his chin.

"I can help," Therron offered. The three of them looked at the elf with expectation on their faces. "I know a way to, erm, redirect him."

Rowan's eyes rounded and his mouth drooped. "So it's true? The legends. They're real?"

Therron held up a hand. "Don't ask me how it's done, for I won't show you. Just trust me, please?" His gaze was rooted on Rori and her insides blazed.

Questions, so many questions sprang to her lips, but the look on Therron's face said he wouldn't answer them any time soon.

A fierce wail stopped her from responding. She grabbed her head and crouched low. The image of Cian standing before a doorway.

"He's coming." The words sputtered between gasps of air.

The three of them became a flurry of action as they sprinted from the room to Rowan's study. Tug ambled into the room and Rori gave her friend a warm smile. Meg sidled next to the giant and they all watched Therron with tempered anticipation.

The elf stood before Rowan's bookcase and swirled his right

hand in a circle, his left at chest level, two fingers held up. The words he spoke made the hairs on her arm rise and a shiver snaked its way down her back. Black magic.

She listened, keen to know the words he used, but he spoke too low even for her fae hearing.

The air began to undulate and shift, spinning in a circle with his hand movements. Quicker and quicker he went until there was a vortex not more than two feet in front of him. Rowan's bookcase disappeared into blackness. Rori unconsciously took a step backward. From her peripheral, she saw Rowan did the same.

Time slowed and they waited. The vortex continued and Therron stood firmly planted in front of it. Rori inched her way closer and placed a hand on his shoulder. He acknowledged her touch with a slight tilt of his head.

With a long, steadying breath, she opened her magic and let it flow through Therron to the spinning air and beyond. She reached inside the blackness to find her brother.

"He's just there," Therron whispered and Rori felt what she couldn't see. Therron's magic had made a net around her brother and was pulling him toward Rowan's study.

A moment later, a huge black dog lunged into the room, startling them. Rori gasped and clutched Therron's tunic, but held her magic in place. The creature stumbled forward and collapsed in a heap at Tug's feet.

"He's injured." Tug bent and picked up the mass of black fur.

"We'll see to him as well. Cian first," Meg assured them.

A moment later, Cian's face emerged from the vortex, eyes wild, hair sticking up at all angles.

"The bloody hell is this?" He clutched his side where a crimson stain covered most of his shirt.

Tears of relief stung her eyes and she brushed past Therron to her brother. "Cian." She wrapped him in a hug and cried against his shoulder. Gods help her, she cried like a troll baby right there in front of everyone.

"Let's get them to the surgery theater." Rowan led them out of the study and down the hall.

Rori glanced over her shoulder at Therron. He was closing the vortex with both hands. Sweat rolled down his temples. He'd saved Cian's life.

He joined her and held Cian aloft as they dragged more than walked with him to the room. Once there, Rori lay her brother on the soft bedding and sat beside him.

"I saw you with a woman. Did she do this?" Even then, Rori was conflicted about hunting that bitch down and killing her or staying with Cian until he recovered.

"It wasn't Nikala." The way he said her name made Rori's nerves tense. Whoever Nikala was, she meant something special to Cian.

"Rori, you can interrogate him later. Right now, we've work to do." Meg shooed them from the room and Rori promised Cian she'd be right outside the door.

They crowded in the hall and Rori tapped her fingers on the wall.

"I seem to recall being here not too long ago waiting on word about you." Therron broke the silence.

A flippant reply sprang to her lips, but then she looked at him and saw the concern etched in his forehead. The tiny crinkles at the corners of his eyes where worry rested. He was scared. Not just for Cian, but for her.

She did something completely not in her character and leaned into him. His arms wrapped around her and she breathed in his scent of forests and stone and spice. Tug's big arms circled them both and she giggled against Therron's chest.

When Meg and Rowan finished with Cian, she'd get answers. For the moment, she was exactly where she needed to be—with the people she loved, and who loved her.

❈ 29 ❈

Nikala stared out at the skyline. London was glorious at night with all the twinkling lights from streetlamps to office buildings. She loved seeing the city from this height. From up here, she believed in the possibility of others. From this distance, she was removed from the filth and dangers of the streets.

She cracked her neck and looked toward Chelsea, where Malcolm was murdered. Cian hadn't killed him. Even though she knew the truth, her heart wasn't ready yet to accept the alternative. There was no reason to eliminate Malcolm. He was Hunter's funding. Surely he still needed Malcolm's money. Although, the extravagant mansion shot a hole in that theory.

Nikala tapped her fingers on the windowsill, her mind spinning. The papers she found in Malcolm's safe were spread across his desk, spelling out what was to happen to SIRE in the event of his demise. She shuddered at the realization Malcolm knew something would happen to him—sooner rather than later.

While she'd been off doing his dirty work, he'd been plotting and planning behind her back. The sneaky bastard. He'd suspected Hunter of treachery long before today. She unfolded the letter he'd written to her and read it again. Although she'd already memorized the words, she reread them in the hope she'd gain more understanding. More closure.

Dearest Nikki (Nikala, I know how much you hate the nickname, please indulge me this one last time),

Long ago, I let someone convince me to leave home for reasons I won't bore you with here. I left the woman I cherished more than the sun loves the moon, and I left my friends and family. I came here to rebuild my life, but it was never complete without my starshine.

Then you came into my life and I thought perhaps I had a second chance, but I soon learned that was not to be.

Nikala's hands shook as she read. Malcolm had never once told her who her mother was. She looked out the window at the stars dotting the horizon. Was she in London? Had he met her on a business trip and she'd died?

The life I started building here benefited someone else as well and they abused our friendship through manipulation so complete it took me years to fully comprehend what they'd done. By that time, it was too late. I'd already lost you.

Her snort echoed in the silent office. The victim stance didn't sit well. Malcolm was too cunning to be taken advantage of so completely. Unless there was something else, a reason he was easily fooled. She scratched her chin and read on.

My darling, perfect daughter. I destroyed you for a dream. A dream of a more perfect world, where one can love whomever they wish without penalty. A world where our kind can live side by side with others in peace.

And now I see what I helped to create and what he truly is—a madman bent on destroying this world and ours. I once believed in his wild ideas and experiments. I once believed he twisted you and broke you so that all our kind would be immortal. I was wrong.

Interesting. So Malcolm at least thought she could be killed.

She wished he'd given Hunter the memo before the asshole shot her.

My last wish is that you can somehow right the wrongs I made. Turn his experiments against him and help our people when the time comes.

I hope one day you can forgive me.

My eternal shame. My eternal regret. My eternal love.

Your loving father.

There was no date on the letter, and it wasn't signed. She folded it into a neat square and tucked it inside her back pocket. As far as she knew, it was the first time Malcolm had ever put in writing that she was his daughter. She doubted whether even Yash or Jude knew.

Certainly, Hunter knew. He'd used Malcolm as a weapon on her too many times not to have known. Taunting her about being sold to the highest bidder. Or, on many occasions, he'd claimed that perhaps Malcolm wasn't really her father and she'd been found in a back alley, the product of an illicit affair, an unwanted consequence. His mental games were as much or even more of a torment than his physical abuse. Skin healed; the mind remembered.

He was out there, somewhere. She hoped it was on a train back to Scotland. At some point she'd have to deal with him, but not yet. She was too raw from everything that had happened and from Malcolm's letter.

She leaned her forehead against the cool glass. If only Cian had stayed. For a day or a week. Long enough to explain to her what being a faerie meant. Could she fly? Did she need to pollinate flowers? What did it mean to be fae? She was being selfish. As much as she wanted him to stay, he needed his people. *His* people. Were they now her people? He'd said there were healers in Faerie and gods knew, he didn't look good when she left him.

Two days ago, she thought she knew exactly who she was and lived as much on her terms as Hunter and Malcolm would allow.

Now, she had no idea who the woman in the mirror was or where she belonged.

"I thought I might find you here," Hunter's smooth, gravelly voice said from the doorway.

Ice trickled over her skin, burning with its intensity. She thought she'd have more time before he showed up. But that wasn't Hunter's style. Of course he'd pounce when she was vulnerable.

"What do you want?" She didn't turn around. Couldn't look him in the eyes. Not yet.

"Did you destroy my lab?"

"No. I told you, I was at the pub. I don't know who did." She turned then and faced the man who killed her father. "Why does it matter? The amulets are gone. You can't get more."

His face brightened and he stepped closer. "You still believe in my work?"

Pain, sharp and cruel like a knife piercing her heart, stunned her into silence. *His work.* She was as much a product of his work as Yash and Jude had been. He was the madman Malcolm wrote about.

"Come with me," he said when she didn't answer. "Return to Scotland with me, where we can work side by side like we used to. Only now, you'll be my assistant instead of my experiment."

The way his eyes danced and cheeks brightened, he truly believed she would be excited for the opportunity.

"No, I won't join you." She crossed her arms over her chest. "I'm glad your lab was destroyed. I'm happy Acelyne is dead because now you can never torment our kind again." The words were strange on her tongue. *Our kind.* What did that really mean? To what purpose was any of this? His experiments and enhancements, they were just so he could play God.

His eyes became hard and mean. His disfigurement turned rosy with his rising anger. Nikala had seen this side of Hunter too many times not to be afraid. But unlike all the other times, she wouldn't shrink from him.

"Who the hell do you think you are? You're nothing but a throwaway. A scrap of flesh no one wanted. I made you who you are. I did that!" Spittle formed at the corners of his lips and his hands gesticulated wildly. The tiny scars on the backs of his hands —the ones he got from the same potion that destroyed his face— rose in crimson webs, reaching to his wrists.

"You made me a monster. A killer without a conscience." She strode to face him, their bodies inches apart. "I was loved by my father and you destroyed that. You lied and deceived and manipulated to get what you wanted. Then you broke me again and again for your sordid pleasure. I wanted to die every day for the last twenty years, but you wouldn't let me. I don't know how, exactly, but I know you made it impossible."

Shock shuttered over his features and he stumbled backward. "You ungrateful bitch. I made you immortal."

"At what price, Hunter?" She returned to her place behind Malcolm's—no, her desk. She drew on strength from Malcom's letter. He'd loved her. He wanted her to fight for their kind. *My last wish is that you can somehow right the wrongs I made. Turn his experiments against him and help our people when the time comes.*

Nikala reached into her waistband and removed the gun she'd used to kill Yasheda. She held it steady, pointed at Hunter.

"Do it. I dare you." His mocking tone and quirk of his lips sent warnings through her mind.

She pressed the trigger, but her fingers wouldn't budge. Pain, cruel and twisted like a serrated knife ripping across her skin over and over, tormented her psyche. The harder she tried to pull the trigger, the harsher the agony.

"Pathetic."

Nikala lowered the gun and the pain stopped. "What did you do to me?"

"Call it insurance." That stupid grin returned and his eyes lit with excitement. "I can show you the wonders of cerebral manipulation. We'll be unstoppable, Nikala. Come with me now." He held out his hand, fully expecting her to accept his offer.

"Leave, Hunter. Leave now and don't ever come back." Her legs shook and she pressed them against the solid desk to hide her nerves.

The grin disappeared and darkness covered his features. "How dare you dismiss me. You have no authority."

She'd long ago grown accustomed to his mercurial moods, but it still was unsettling to see the speed with which he could flip from pleased to pissed.

Nikala held up a paper. "This says I do. Malcolm left everything to me. Including that monstrous house you bought in Chelsea. You really shouldn't have borrowed the funds through SIRE."

Hunter sputtered and shook, his anger at full tilt. She kept a hand on the gun, hoping if her life were in danger she could break past whatever fuckery he'd done to her brain.

"Technically, I own your manor house in Aberdeenshire, but I'm not a total monster. You can live there for now." At least, until she decided what to do about him. Cian said something about turning him over to the queens, but she didn't know any queens and doubted the reigning monarch of Great Britain would be interested in a mad scientist. Because she couldn't kill him, this solution at least meant she could keep an eye on him.

"You'll regret this, Nikala." Hunter fumed and worked his jaw like a cow its cud. "I created you. I know how best to destroy you."

She crossed her arms over her chest. "What do you think I was doing all those long, lonely years? I was studying you, Hunter. I know your weaknesses as well as my own."

He pivoted and stormed from the office. When she heard the lift doors close, she sank into the huge, comfortable chair that had belonged to Malcolm. His scent was embedded in the leather and she inhaled deep, recalling the few good memories she had of him to imprint them on her heart.

Nikala spun the chair to face the window and gazed at the stars. She'd survived facing Hunter. Somehow, she'd found the courage to confront him. Not only that, but to deny him. A giggle burst up from her midsection and out, surprising her with its gaiety.

"Celebrating, are we?" a female said from the doorway.

Nikala spun to face the intruder, the gun at the ready.

"Now, now, there's no need for that." Maxx entered the office and closed the door behind her. She put a finger to her lips and a moment later, an ochre film worked its way from her outstretched fingers to the floor, and up the walls to meet in the middle of the ceiling. Once the room was ensconced in her magic, Maxx smiled warmly. "I thought he'd never leave."

"What are you doing here?" The last Nikala had seen of her, she was running away in the alley.

"I thought you might like to talk." Maxx indicated the sofa. "Join me, please."

Nikala cast a worried glance to the door and took a seat opposite Maxx.

"Don't worry about her. Hunter made certain she wouldn't see or hear anything."

"Is she dead?" No stranger to killing, Nikala had had enough for one day.

"Just sleeping. She'll wake with a wicked headache, but no more harm than that." Maxx adjusted her saffron coat and smoothed her hair. She looked completely different from the hoodie-wearing stalker she'd been earlier.

Nikala wished they had tea or something to settle her stomach. A moment later, a tray complete with a pot of tea, cream, sugar cubes, and biscuits appeared on the table in front of her.

"Did you do that?" Nikala tentatively put a finger on the teapot. Heat seared through the pad of her finger.

"Of course. You'll be able to as well, in time." Maxx reached into her pocket and withdrew two amulets. "Malcolm gave these to me for safekeeping. I believe you should have them."

Nikala reached for the pendants, a tremble in her hands. "Why just the two?"

Maxx's shrug moved the coat at a comical angle. "I've no idea."

The amulets sparkled beneath Maxx's wall of magic. A wave of guilt washed over her and she removed the pendant she'd hidden in her bra. She'd lied to Cian when she told him Hunter had the amulet. She should've given it to him, but the idea of being separated from the amulet filled her with horror. She placed it in her palm alongside the others. It was more ornate than the other two and it occurred to her that they were decorated specific to the contents inside.

"I told Cian Hunter had taken this one. He's going to hate me when he returns." The confession came unbidden, but Maxx had given her the other two pendants; surely that deserved a little trust.

Maxx folded her hands over Nikala's. "Not if you tell him the truth and keep these safe. Hunter can never get hold of them, do you understand? Never. If you think there's a chance he'll take them, promise me you'll destroy them before that happens." Maxx held her gaze. "Promise me."

"I, erm, I promise." She knew Maxx was right. Without the amulets, and what was inside, Hunter couldn't continue his experiments. Nikala tucked the three amulets inside her bra where they'd be safe until she found a more permanent solution.

Maxx poured them tea. "How much did Cian tell you about the fae?"

"Not much. There wasn't really time." Nikala glanced at the magic surrounding them. "Are you a faerie?"

"Pureblood, from one of Faerie's oldest families." A note of pride filled her words. "I can answer most of the questions you might have, but there's something I'd like to present to you first. With Malcolm gone, blessed be his bones that rest in the dust, I would like to offer my services in an official capacity. No threats, no blackmail. A proper job. Working for you."

Blackmail? Nikala would sort that out in a minute.

"Do you know the inner workings of Malcolm's empire?"

"I do indeed. I wasn't just his courier. When a job was too messy for you, he'd send me."

Nikala gasped. Malcolm had sent her on some pretty traumatic missions. She shuddered to think what Maxx had to endure.

"What do you know about the Dawn Project?"

Maxx took a sip of her tea and set down her cup before answering. "Starting with the difficult interview questions first. I like your style."

Although her tone suggested she was joking, seriousness clouded her eyes. Nikala waited impatiently for Maxx to answer.

"The Dawn Project was Hunter's prototype. His first experiment, you might say."

"If that was his first, then it was more than twenty years ago. Why were he and Malcolm discussing it again?" Nikala took a bite of a biscuit and sipped her tea, her mind spinning.

"Because the Dawn Project is what started Hunter down this path. He's compelled to finish what he started and that means fully exploiting his first experiment."

A sliver of jealousy slipped beneath the cool veneer of indifference she'd perfected over the years. "Do you know who or what that is?"

Maxx nodded, her eyes growing misty. "Aurora MacNair. Cian's sister."

The sliver of jealousy twisted in her heart and wrenched free. *Dawn. Aurora.* "Does Cian know?"

"No one knows but you, me, and Hunter. Acelyne and Malcolm are beyond giving away secrets."

Nikala stood and paced the office, her boots making light thuds with each step. She had to warn Cian, but how?

"You can go between the worlds, right? You have to tell Cian. Let him know his sister isn't safe."

"I've already warned Rori not to come to the human realm, but that girl's as headstrong as you are." Maxx stood and dusted crumbs from her coat. "With Cian gone, you need someone here to look out for you. I'll send a message to a contact I have in Faerie, but I won't risk both our lives chasing Cian down."

"You can do that? You can send messages back and forth?" Nikala reached for a pen and paper.

"I can. You can't." Maxx went to the door and turned. "The fate of both Faerie and the human realm rests on your shoulders now, Nikala. I do hope you don't let us down."

With that, she left the office and the ochre lights dimmed until Nikala stood alone in the darkened space. Someday she'd break the hold Hunter had on her and she'd kill him. Maybe Maxx would know how, or Cian, but she'd be free of him for good.

"I promise you," she said aloud to the stars, hoping Malcolm could hear her, "I will right the wrongs we both made. I will help our people." Somehow. Someday.

She retrieved the more ornate amulet and held it in her fist, close to her lips.

"If you can hear me," she whispered to the glass, "I could really use your strength and wisdom right now."

An image of a field of wildflowers filled her mind and Nikala breathed in the scents of a summer's day. A warm, floral breeze ruffled her hair and she closed her eyes to bask in the sun. Standing in the middle of the field was the woman with strawberry-blonde hair. She held her hands out to Nikala, beckoning her close.

She ran to the woman, sure in her steps. A comfortable

warmth covered her and she knew she was where she belonged. Where she was loved. She was home.

Their hands clasped together and the woman's smile outshone the sun and stars in the sky. Like starshine.

I am Mairead, the woman said. *I am your mother.*

ABOUT THE AUTHOR

Tameri Etherton is a *USA Today* Bestselling and award-winning author of dangerous fantasy and magical ever afters. She grew up inventing fictional worlds where the impossible was possible.
It's been said she leaves a trail of glitter in her wake as she creates new adventures for her kickass heroines, and the rogues who steal their hearts.
She lives an enchanted life traveling the world with her very own prince charming and their mischievous dragon, Lady Dazzleton.

Read More from Tameri Etherton and explore the Aetherverse at
www.TameriEtherton.com

AUTHOR NOTES

This is one of my favorite parts to writing—being able to thank those who make this incredible journey memorable. First, I have to thank my readers because without them, the stories wouldn't have the vibrant life that they do. I'd also like to thank my Dazzling Dragons—reader group extraodinaire.

To Jessa Slade for always being willing to kick my authorial ass!

No book is ever finished, but Faith Williams at the Atwater Group does her best to make sure mine are as polished as possible. I owe her a debt of gratitude for her editing skills.

Thank you to Lori Grundy who made gorgeous covers to reflect what I saw in my mind.

And finally, my husband David. My favorite person on this planet and all the worlds. You are my everything.

Who will rise? Who will die?

A madman hunts fae, a life falters beneath the glass. With relations between Faerie and the human realm growing more tense each day, loyalties must be drawn, alliances made.

Nikala's world crumbled when Cian disappeared through the doorway back to Faerie. As she struggles to hold the reigns of her father's business, and of her heart, she begins to lose hope of ever seeing the mysterious fae again.

When she unwittingly uncovers the truth of her mentor's plans—that he controls not only her mind, but has programmed her to be a ruthless killer of his enemies, including Cian and his sister Rori, she must fight Hunter's control to save those she loves. Can she conquer her murderous impulses? Or will his experiments leave her defenseless against his whims?

Cian and Rori now know who kidnapped the fae, but they don't know why. It's not just the faeries' lives that are at stake—creatures known and foreign are also victims of Hunter's devious schemes. With their future uncertain, Rori and Therron must work quickly to find the shadow man who controls the destinies of those not just on Cilachaem, but also Earth.

But shadows aren't meant for the light and Hunter doesn't want to be found. What he needs, however, is Cian dead and Rori's blood.

As Cian, Nikala, Rori and Therron race to find answers, dark secrets emerge about pasts that were best left forgotten. Their destinies are forever entwined. Their lives hang in the balance.

Their legacies will either save or destroy both worlds.

Otherworldly portals. Mysterious powers. Evil hungrily awaits her return.

Taryn's simple life is all she's ever known. Living above a busy London pub with her grandfather, they're ripped from their reality and plunged into a strange world to jumpstart an ancient prophecy. And when he's killed defending her from a vicious intruder's magic, Taryn's left nearly alone… and forced to trust a rugged savior.

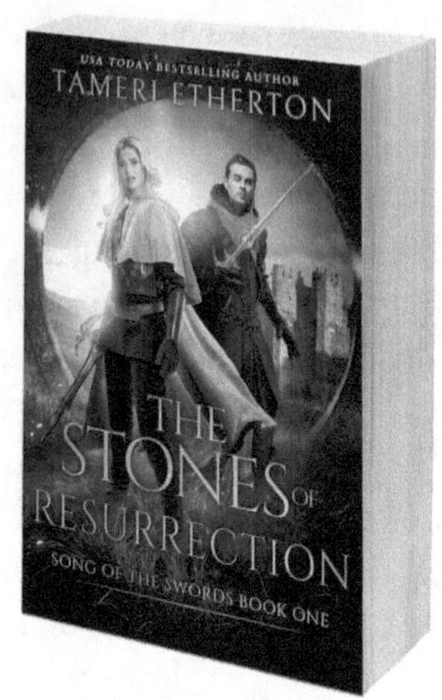

Rhoane has one job. Sworn to protect the young woman who has returned to fulfill her destiny, the assassin dare not let his feelings get in the way of her training. But he knows the time will come when she accepts her power and recognizes he's her fated mate.

As Taryn learns her life on Earth was a lie, she must unlock her hidden talents to save an entire world from destruction. And though Rhoane will show no mercy to anyone who stands in her way, he fears her biggest threat comes from the family she has never known.

Will the destined pair rise to stop the annihilation of a vast kingdom?

The Stones of Resurrection is the enthralling first book in the Song of the Swords fantasy series. If you like ensemble casts, intense action, and dark family sagas, then you'll love Tameri Etherton's epic tale.

Essence of elegance by day. Rampant with desire by night. Can she keep her deadly secret while she wins a prince's heart?

Lady Rainne Dequette hates her ugly magical curse. Transforming from dignified elf to reckless ogress every evening, she's resigned to dispatching bandits after sundown instead of dancing at magnificent castle balls. But when her epic skills with a blade save a handsome royal from ravenous wolves, revealing her shameful form could get her killed.

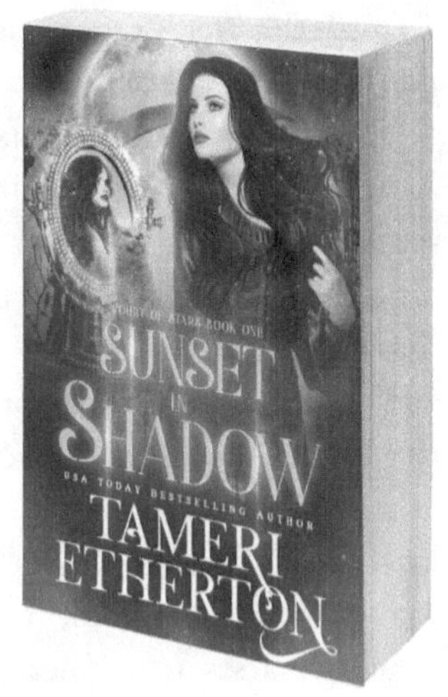

Prince Theo Mistwalker would rather be in his grand library than combing the forests for his wayward brother. But after he's attacked, he's smitten by the swashbuckling rescuer who plants an alluring kiss on his lips before vanishing into the trees. Though his loyalty weakens while he heals in a local duchess's home and develops feelings for her beautiful elven daughter.

After Rainne confesses her burden to the noble man she's fallen for, she has no choice but to deal with her self-hatred or risk losing her one shot at happily-ever-after. And to be with the woman of his dreams, Theo must embark on a dangerous quest to break the spell.

Can they find a way to end Rainne's torment and surrender to their destined passions?

To unleash her dragon, she must confront her past.

In the seven years since Amaleigh failed to assassinate her best friend, she's been on the run jumping from world to world. All she truly wants is to stop running and find a place to call home. And maybe be kissed by someone who doesn't leave her feeling indifferent. Love doesn't come easily for her, yet unlocking her cold, dead heart might be a start to unleashing her inner dragon. That would mean trusting another and there's only one person she's ever trusted—the same man she couldn't kill.

Prince Gwilym knows he shouldn't risk Amaleigh's life by asking for help, especially since he's the reason she had to escape Eidyn. Now his life is in peril and she's the only person he trusts. He wouldn't blame her for not daring to return to the city that celebrated the slaughter of her kind and cast her aside.

Can she survive the very place her parents were murdered, or will palace intrigues claim another victim? If she fails Gwilym, she might lose her chance to come to terms with her past, and open her heart.

Forced to make a desperate choice, she must put aside her hatred for the man who murdered her family and sentenced her to a life of crime and loneliness.

To save those she loves, she must become the Dragon Mage the king fears most.

www.ingramcontent.com/pod-product-compliance
Lightning Source LLC
Chambersburg PA
CBHW062017190726
48284CB00012B/494